The latest in the LE CHAT ROUGE series…

"I wouldn't tell anyone." Sera folded her arms over her chest, partly to hide the shiver that went through her at the mention of Jeremy's name. The gun had been heavy in her hand, the retort more than she'd expected. After the first shot, he had charged her like a bull, rage in his eyes, and in that moment she'd seen her own death.

"It's precarious here," Marc said, interrupting her bloody reverie. "Did Jeremy ever tell you about his boss?"

"Nothing. Why?" What could Marc possibly be driving at?

Marc clasped her hands tight. "Watch yourself while you're here, if you won't come back to Paris with me."

"I always do."

"And stay clear of Mayson. Don't say anything about Le Chat Rouge, or about Royale. Don't invite Mayson, or any of them, to speculate."

The pieces fell into place. "Mayson is…"

"Jeremy's boss. Yes, he is. And though he can be kind, he's every bit as much of a gangster as Royale."

Sera sucked in a breath. Sanctuary wasn't a sanctuary after all.

THE LONDON GAME

ALYSSA LINN PALMER

DEDICATION

For all the artists and the dreamers.

CONTENTS

ACKNOWLEDGMENTS

Many thanks to all those who assisted me with this book, including Shelley Kassian, editor extraordinaire, Cathy Pegau, my fantastic critique partner, and all those family and friends who have given me support. A huge thank you as well to the tour guide at Highgate Cemetery in London, the book lover's fantasy Foyles bookshop, and the beautiful town of Chartres, France, for being such an inspiration.

CHAPTER 1

The train glided smoothly away from the platform at Gare du Nord, sailing past graffiti-covered brickwork and out of Paris. If Marc didn't think about the past, he knew he could pretend this was just another business trip, but with Sera at his side, her fingers clutching his, her lips a thin line, and her eyes brimming with tears she tried to hide, the past was impossible to forget. He would have changed everything if he could have, standing up to Royale, and giving up his family's connections to crime. He lifted her hand, pressing a kiss to the back, and she turned to look at him.

"Think of England as an adventure," he said, his voice low. "Paris is only a train ride away."

"I know." Sera's chin trembled. "It seems so final, like we can never return."

"Are you regretting this? Us?"

"No, not us." She managed a smile. "Never us."

"It will be a new start."

Sera tried hard to keep her smile, but Marc saw the edges crumple, the quiver of her lips. He pushed up the armrest that separated their seats and gathered her under his arm. She tucked herself against his side the way she always had done, before their earlier break. Though they were heading into something entirely new, he felt content with Sera at his side. Her head rested on his shoulder, her dark hair spilling over his arm. He regretted when the attendant came by with their meals and she had to move away so they could eat. He had wine with his meal, but she politely declined, pouring herself a glass of water. When she looked away, the attendant, an older man with an almost fatherly air to his poise, passed a second bottle to Marc, giving Sera a kindly glance.

"Le vin might give her some joie de vivre," he said in a low whisper. Marc set the bottle on his tray, hoping that would be so, though he doubted wine would bring Sera much cheer. "Merci."

The man waved Marc's thanks off with a smile before continuing on to the next passengers. "De rien."

Sera seemed not to notice the exchange; her gaze went to the window again, her food sat untouched, and her glass of water was empty. Marc broke the seal on the wine, unscrewing the lid. He poured some of the Beaujolais into Sera's glass and the remainder into his own. He knew she pined for Paris already, having never been away from France in her life. She looked down at her tray, then over at him.

"You'll feel better if you eat something, have a drink," Marc said. Sera hadn't eaten since last night and it was nearly two o'clock now. She'd done the same when they had traveled to Marseille to see her mother and he wished her anxiety would subside.

"One glass of wine, and some food."

Sera relented, taking a minute sip of the wine. Though the train hardly swayed, she held the glass carefully. She took another sip, a longer sip, and Marc lifted his own glass.

"To new adventures," he said. She nodded solemnly, and drank again before setting down her glass. Marc watched her reach for her cutlery, then pick at the couscous before tasting a small forkful. Then another. He took a deep swallow of his wine, almost draining the glass, before he tucked into his own meal. Beside him, Sera ate slowly but steadily, and when the attendant retraced his steps through the cabin, he smiled at Marc.

The attendant collected their trays last, sliding them into their spots in his trolley. Another attendant came behind him with a silver-coloured tray with sugar and a small carafe of milk. In her other hand, she held a steel carafe.

"Un café, monsieur, madame?"

Marc gave her his cup and took a packet of sugar while she poured. He removed his full cup.

"Madame?" the attendant asked again. Sera glanced away from the window and set her cup on the attendant's tray, lifting it when it was full and placing it back onto her own tray. She dressed her coffee with a generous dollop of milk and took a packet of sugar.

"Merci."

The attendant continued on her way and Sera dumped in the entire packet of sugar, slowly stirring her coffee. Marc put a bit of sugar in his own cup, wondering if Sera would be amused or annoyed if he offered her the remainder for her cup. Sera shifted on the seat until she was beside him once more.

"Feeling better?" he asked.

"I want this to work," she said, "but what if I'm not good enough?"

"Once the club owners hear you sing, you'll be in demand all over London," he replied. "I'm the one who should be worried—you'll be famous and put me aside."

Sera looked up at him in surprise, but he winked at her and saw her realize he'd been teasing.

"Everything will be fine," he reassured her. "This will be our new start."

Once out in the terminal at St. Pancras with their luggage, Sera let Marc lead her through the crowd. They emerged onto a side street lined with black cabs and soon joined the queue. A pair of women ahead of them gossiped and Sera gave up trying to follow their conversation. Her courage slipped, and she wondered again why she had ever thought that leaving France was a good idea.

Marc squeezed her hand and they moved forward to the next free cab. Sera ducked inside the cab and sank back onto the seat.

"Where to, madam?" The cabbie leaned over and gave her a friendly grin as Marc lifted their bags inside. She puzzled over what he'd said, trying to decipher the words through his accent.

The cabbie tried again. "What is your destination, madam?"

Sera looked at him helplessly, but then Marc swung in and onto the seat next to her, closing the door.

"Claridge's please," he said. The cabbie whistled.

"Yes, sir." He pulled away from the curb and into the traffic crush of Euston Road.

"A hotel?" Sera asked. She knew he had made arrangements, but Claridge's? How long did he plan for them to stay there?

"For now. Just for a few days until we can look over some apartments," Marc said. "Let me treat you. You'll like it, I'm sure."

Sera couldn't argue, not when he put his reasoning like that. Marc liked his luxuries and she couldn't deny him the pleasure. But they couldn't live in the lap of luxury forever. Marc had passed the running of the firm over to his second-in-command, Guillaume Fournier, and his income would be reduced. They would have to make their own way.

"Have you been to London before?" The cabbie glanced at them in the rear-view mirror and Sera looked to Marc. He translated, but replied to the cabbie.

"Many times, but her first."

Sera let her gaze wander out the window, ignoring the conversation that she couldn't understand. Marc and the cabbie chatted amiably. Marc nudged her.

"He's curious to know what you think of London."

Sera shrugged. She had not seen much of the city yet, only the rail station and now this cab. "Tell him it's nice so far," she said finally. Marc said something to the cabbie, but she wasn't entirely sure that he had translated what she had said.

"I elaborated," Marc explained. "We're almost there. You can shower, rest, and then we'll go for dinner."

Sera quailed at the thought of having to order her meal in English, or trying to make small talk with the wait staff, but she put on a brave face.

The cab slowed and soon pulled up in front of an elegant old hotel. Sera peered out the window at its beautiful front doors and the bevy of uniformed doormen. One stepped forward to meet the cab, opening the door. She took the proffered hand and the doorman helped her out. Marc paid the driver and then followed her outside.

"Monsieur Perron." A man who appeared to be the head doorman strode over. "Welcome back to Claridge's." His French was flawless. He shook Marc's hand while the second doorman handled their luggage. The man turned to her.

"And Madame Durand, it is a pleasure to meet you. I wish you a very pleasant stay at our hotel."

"Merci beaucoup." Sera's nerves quieted. They knew Marc and knew she spoke French. She felt some of the tension that had built up leave her.

"Edwards will assist you to your usual suite," the doorman said to Marc as he led them inside, tipping his hat. Sera hardly noticed the courtesy. Light gleamed off the polished columns in the lobby, gave the ceiling a pleasant glow, and made the buffed marble floors shine. The expanse awed her.

"Beautiful, isn't it?" Marc rested his hand on the small of her back and ushered her towards the desk.

"It's as lovely as the George V," Sera replied. She noticed a uniformed butler, with his waistcoat and shirt carefully starched, waiting off to one side. A young porter waited beside him with their luggage.

"It's good to see you again, Mr. Perron." A cheerful young woman greeted Marc at the desk, and again, spoke in flawless French.

"Sera, may I present Ruby. Ruby, this is Sera Durand."

"Enchantée, madame." Ruby flashed Sera a brilliant smile. She passed over the key to Marc. "Enjoy your stay."

The butler stepped forward. "It's good to see you again, sir. It's been awhile since the last time."

"Business kept me elsewhere," Marc said easily in English. He introduced Sera, switching effortlessly between languages.

"How do you do, madam?" Edwards gave her a kindly smile and a short bow. Sera felt at ease with him immediately, even though he didn't seem to speak French. He had laugh lines around his eyes and his smile seemed genuine. He led them towards the elevator, speaking to Marc all the while. She tuned him out as they passed by, while looking at the beauty of the hotel.

Once inside the suite, she still found herself gaping. The room was cosy and beautifully appointed, and she felt at home in a matter of moments. She knew she would miss this place once they left.

"Do you want anything to eat from room service?" Marc asked her. Edwards looked expectant and she realized he was waiting for her answer.

"Thé?" Tea was all she could handle right now. She addressed Edwards, who nodded, and Marc added a meal request of his own. Edwards withdrew.

"You always stay here?" she asked, moving from Marc's side. She crossed the small sitting area and leaned against an Art Deco-styled desk in pale wood, looking out the window and down into the street.

"Always," Marc said, coming up behind her. He lifted her hair off the back of her neck and bent to kiss her nape. She shivered. "I have always wanted to bring you here." He lowered his voice. "And if Edwards wasn't coming back in a few minutes, I would show you just how comfortable the bed is."

Sera turned in his embrace. "As soon as he's gone, show me," she said.

"You needn't even ask."

Sera lifted her face towards him and he kissed her hard, just as she liked it. The desire rose in her and she clung to his lapels, her knees weak. She responded ardently to his kiss. At a knock on the door, they broke apart.

"Enter!" Marc released her and she steadied herself against the desk, smoothing her hand over her hair, hoping she didn't look frazzled.

Edwards entered with a cart, which he left in the entryway. He lifted a tray with a full tea service and placed it on the coffee table. She gave him a grateful smile and sat down in the comfy armchair. Edwards returned to the cart and carried a tray with a covered plate and a basket with a folded napkin that she supposed must be bread. He set it on the desk and returned to the cart for the rest of the items. She could hardly believe that he had managed so much in so little time.

"You're a miracle worker, Edwards," Marc said, translating his statement in an aside to Sera.

"D'accord," Sera agreed.

"At your service, Mr. Perron. Would you like your bags unpacked?"

Marc declined and he escorted Edwards to the door. Sera leaned forward, reaching for the teapot. She poured herself a cup and added sugar and a splash of cream. She lifted the cup and sat back in the chair, letting out a sigh. She was here in London. For real, no turning back.

Marc came back into the room. "Are you sure you're not hungry? There's enough food for two, knowing Edwards." He went to the desk and lifted the silver cover from the plate. Steam rose from the roast beef, mashed potatoes, and vegetables. Marc unfolded the napkin and Sera caught the scent of fresh bread. Her stomach growled.

"Maybe I am a bit hungry," she conceded, taking another sip of her tea. She rose from her chair and came over to the desk. Marc pulled her down onto his lap.

"Eat with me," he said, kissing her cheek. She leaned back against him and placed her teacup beside his plate.

"Are you sure it's food you want?" she asked, taking a bun from the basket and tearing it in two. She picked up the knife and dipped it into the pot of whipped butter, spreading a generous amount on the bread.

"Food, and you."

"Food first." The half a bun disappeared quickly. Sera buttered the other half. Marc reached around her for his fork and took the knife from her hand. She shifted to the arm of the chair as he cut into the roast beef.

Marc ate quickly, feeding her bites in between. When the plate was clear, he sat back in the chair, satiated. Sera rose.

"Going somewhere?"

"I need a shower," she said, glancing at him over her shoulder.

"I'll join you in a moment," Marc said. She saw him take his phone from his pocket as she turned the corner and headed into the bathroom.

The luxurious space was more than Sera had imagined. Chrome fixtures gleamed; the light glistened on the strip of black bisecting the light teal-coloured wainscoting, the white old-fashioned sinks pristine. She stripped off her clothes, leaving them in a pile on the floor and turned on the taps of the bathtub. The edge of the tub was set high off the floor. She steadied herself on the glass half-screen as she entered. When the water hit her skin, she closed her eyes and let it stream over her, warming her tired body.

She stood in the shower for a long time, listening to the patter of water on the tub, splattering on the screen.

"Are you trying to use up all the water in the Thames?"

Her eyes snapped open. Marc leaned against one of the sinks, giving her an amused half-smile. Steam misted the air and covered the mirrors. She pushed her hair back and stepped forward.

"Coming in?" she asked. He took a towel from the rack and held it out for her.

"Not yet—you're too lovely to stay there—I have a bed to show you."

Sera turned off the water and left the tub, letting Marc wrap her in the towel. He was gentle, almost too gentle, and she wondered at it.

"I won't break," she said. She dried her face on a corner of the towel.

"I know." Marc's voice was uncharacteristically gruff and she glanced up in surprise. His gaze was troubled and his dark blue eyes were intent on her expression. She cupped his cheek, making sure he paid attention to her next words.

"I'll make you a wager," she said. His stance changed subtly, and she stifled her smile, knowing she had provoked a reaction. "No more treating me like spun glass."

"And what will be the forfeit?" Marc wrapped an arm around her waist, pulling her close. His free hand slid through the folds of her towel and roamed over her bare skin.

"If you lose, you can sleep on the sofa," Sera replied.

"But if I win?"

Sera dropped the towel and it puddled at her feet.

CHAPTER 2

Marc woke early, as he often did. The morning sun brightened the room even through the curtains. Sera slept on beside him, her face peaceful. As he leaned over to stroke her hair, he caught himself. That would surely cause him to lose their wager, and he had no desire to sleep on the sofa, not when he could be here beside her.

He'd woken in the night from a vivid dream, one where Jeremy Gordon had Sera by the throat, his knife flashing against her pale skin. Her steady breathing in the darkened room had brought him back to reality, reminding him that the dream was just a bad memory. He'd almost lost her.

Sera shifted and turned away from him and he rose from the bed, careful not to wake her. In the sitting room, he lounged on the sofa in his jeans, unplugging his phone from its charger and flicking through the messages. Someone had called from the firm, and he listened to the voice mail message.

"Call me, s'il vous plaît." Fournier's voice was terse and rather unlike him. Marc frowned. He'd only been away from Perron et fils for a month and Fournier was never so serious. He rang Fournier's private line at the firm, but as he expected, there was no answer. It was too early. He tried his mobile and after two rings, Fournier picked up. "Monsieur Perron? Merci, mon Dieu." That was more like the Fournier he knew, colourful and brash.

"What is so important, Fournier?" Marc kept his voice low. He rose from the sofa and went to close the bedroom door. "You were only to call me in the most dire emergency."

"We had an unexpected visitor last night, monsieur," Fournier said. Marc thought he heard a tremor in the man's voice, but he dismissed the angst as a connection quirk.

"And this is an emergency?"

"He said you owed him a Monet."

"Did he?" Marc kept his voice level.

"Aurore doesn't have any Monets on file, and you know as well as I do that masterpieces are rarely available on the open market. What were you thinking, dealing with this bastard?" As if realizing he'd stepped over the line with his boss, Fournier cleared his throat and added, "Monsieur."

Marc paced to the window. "I was thinking he'd understand the wait." In truth, he'd been hoping that money would satisfy Royale, and that he'd forget about wanting a Monet.

"He demanded to speak to you, and he was incredibly rude to Aurore when she wouldn't give him your whereabouts."

"Buy her a bouquet for me," Marc said. "Something expensive. I'll call Royale."

"Merci, monsieur." Fournier sounded relieved. "I will."

Before he called Royale, Marc went to check on Sera. She slept still, burrowed into the covers, her hair strewn over the pillow. He turned back, closing the door behind him.

"Monsieur Royale has been expecting your call," Royale's secretary, Françoise, said, her usual primness seeming especially sharp. He wondered how much she knew of Royale's business and who she really was. He'd never met her, not once. She put him on hold and while he waited, he paced over to the desk, glancing out the window. He shouldn't have to be talking to Royale—he'd meant to leave this all behind.

Maybe he'd been listening to too much Édith Piaf. There was no such thing as 'La Vie en Rose'—only in the song.

"Perron." Royale's stern voice came on the line. "I had not heard that you'd left Paris. Or left your business. You still owe me."

"You and I both know that there are no Monets up for auction in the near future," Marc replied. "When one does come up, I'll be in touch."

"I'm afraid, I can't wait that long," Royale said. "My wife's birthday is in a few months and I promised her. You know how I hate to break my promises."

"Have you considered commissioning a copy? I could recommend a few artists who are skilled in reproductions."

Marc heard Royale chuckle. "If only that would work. But you see, imitations are unsatisfying, rather like being given money instead of vengeance. It seems that Jeremy Gordon's boss didn't consider our offering sufficient. He misses his favourite hit-man."

"How unfortunate." Marc paced the length of the sitting room. He wanted a cigarette.

"He'd like me to investigate to find out who killed Gordon. Of course, I have no idea—at least for now, but I can't hold him off forever."

Royale knew very well who had killed Gordon, or rather, who Marc had let him think had killed the English hit-man. In this, he would protect Sera. "A Monet for your silence?" Marc let his derision show in his tone.

"A rather good deal, don't you think? Mayson wants to know about everyone who was there when Gordon died, and he's not bothered if he hurts a few innocents along the way."

"I would expect no less from a gangster."

"He's quite a proper gangster," Royale agreed. "Jean admires him a great deal, aside from his Englishness of course. He happened to mention that Gordon was seeing a lovely chanteuse. He didn't mention her name, but Mayson will likely want to know who she is."

Marc wanted to reach through the phone to throttle Royale, and watch the man's eyes bug out as his substantial cheeks went purple and his heavy body flailed, desperate for oxygen.

"He wants to speak with her," Royale continued, ignoring Marc's silence, "and find out what she knows, have her tell him about Gordon's last days. He was disappointed when I told him she'd quit, and I hate disappointing my friends."

"I doubt Mayson is your friend," Marc said, recalling a conversation he'd overheard where Jeremy Gordon talked to someone about the possibility of murdering Royale. Mayson surely would be the brains behind that operation.

"He and I have an understanding."

"I can't get you a Monet in that time frame."

"What has happened to the man who could provide whatever a client asked for? Your uncle would be disappointed in you, giving up the business for a woman."

Marc heard footsteps behind him. He whirled, startling Sera. She began to speak, but he laid a finger over her lips.

"No response? You've become a coward, Perron. What a pity. I thought you had such promise."

"I'll consider your proposal," Marc said. Sera gave him a puzzled look.

"That's better. Call me with an update in a few days. My wife loves the water lilies, but they're too big for our home, so I'm sure you can find something smaller."

"And Mayson?"

"He'll be disappointed that no new information has come to light."

"Appreciated."

Royale rang off and Marc put his phone on the desk, removing his finger from Sera's lips.

"Who was that?" she asked.

"Fournier."

"I thought he knew you weren't available?"

Marc drew her into his embrace. "You know Fournier—he just can't help himself sometimes." He rubbed her back through the terrycloth of her robe.

"Marc, you promised."

"I know, but I also promised Fournier I'd be available if he needed me." Marc kissed her, parting her soft lips, stilling any protest. "He didn't need me while we were in Marseille," he reminded her. "Please don't begrudge him a bit of my time now."

"All right. I know it's your family business. I can't imagine what such responsibility is like."

"It won't interfere with our plans," Marc vowed.

There was a knock at the door and Sera turned in surprise.

"Breakfast," Marc said, calling out, "Come in."

Edwards pushed a trolley into the sitting room, laden with a fresh tea service, which included two covered plates, a carafe of ice water, and another of orange juice.

"Good morning sir," he said, "and madam." He began to set up the meal on the coffee table, carefully laying out each plate, cup and saucer, and their accompanying cutlery. "Ms. Smythe will be here at eleven to take you on the tour of the properties. She will meet you in the lobby."

"Thank you, Edwards." Marc took the folder Edwards offered, emblazoned with the logo of the estate agent. He flipped it open and glanced through the pages.

"You arranged for all this?" Sera asked, taking the folder from Marc and sinking onto the sofa to closely study each listing.

"With Edwards' help," he replied. "I think we'll find some-where to live." He dug into his pocket, extending his hand to Edwards, proffering a tip.

"It's a shame you can't stay here permanently, sir," Edwards quipped. Marc chuckled.

"Even I can't afford that, I'm afraid."

Edwards grinned, then politely withdrew. Marc sat down next to Sera and poured a cup of coffee from the carafe, adding a dollop of cream. He set the cup and saucer in front of her before pouring his own cup.

"Is there anywhere that looks worthwhile?" he asked, leaning in to glance at the contents of the folder. Sera pulled a sheet free.

"This one is the cheapest," she said. "Marc, these flats are all so expensive. I can't possibly afford to live in any of these."

"We're in this together," he reminded her. "Besides, I want a place that's been soundproofed, and they're hard to find."

"I hadn't thought of that. It'll be easier to rehearse."

"And we won't have to deal with noisy neighbours," he replied.

Sera laid the folder aside and reached for her cup. "I could get used to this kind of place," she teased.

"If we stayed here at Claridge's, we'd end up bankrupt and not even Fournier could save us."

"But what a life." Sera laughed, and he loved hearing the joyous sound, as beautiful as her singing. In the last month, Sera seldom seemed to feel joy as she recovered from Jeremy Gordon's predation. While travelling to Marseille to take care of her aging mother, the burdens had been too great to render a smile. When they'd first been together, over five years ago, her laughter had come easily and often. He liked her return to happiness and he'd do anything to protect it.

"Perhaps we'll become famous and then we could stay here all the time," Marc said. "Or we could tour the world."

"The world?" Sera drained her cup and leaned forward to pour another. "I'll be happy with enough to live on. The world can wait." She lifted the silver cover from her plate and her eyes widened.

"You don't have to eat it all," Marc said. The plate held fried eggs, sausages, bacon, grilled tomatoes, and mushrooms. He lifted the cover from his own plate to reveal the same.

"Are you sure you can?"

"I'm hungry after last night," he said with a wink, picking up his fork and knife.

The estate agent, Joan Smythe, was cheerful when she met them in the lobby. She shook their hands and greeted them in proficient French. Sera let out a breath of relief. She'd envisioned a day of tagging along while Marc and the agent chatted in English.

"Now, I can understand why Edwards recommended you, Ms. Smythe," Marc said.

"Do call me Joan," she trilled. "There are so many French people moving to London that it's always prudent to speak another language." She matched Sera's pace as they walked to the door. "Now, it really will be you and I choosing your residence," she confided in a stage whisper. "In my experience, most men don't really concern themselves much with setting up house."

Sera thought of Marc's flat in Paris, with its modern furniture and carefully curated art and literature. "You might find yourself mistaken."

"Well, they do like a certain cachet in their properties, but where it really counts, the everyday living, that's where we ladies put our foot down."

They emerged from the hotel and a doorman stood beside an idling silver Mercedes-Benz. "That's mine," Joan trilled again.

"The congestion fee is expensive, I'll admit, but it'll be the easiest way to see all the properties we have lined up for you."

"As long as they're all close to the metro," Sera said. The likelihood of her driving was low; living in Paris, she'd never had to learn.

"Yes, of course. All the properties have good access to the Tube," Joan replied, putting some emphasis on the last word. Sera felt her cheeks flush as she ducked her head to climb into the car, and then she slid to the far side of the back seat. Marc settled beside her and put his hand on her knee.

Joan got into the driver's seat. "We'll start in North London," she said, "at a house in Islington. It's a bit close to the Emirates Stadium…"

"Ready for this?" Marc asked. Sera met his gaze. Was she ready? Leaving Paris was a huge step, and picking out a place to live in England made the transition all the more real. "It's mostly up to you where we stay," he remarked. Joan prattled on in the front seat, but they ignored her.

"You'll get some say," Sera replied, squeezing his hand. "You're the pickier one, anyway." She wouldn't think about the permanence of their situation, not yet. Better to pretend this was just a speculative jaunt.

"I am not," Marc chastised her, giving her a nudge. Sera kept a straight face, though she wanted to laugh.

"You are so, and you know it."

"It's delightful to see a couple so in love as you two are," Joan said, smiling into the rear-view mirror. She really did seem delighted; her eyes twinkled behind thin-framed glasses, with laugh lines crinkling at the edges. "I do envy you, of course, but I won't bore you with my life story."

Joan pushed a lock of her light blonde hair behind her ear. "But I want to hear all about you—such an exciting time it must be, to move here from Paris."

Sera didn't know what to say, but it didn't seem to matter as Joan kept up a running commentary, even answering some of her own questions. She'd never known anyone to talk so much, and almost wished the woman didn't speak French. Marc interjected a few comments about the weather, and business, but for the most part they were a captive audience.

"Here we are," Joan said, pulling into the only parking spot on the residential street. "It's just up ahead. End of terrace, reasonably sized…"

Sera tuned her out, emerging from the car and onto the uneven pavement. She paused on the sidewalk, looking up and down the street. Terraced, brick-fronted houses lined both sides. Some appeared well-kept, while others seemed a bit worn and in need of repair. Most of the front gardens were cluttered with garbage bins and off-street parking.

How dreary. She stifled a sigh. It seemed so utilitarian, utterly devoid of charm. Marc took her hand and they both followed Joan.

"We don't have to see this one if you don't want to," he said.

"We might as well. We're here."

"You'll say no, I'm almost sure of it," Marc said, "no matter how nice it is inside."

"Will I?"

"I can't even imagine us living here," Marc said in a low voice, so that Joan wouldn't hear. "Not my style, or yours."

They stopped in front of the house for let. It looked passable from the outside; its brick and trim were well maintained, and the small patch of grass was mowed and green. Once inside, its plainness seemed to echo the street's, with wall-to-wall beige carpeting and bare walls painted a similar shade. The furnishings were nice, but they looked as if they should be in a showroom rather than a home.

"The reception area is quite large, as the owners had the wall knocked out." Joan gestured, droning on and on. Sera let go of Marc's hand and paced through the room and into the kitchen. Plain again, but she could forgive neutral tones in a kitchen. She retraced her steps and headed upstairs, leaving Marc and Joan discussing the location. The first floor was more of the same dullness, the master bedroom dominated by a bed and built-in wardrobe. The second bedroom was empty, to her surprise.

"It could be our music room," Marc said, coming up behind her.

"So that's why you wanted soundproofing," Joan said from the hallway. "Edwards didn't mention that you were a musician."

"Sera's the true talent," Marc replied. "I'm more of an amateur."

"And what do you think of the property?" Joan asked. She directed the question to Sera, and Sera hesitated. It was nice enough, just not to her taste. It had no character, held no appeal.

"I'd like to see some of the other places first, but I don't think this is for us."

"It's not my favourite property either," Joan confided. "I think you'll like the next one much better."

They retreated to the car and Joan took them to their next flat. They drove down a small high street with a pharmacy and several fast food restaurants, a grocery store, and other shops.

"Archway tube station is over there," Joan said, gesturing to a grey building with the iconic sign. "The property is a short walk away, a little ways up the hill. And the Northern line connects to the Overground line and King's Cross station."

The names meant nothing to Sera, but Marc nodded. "That will be useful, however, I would prefer to be on the Piccadilly line."

"We're in the Highgate area now," Joan said, pulling into a spot near the top of the hill. She took them past two churches and a pub that looked like a small castle's keep. "I'm afraid the property is mid-terrace, but it is fully soundproofed. It isn't nearly as large as the last one, but it is a very nice space."

Joan unlocked the door and they found themselves in a hall painted a light green, with clean white wainscoting. A long staircase with a dark green carpet runner and a nicely polished wood banister caught Sera's eye. She hardly noticed the door on the left.

"It's a second floor flat," Joan said, almost apologetically. "But it has a lovely view."

"I like it better already," Sera remarked. The hallway alone had more personality than the entirety of the last house. She preceded Marc up the stairs, following the estate agent. The risers creaked slightly under their feet. On the second floor, Joan opened the single door with a peephole. She pushed the door wide and stepped over the sill.

A pale blond hardwood floor stretched the length of the entryway, leading into a reception room with a dark upholstered sofa, a cosy overstuffed chair, and a simple coffee table. A print of Seurat's 'Sunday Afternoon on the Island of la Grand Jatte' hung over the sofa and an area rug in similar shades of blue broke up the expanse of hardwood. Behind the chair, a bay window let in the afternoon sun, warming the light grey walls.

Sera liked it already. She could see green from the window, and she ignored everything else, walking over to peer out. Trees stretched as far as she could see and for a moment she didn't feel like she was in London at all. It was perfect.

"That's Waterslow Park," Joan said, coming over to stand next to her. "Lovely walks, but the cemetery's right there too." She gave a dramatic shudder. "Spooky place."

"I don't mind." Sera wasn't worried about the dead. The living were more dangerous. She'd often walked through the cemetery in Montmartre, especially when she needed a bit of quiet. Cemeteries were peaceful places.

"Come see the rest of the flat," Marc said. Sera turned from the window, but she knew she wanted to live here, no matter what the rest of the place was like.

They went through the remaining rooms in the flat; the master bedroom was on the small side, as were the kitchen and the bathroom, but the size didn't really matter.

"The second bedroom is a box-room," Joan said, opening the door to a room not much bigger than a closet. A skylight had been put into the ceiling and the sun on the pale walls made the space seem larger. Joan retreated into the reception room, but Sera lingered in the doorway.

"You've made up your mind, haven't you?" Marc said, leaning against the wall beside her. He'd removed his leather jacket and folded it over his arm, and it brushed against her dark cotton shirt.

"Maybe," she replied. "What do you think of it?"

"It'll do. It's a bit further out than I'd considered, but the area is nice enough. Let's look at the rest before we decide."

"If I have to," she said, taking his hand. "It is beautiful here."

Back at the hotel, Sera flopped onto the sofa with a sigh, kicking off her black derby shoes, not bothering to undo the thin laces. She seemed exhausted, her face pinched and pale. Marc caught himself before he said something. He wouldn't baby her. Their wager was still on.

He took a seat beside her and when he put his arm over her shoulders, she leaned into him. "Ready for dinner?" he asked. They had stopped for a coffee and cake in between viewings, but that was hours ago.

"Dinner?"

"We could go down to Covent Garden, see a show and have a meal."

"I don't think I could stay awake for a show," she replied. "But dinner sounds nice."

"I know a good Indian place," Marc said. "It'll be a change of pace."

Sera bent forward and grabbed her shoes, undoing the laces in order to put them back on. "I'm starving."

At the curb in front of the hotel, Marc paused.

"A cab, sir?" the doorman asked.

"I think we'll take the Tube to Covent Garden," he decided.

"Bond Street station is closest, just a block north," the doorman replied pleasantly, "though you'll have to switch at Holborn onto the Piccadilly line. Have a good evening."

Sera took his hand as they strolled along Brook Street and Marc realized it had been a long time since they'd had a normal evening out. "How far is it from here?" she asked.

"Only a few stops," he replied. "We'll pick up Oyster cards as well."

"Oyster?" She giggled.

"Like our Navigo," he said, squeezing her hand, "but why they call it an Oyster, I don't know."

At the ticket desk, Marc paid for two cards. Sera hung back until he drew her up beside him. "Feeling shy?" He'd never seen her so timid, even when they'd first met in that tiny, crowded bar on the Left Bank.

"I can't understand them much at all," she said, her voice soft.

"You'll get better with practice," he said. He hadn't considered whether or not she knew much English and he should have. Nor had it occurred to him that she might not be comfortable. "Didn't you and Sophie speak English occasionally?"

"Sometimes," she admitted, "but Sophie's a friend, and it's easier with a friend. I just don't want to make any mistakes."

"You will, but it won't matter."

They went through the turnstiles, scanning their cards, and walked down the tunnel to the platform. The display flashed "01" and he could hear the rumble of the approaching train. When they boarded, the train was already crowded, and he found them a spot near the door where Sera could lean against a padded bolster. Her head just brushed the low curved ceiling, and Marc took up a spot in front of her where he could stand without bumping his head.

"How about another wager?" he suggested. Sera raised a brow.

"Another one?"

"I'll wager," he said, "That you can't speak English for the remainder of our evening."

She pursed her lips, affecting an annoyed expression, though he could see the amusement in her eyes. "What is the forfeit?"

"If I win, then I get to pick where we live," he said, holding back his smile. Choosing which flat to rent would be the one thing that would convince her to take up his challenge. In the car, they'd debated the virtues of each flat, and he'd pushed hard for a luxurious third floor flat in South Kensington, knowing all the while that she was still stuck on the small flat on Highgate Hill.

"That's not fair," she retorted.

"But if you win, you can choose where we live, and I'll take you somewhere I know you'll love."

She pondered his proposition for a long moment, but was interrupted by the announcement, "Holborn Station." They disembarked and followed the signs to the Piccadilly line platform, where a train was just pulling in. Once aboard, she refused to speak. The train slowed again, and the recording announced, "Covent Garden."

"I agree," she said, her English strongly accented.

"And you can't just spend the entire evening silent," he said, also in English.

"Mind the gap," the recorded voice intoned. They shuffled off the train along with most of the other passengers, not gaining another chance to speak until they had taken an elevator to the surface.

"Are you sure about this?" Sera asked him as they exited the station, putting her arm through his. He tucked her hand into the crook of his elbow and held it there as they walked.

"Absolutely."

Sera didn't speak much as they walked, but he didn't press. She was too busy looking around at all the shops, theatres, and restaurants. He was in no rush. She still had all of dinner to get through. He directed them down a smaller side street and even though they were a block away, he could smell the spicy food.

"Mmmm." Sera inhaled deeply. She began to speak, then paused, catching herself. "Delicious."

They joined a short queue and when they reached the front, the host smiled warmly. "For two?"

Marc didn't answer. He looked pointedly at Sera. "Yes, two," she said, and he saw the awkward blush pinken her cheeks.

"Right this way." The host led them to a small table by the window. "Your server will be with you in a moment." He laid the menus on the table. Marc pulled out Sera's chair, then seated himself across from her.

"So far so good," he said, amused. Sera shot him a look and he knew that if they hadn't been in public, she might have smacked his arm.

"So you say." She enunciated every word, and then picked up her menu. He watched her brow furrow in dismay and she pursed her lips. He browsed his own menu and quickly decided what he wanted to order. Still, Sera perused hers with her mouth turned down in a frustrated moue.

A young woman wearing a black half-apron and the restaurant's uniform shirt stopped at their table, smiling warmly. A long dark braid hung down her back, and gold bangles clicked together on her wrist.

"Good evening," she said. "May I get you something to drink while you decide what to order?"

"Sera?" Marc nudged her foot and she looked up from her menu. "What do you want to drink?"

"I would like…" she began, her eyes skimming down the list, "A glass of white wine." She pointed to one and the server made a notation on her pad.

"And you, sir?"

"The same." He waited until the server had retreated, and then spoke. "You'll have to say more than that, ma chère."

"I will. Why do you get to speak French?"

Marc shrugged, then continued in English. "My dear. What will you have to eat?"

Sera's brow furrowed again as she looked at the menu. He wanted to stroke his finger over the wrinkles and smooth them away. She murmured words to herself, trying out the sounds, her finger hovering over a line on the menu.

The server returned with their wine and filled their water glasses. "Have you decided?"

Sera looked up, a nervous smile crossing her features. "I would like the…" and she paused to read the line on the menu once more, "…butter chicken, please."

"And any rice with that? Or naan bread?"

Marc knew the quickly asked question had overwhelmed her, as she stared at the server in silent confusion. He waited while Sera regained her equilibrium, and she spoke sooner than he expected.

"Bread, please." She folded her menu and handed it to the server.

"And yourself?" The server turned to him and he handed her his menu.

"The lamb curry and a side of dhal with garlic naan bread, please."

When the server left, Sera slumped a bit in her chair, resting her forehead on her hand. She didn't move for several long moments and Marc reached across the table to cup her cheek and gently dislodge her hand. Though her smile had fled, to his relief, she wasn't crying.

"I don't know if I can do this," she whispered in English. Instead of taking her into his embrace, as he wanted to do, Marc pressed a kiss to her hand, once on the back, and then he turned her hand over and pressed another to her wrist. Finally, he pressed a third kiss to her palm.

"I know you can do it," he said, holding her gaze. "Have courage, Seraphina." The use of her full name brought back her smile, slight though it was. He lowered their hands to the table, and with his free hand, picked up his wine glass. "To us."

Sera picked up her glass. "To us," she echoed. They drank. The server came by with their food and Sera let go of his hand. Marc laid a napkin in his lap as Sera thanked the server. When he glanced up again, a movement from the corner of his eye caught his attention and he turned slightly in his seat, looking out the window into the darkened street. People passed by, but he wasn't sure what, or who, had caught his attention. He studied the passers-by, then turned back to his meal. It was nothing.

CHAPTER 3

Sera was exhausted. Her head ached from concentrating, and all she wanted to do was crawl into bed with a cup of tea. They returned to the hotel and went straight upstairs, to her relief. She took off her shoes and left them in the entryway, walking straight into the bedroom. A bed had never looked so inviting. She sank onto the crisp white duvet, letting her body go limp. She heard Marc talking to someone in the hallway, probably Edwards.

A pain throbbed behind her eyes and she closed them, trying to ignore the ache as best as she could. She had paracetamol in her bag, but even getting out of bed seemed like too much of an effort. The mattress dipped and she felt Marc's warmth settle next to her. Soon, she smelled the spicy scent of his cologne. He gave her nose a gentle tweak and she opened her eyes.

"Edwards is bringing some tea," he said. His fingers ran over her forehead, massaging her temples before sliding into her hair and stroking her scalp. Sera closed her eyes again, this time bliss-fully. "I hope this doesn't qualify as treating you like spun glass," he said, laughter in his voice.

"No, it doesn't," she murmured. "Don't stop."

Sera heard the clink of china in the other room, then footsteps.

"Thank you, Edwards," Marc said, his finger movements continuing.

"Goodnight sir, madam," she heard Edwards say. She murmured a goodnight.

"Open your eyes," Marc said, his voice as soft as his touch. He leaned over her and when she opened her eyes, he began to undo the buttons of her shirt, one by one.

Marc drew the panels aside, baring her breasts in their delicate lace bra to his gaze. He bent his head and his lips ghosted along her sternum, then over her breast, his teeth lightly scraping her nipple through the lace. Her breath caught in her throat. Marc lifted his head.

"Does this help?" he asked. Before she could speak, he added, "English, remember."

"Yes." Her voice wavered as he bent his head again and paid the same attention to her other breast. He undid the front clasp of her bra and then his mouth settled on her nipple, hot and wet, sucking hard. Sera arched her back, pressing up towards him.

"Patience," he murmured against her skin. His fingers stroked down her side, over her ribs, slipping under the waistband of her trousers. She laced her fingers through his hair, but he took his time, trailing kisses down her belly until she quivered with need.

Only then did he undo her trousers, hooking his fingers into the waistband and dragging them over her hips and lower still. She lifted her buttocks off the bed and Marc pulled her trousers right off, dropping them on the floor. He laid his hand on her leg, his thumb stroking the soft flesh of her inner thigh.

"What would you like me to do?" he asked—still in English—as he placed a kiss on her belly just above the lace of her underwear.

Sera knew what she wanted, but she didn't have the words to voice her appeal. "I want you to…" She tried to think of a way to say it using words she knew, but her mind was blank. She groaned in frustration.

Marc chuckled as he traced a finger around her belly button. "I never thought I would have to teach you how to talk dirty again."

Sera remembered the first time almost as vividly as if it had happened only yesterday, though in truth it had been at least half a decade. Dirty talk was almost as mortifying now, as she'd always found it embarrassing, even though her body ached for release.

"Tell me," she pleaded.

"Anything for you," he replied. "You already know touch,"—he caressed her belly again—"but I don't think touch is what you want."

He shifted on the bed, moving lower, drawing her underwear down her legs, and dropping them to the floor. His warm breath fanned over her thighs. "What you want to ask me," he said, parting her legs with his hands, his thumbs resting in the hollows of her inner thighs, "is if I will lick your pussy." He glanced up, their gazes locking, his mouth hovering over where she most wanted him to be.

"Please, Marc, lick my pussy," she begged.

"You're a fast learner."

Marc's tongue teased her as it dipped between her legs, tasting, but with little pressure, at least at first. He flicked her clitoris and she nearly came off the bed with a gasping moan. He held her down, his strong musician's hands on her hips, sucking her clit into his mouth, teasing the sensitive flesh.

"Please, more," she managed to gasp out, barely remembering to say the words in English. Two fingers slid into her and her head fell back against the duvet. He added a third finger and pressed up into her most sensitive flesh while his mouth laved her clit. The sensations took her over the edge, her hands grasped at the duvet, her entire body went rigid. The pleasure rolled over her and she collapsed bonelessly on the bed.

Marc shifted, and moved up the bed beside her, and she felt the rough denim of his jeans on her bare skin. She reached out, and fumbled with the hem of his black t-shirt where it tucked into his jeans, rolling onto her side to face him.

Marc sat up and pulled his shirt over his head, then lay back down beside her. "Better?"

"Yes." Sera moulded herself against him, scratching her nails lightly down his back. She brushed her lips over his, softly, her tongue darting out to taste him. He cupped the back of her head and deepened the kiss. She could taste herself on his tongue.

Sera hooked her leg over Marc's, pulling him closer. She fumbled with the button on his jeans, finally pulling down the zipper. Marc broke off their kiss and helped her, shoving the jeans down his legs and off, along with his briefs, but then he held back.

"Tell me what you want," he said, giving her that amused half-smile of his.

Sera didn't bother with words. She wrapped her hand around his cock, stroking him from root to tip, running her thumb over the head. It was her turn to smile when she heard his sharp intake of breath.

"What do you want me to do?" she asked him, and she couldn't hold back her laughter. Marc thrust into her hand with a low moan.

"You're beautiful when you laugh," he said hoarsely—and in French. She knew she'd captured his attention then. She laughed again, delightedly, and used her leg over his to pull him on top of her, guiding him between her legs.

"I want you," she said, still in English. He penetrated her, sheathing himself in her wetness. She wrapped her legs around his waist.

"Pour toi, toujours," Marc rasped, abandoning English altogether.

Marc pulled out his phone and looked up the number for Dawson, one of his auction house contacts. If anyone would know of a

Monet for sale, he would. Dawson had as much experience in the industry as Marc, and he knew everyone there was to know in England's auction world. He finished his coffee and dialled the number.

"Dawson speaking."

"Hello Dawson. How are things?"

"Perron, how are you? I'm still disappointed that you didn't let me manage the baroness's estate sale the other month. It went off so well."

"She was too nice to work with," Marc replied. "You know how it can be with aristocrats."

Dawson chuckled. "I do. Have you called to make up for my lower income?"

"Possibly." Marc paced the sitting room as he talked, hoping against hope that Dawson would have a lead. "Have you heard of any Monets coming up for auction in the next couple of months? Anything at all?"

Dawson gave a low whistle. "You're asking for the moon, you know."

"I'd settle for the stars," Marc replied, "but they've built rockets to the moon, after all. Is there nothing? No studies, no sketches even?"

"Let me check." Marc heard the clack of computer keys, and Dawson hummed to himself as he searched. "Nothing in my database, and I don't see anything listed for the other houses either. I would have heard."

"That's what I thought."

"You know as well as I do that Monets rarely come up for auction."

"One of my clients has a hankering, so I'm making inquiries." Marc gave a wry chuckle, though in truth a chill ran through him. "He knew it was unlikely, but he's persistent."

"He'd better be rich then!" Dawson quipped. "I'll keep it in mind, and let you know if I hear of anything."

"Much appreciated."

"Not a problem. Just keep me in mind the next time you have a big sale."

"Of course. I'll let Fournier know too."

"He's taken over for you, hasn't he? I was surprised to hear of the changes." Dawson sounded puzzled.

"I had to step back for awhile," Marc confirmed, "but I'm keeping a hand in the business."

"Glad to hear you haven't thrown in the towel just yet." There was a muffled voice on Dawson's end of the line. "Must dash, I'm late for a meeting. I'll let you know if I find anything."

Marc hung up and slumped back onto the sofa. His legal avenues for finding a Monet were closing rapidly. He rubbed his eyes. There would be no getting around trouble now.

Sera emerged from the bedroom, yawning. Marc placed his phone on the coffee table and held out a hand. She walked over and settled sleepily onto his lap, all warmth and softness, her hair in a dark tangle, brushing his chin as she laid her head on his shoulder. He held her close.

"Don't you ever sleep in?" she chided, stifling another yawn.

"I could be convinced to come back to bed," Marc replied.

Sera squirmed on his lap, the terrycloth robe parting to reveal her bare thighs. "Is that so?"

His phone vibrated on the table, rattling his empty coffee cup in its saucer. Marc reached out to grab it, but Sera got there first. She frowned at him and held it out.

"Tell Fournier to stop calling," she said. "He knows better."

"This won't take long." Marc replied, answering the phone. "What can I do for you, Fournier?"

Sera slid from his lap, shooting him an annoyed look, and left the room. He heard the bathroom door close.

"I'm terribly sorry to bother you, monsieur, but a new client of ours has specifically requested you."

"A new client?"

"She's a friend of the baroness; her name is Mrs. Gillian Lancaster," Fournier explained. "And when she heard of how well the baroness did with her estate sale, she asked for a referral. Her husband died recently and she has to liquidate their estate in order to pay off mortgages and tax bills."

"It's a large estate?" Marc asked. He heard the water running, and he wanted to be in the bathroom with Sera, not talking to Fournier.

"Substantial," Fournier confirmed. "A collection of paintings, some sculptures, and a forest's worth of vintage furniture. She's able to keep the entailed family lands, but her husband had purchased a larger estate and furnished it lavishly, to their detriment."

"All right. Have Aurore schedule a meeting with Mrs. Lancaster and then send me the details."

Fournier cleared his throat. "I took the liberty, hoping you would be free later this morning, as she was most insistent. Aurore will send you everything you'll need."

"I see."

"I am sorry, monsieur, but it's a large estate, and as you're in London already—"

"I'll manage," Marc interrupted, "but never again, Fournier, not like this. You're lucky I'm not in the office."

"Yes, monsieur." Fournier sounded properly chastised.

"Aurore is sending the information soon? I'll need to review it before I go," Marc reminded him.

"Aurore is working on it right now. Thank you, monsieur."

Marc hung up and placed the phone back on the table. Sera had turned off the water in the bathroom, so he assumed she must be out of the shower. They needed to talk. His phone vibrated once with a message from Aurore and he skimmed the details. He had three hours before his meeting. Long enough to prepare.

He went to the bathroom door, but couldn't hear anything except an occasional drip of the tap. He knocked.

"Come in."

Sera lay in the bath, her head resting on a towel placed on the edge of the tub, her hair up in a bun. The water covered her body to her shoulders and he thought she looked like a mermaid, reclined as she was.

When he didn't immediately speak, she opened her eyes. "What? No excuses?" Her sharp tone seemed to fill the space, echoing off the tile. Marc stepped forward and hunkered down by the tub so that they were eye to eye.

"No excuses," he replied. "Just reality. The firm is still mine, even though Fournier manages it. This client will be a good one for the firm and she asked for me personally."

"She?" Sera's brows rose.

"She," Marc replied, "happens to be a Mrs. Lancaster, who is in her early seventies. "If that's what you're worried about."

"So your pretty words in the church were just words?"

"This is a legitimate client," Marc pointed out. "A wealthy old woman. Not a gangster or a thief. And dealing with her estate doesn't mean that I won't be with you."

Sera dropped her gaze. "That's something at least."

Marc dipped his hand into the water, entwining his fingers with hers where they rested on her knee. She glanced up at him and he saw the worry in her eyes, the concern for him.

"Forgive me?" he asked. She cupped his cheek with her free hand and the water ran down his cheek and dripped onto the floor.

"I don't want to see the business overtake you," she said. "Work was your life and you forgot everyone else, and about me."

"I never forgot you."

She nodded once, to herself. "Do you have to leave soon?"

"I have an hour or two before I need to leave, and I have a file to review," he replied. "We can have breakfast before I go."

A glimmer of a smile crossed her features. "Time for that later." She dipped her hand into the water. He tried to pull away but she kept hold of him, soaking his face and t-shirt with water.

Marc started to laugh. "Remember that you started this," he said, rising to his feet. He pulled off his shirt and undid his jeans, shoving them down his legs and off. "Now that you've gotten me all wet, you'd better share your bath."

"And if I don't?" she challenged. Before she could splash him again, he rested his hand on the cold-water tap. She stuck out her tongue. "You wouldn't."

"Try me." Marc slowly turned the tap and she sat forward, grasping his hand with both of hers. He let go of the tap and stepped into the tub behind her, lowering himself into the hot water. He relaxed back against the edge of the tub and stretched out his legs on either side of her.

"You…" Sera's hand sluiced over the surface of the water, soaking him. He grasped her wrist and pulled her against him, water sloshing over the edge of the tub.

"That wasn't very nice," he chided her, a teasing tone to his voice. She relaxed against him and he wrapped his arms around her.

"No, but it was still fun," she said. "And you're here with me, naked in a tub, in one of the most exclusive hotels in London. I don't see what you have to complain about." She delivered her words with a cheeky smile.

"I'm not complaining," he assured her. "Not at all."

She rested against him, her back to his chest, and he slid his hand into her hair, tilting her head back towards him. Her lips parted in expectation and he took her mouth in a bruising kiss. She sank into him, letting him ravage her mouth, her arm draping around his neck as she kissed him back, desire battling desire. Using his free hand to shift her position on his lap, his cock slid between her thighs. She arched into him, her hips moving against his pelvis, and he thrust inside her, drawing a gasp.

Marc loosened his hold on her hair and his hand drifted down her neck and shoulder and lower to cup her breast, catching her nipple between finger and thumb. Sera's wet hand came up over his and directed him lower still, between her legs. Her head dropped back to his shoulder and he felt her lips brush his jawline.

He turned his head and they kissed again. Sera moaned into his mouth as he thrust deep inside her, rocking his hips, his thumb pressing her clit. He grasped her hip, keeping her angled against him just right. They were making a mess of the floor, but neither of them cared. It felt too good.

Sera's nails sank into the skin of his upper back, but the pain only made it better, arousing him more. She whimpered and keened, meeting his thrusts, tightening and relaxing around him until he was nearly out of his head with pleasure. He nibbled along the length of her neck and shoulder.

"Marc," she begged hoarsely. "I'm almost—"

Marc bit down on the sensitive skin where Sera's neck met her shoulders. Not hard enough to mark her skin, but with enough pressure that she bucked against him crying out, tightening around him even further. Soon, an orgasm overtook her. He thrust again, feeling that shiver just before he came, clutching her to him.

When they came back to themselves, they were both breathing hard and the water had cooled. Sera lifted herself off of him and her arms shook as she braced herself against the side of the tub, rising to her feet. Marc pushed to his feet and stepped out of the tub, holding out his hand. With his help, Sera stepped out onto the bathmat, now half-soaked with water.

There were puddles around the tub, puddles neither of them had noticed. Sera leaned against him, stifling a giggle behind her hand as he slipped an arm about her waist.

"Oh dear."

"The cleaning staff won't mind," Marc said. He took a towel from the rack and draped it over her shoulders. "They've seen worse."

CHAPTER 4

Marc took his dark pinstriped suit from the closet and laid it over a chair. He dressed quickly and methodically, shrugging into a crisp white shirt and doing up the buttons, and pulling on his socks and trousers. He affixed his silver cufflinks to his cuffs, then studied the small selection of ties he'd brought with him from Paris. Sera came into the bedroom, clad in a black top, and a slim-fitting, over the knee black skirt, with her hair falling over her shoulders. She was elegant and chic, completely Parisian in this most English of hotels, and he felt a pang for his birthplace, but mentally shook it off. He wouldn't be returning home anytime soon.

"Wear the tie with the accents in purple thread," Sera suggested, coming to stand next to him.

"You think Mrs. Lancaster would like it?" he teased.

Sera smiled. "Of course." She took the tie from the hanger and looped it around his neck, tucking it under his collar. He stood still while she tied it for him, watching her nimble fingers on the silk, making minute adjustments until it lay just right.

"Merci, ma chère." He kissed her gently on the lips and she stood on her tiptoes, pressing closer to him for more. He'd never been one for domesticity, but he would give up a great deal to have her there with him always.

"How long will you be gone?" she asked when they broke apart.

"Several hours."

"I'm going to call Joan Smythe," she remarked. "Since I won our wager last night."

"See if you can get the keys and agreement from her today, and I can arrange for Claridge's to move our things over for us tomorrow. Then we can start rehearsing."

Sera grinned at his last words. "I've missed hearing you play over the past few weeks," she said, lifting his suit jacket from the chair. He took it from her and put it on and she straightened his cuffs and smoothed down his lapels.

"I'm sure Edwards would bring my cello from their storage if I asked," he said.

"I can be patient," Sera replied. "I don't want him to go to any trouble."

"He's fond of you," Marc said. The butler's service had been even prompter than usual; his attention to detail more impeccable, and Marc knew it wasn't the tips.

"Still, I can wait," she replied. "When will you be back?"

"I'll call you," Marc said, "but it should be mid-afternoon. Then I can fulfill the second part of our wager."

"The second part?"

"You haven't forgotten already, have you?"

They went into the sitting room and Marc scooped up his phone, sliding it into his pocket.

"Of course not. Where will we go?" Sera took her phone off its charger and perched on the armchair, pulling the estate agent's folder towards her on the table. She flipped it open and took out Ms. Smythe's business card.

He knew exactly where he'd take her, but he wasn't about to give it away. It would ruin the surprise and he wanted to see her delight. "You'll find out later, ma chère." He came around the coffee table. "À bientôt." Sera paused in her dialling and lifted her face up to him as he bent down. Their kiss was tender but brief, and he tweaked a lock of her hair as he straightened.

"Do Fournier proud," she teased, her voice following him out to the entryway, where he grabbed his leather jacket. He laughed.

"I shall, and I'll tell him you said so." He heard her laugh as he closed the door and headed down the hallway. He took the stairs to the lobby and once outside, one of the doormen hailed him a cab.

Mrs. Lancaster lived not far from the baroness, though her townhouse was on the smaller side. A butler met Marc at the door and ushered him inside, taking his coat.

"The ladies are in the salon, sir," the butler intoned, directing him down the hall. He could hear quiet laughter as they walked, pausing outside a door. The butler knocked before opening the door and then let Marc precede him inside.

"Mr. Perron is here, madam," he said.

Marc paused just inside the threshold, taking in the room. It was decorated in a feminine style with lavender patterned wallpaper, pale wainscoting, and lacy drapes drawn back from French doors that looked out into a small garden. He recognized the baroness, who reclined against a Victorian settee with dark purple upholstery. The woman who sat beside her could only be Mrs. Lancaster. She rose from the settee and came towards him.

"Mr. Perron, how do you do?" She clasped his hand in hers and rosewater perfume drifted to his nose. Her grey hair was perfectly coiffed and she wore only the barest touch of makeup, a bit of pink lipstick and a touch of powder. Her blue eyes were rheumy, but kind.

"It is a pleasure to meet you, madame," he said, "and to see you again as well, baroness."

"Didn't I tell you his manners were lovely?" the baroness said in a stage whisper to her friend. Marc chuckled.

"My reputation precedes me."

"And it's well-deserved, I see," Mrs. Lancaster said with a laugh. "Would you like a cup of tea?" She led him to the settee and he lowered himself to the chair after clasping the baroness's arthritic hand gently in greeting.

"I would, yes. Merci, madame."

Mrs. Lancaster fluttered about him and for a moment, he felt as if he were the client. She poured him a cup of tea, but he declined milk or sugar. Her fussing complete, Mrs. Lancaster resumed her place on the settee. "Mr. Perron, I won't mince words. My late husband was an utter spendthrift"—at this the baroness shook her head—"and he left me in the middle of an awful mess."

"My colleague Fournier mentioned something of the sort," Marc said in a neutral tone, taking a sip of his tea, a strong black tea that was almost bitter.

"The property itself is already listed, but its contents need to be catalogued and sold. "Ellen,"—she nodded to the baroness—"told me you were the very best."

"I'm flattered." Marc gave them a genial smile. "Have any of the art and furnishings been catalogued already, or do you have records?"

"I've had them brought from the house." She indicated a thick binder sitting on a nearby table. "My husband was at least thorough, but that book doesn't cover most of the furniture. Quite a bit came with the place when he bought it."

"I can't promise anything until I review the collection," he warned.

"Of course. Will you come out to the estate? I'll be there later this week, and you could catalogue it then. It might take you a few days, but I'm sure it will be worthwhile. My husband had expensive taste."

"That may be to your good fortune," Marc said, "unless he bought your items when they were at their height of value."

"Good lord, I hope not." Mrs. Lancaster picked up her teacup and took a long, bracing gulp. For a moment he wondered if she was drinking more than just tea.

Marc rose from the settee and took up the binder. He returned to his seat and laid it over his lap, browsing slowly through the pages. The paintings and sculptures were documented with receipts, some from auction houses, some from private collectors. He didn't linger on any one page, but skimmed the pages to take in artists' names and titles of works.

He couldn't discern any particular pattern. Most collectors stuck to a specific period, but the late Mr. Lancaster didn't seem to aspire to any one era. Two pages expressed Modernist works, a further page offered an image from the Renaissance, and a third painting revealed a minor Impressionist work. He paused, then continued to skim the pages as the baroness and Mrs. Lancaster chatted. In his quest to own expensive art, what might the chances be that the unmourned Mr. Lancaster might have had the foresight to purchase a Monet?

If only it was that easy.

He came to the end of the binder. No Monets.

The ladies' conversation stilled and they looked at him expectantly. Marc set the binder aside and lifted his teacup. The tea had gone cold, but he drank it anyway.

"Mr. Perron? Will the collection make money?"

Marc set down his teacup. "It looks promising thus far," he said. "Is this all the art your husband owned?" He rested a hand on the binder.

"I'm not sure," Mrs. Lancaster admitted. "Towards the end, he had become a bit senile, and he couldn't have told you if he'd tipped a waitress a tenner or a fifty."

"Then we'll have to do a full inventory," Marc replied. "I can verify the collection against the records and estimate values." He thought of throwing Dawson a bone. "I have a contact at one of the auction houses who is an expert in furnishings and he may be able to catalogue all the furnishings for you. And we could sell the collection through the house."

"Whatever you think best," Mrs. Lancaster said. "I shall put myself in your hands. Hopefully with the promise of payment, some of the creditors will be reassured."

"We shall do our best," Marc assured her.

"Don't worry, dear." The baroness reached over and patted Mrs. Lancaster's hand. "Mr. Perron is one of the best."

Sera ventured down to the lobby in search of the restaurant, steeling her nerves. Ms. Smythe would be meeting her for tea and to arrange for the keys and all the paperwork, but that wasn't what had her worried. She would have to speak English, and Marc wouldn't be there to help her. She paused at the entrance to the Foyer dining room and almost immediately a maître d' approached her.

"Will you be dining alone, madam?" he asked, and it took her a few moments to comprehend his meaning. But how would she explain that she'd be alone only at first?

"One, then two…later," she said hesitantly, feeling her cheeks flush.

"Of course, madam. Please follow me." He led her to a table for two in the midst of the room, the single free table in a sea of diners. He unfolded the menu and graciously held it out to her after she seated herself. She thanked him. "The waiter will be with you shortly."

She studied the menu carefully, slowly reading over the selections. Without Marc here to act as translator, she would have to try. Under salads, she saw a salmon niçoise, and she felt heartened. That, at least, she knew.

The waiter who came to her table presented a professional image with his brown hair neatly styled, yet he stood awkwardly stiff in his uniform, seeming more youthful than his co-workers. "Good afternoon, madame," he said in French. She gave him a tremulous, relieved smile.

"I'm so glad you speak French," she confessed. He grinned at her.

"It can be hard in a foreign country," he said. "What would you like to have for lunch? Are you all right with the menu?"

Sera ran her finger down the list of teas. "I would have an Earl Grey tea, s'il vous plaît," she said.

"Have you decided on a meal?"

"I considered the salmon niçoise, but I would like your recommendation."

"Everything is good," he said at once, "but my favourite is the lobster salad. The crème fraiche vinaigrette is very refreshing."

"That sounds perfect." She handed him her menu and relaxed back into her seat. The conversations continued around her, most in spoken English so quick that she couldn't even attempt to follow the conversations.

The waiter returned with her tea, laying out the service precisely, arranging the cream and sugar and a small bowl with slices of lemon to one side. He poured the first cup for her, and then retreated. She took a sip and added a small splash of cream.

While she waited for her meal, Sera set the estate agent's folder on the table and took out the page for the flat on Highgate Hill. If she could, she'd skip lunch and go there right now. She loved the hotel, but she wanted to be settled. Then she would be ready to find work.

"Madame Durand, there you are." Joan Smythe's voice trilled, cutting through the general murmur of conversation. She pulled out the chair across from Sera and sat down. "This is such a lovely hotel, isn't it?" She set down her purse and shed her jacket, hanging it over the back of her chair. She didn't wait for an answer.

"I'm so glad you chose the Highgate flat," she said. "I knew you'd choose that one. Did Mr. Perron object?"

"Not at all," Sera replied. She didn't feel like explaining their wager; it was too personal to share.

Joan chortled. "I knew he'd let you decide. Just a cup of coffee," she said to the waiter when he came to their table with Sera's salad.

"Could I have the keys today? I'd like to arrange for our things to be moved over."

"I'll need both of your signatures on the lease before I can deliver the keys," Joan replied. "Is Mr. Perron around? We could get it done straight away as I have all the paperwork with me."

"He's working, unfortunately."

"A pity." Joan clucked her tongue. "After lunch, we can go back to the flat and do the walkthrough. If Mr. Perron could meet us there, we could finish the paperwork."

"I'll call him." Sera pulled out her phone and dialled. It rang, but Marc didn't pick up. She left a short message, and then turned apologetically to Joan. "Hopefully, we'll hear from him shortly."

"So he's not just a musician?"

"He owns an art and antiques firm in Paris," Sera replied. "He has clients here also."

"Antiques? My mother-in-law is obsessed with that Antiques Roadshow—she swears half of what she owns are expensive heirlooms."

The waiter brought Joan's coffee and Sera ate as the woman

talked, hardly needing to interject more than a word or two. When she was finished, the waiter came by and collected her dishes. He laid down the bill.

"It has been charged to your room, madame," he said when she reached for her purse. "Just sign here." He proffered a pen and she signed the bottom of the bill.

"Merci."

Joan finished her coffee. "We'll take a cab to the flat," she said, gathering her things. "The ride shouldn't take us long, though the congestion this morning was so dreadful I left the car behind."

Sera rose, scooping up the folder and her purse. "Is it nice out? I should grab my jacket from the room." She should have thought to bring it with her.

"Best to have it, just in case. London's weather is unpredict-able." Joan followed her upstairs, and into the suite, she exclaimed over the luxury while Sera grabbed her black mid-thigh jacket from the closet and slipped it on. She took a light scarf striped in shades of blue and wound it about her neck. They retraced their steps, exiting the hotel, and a doorman flagged down a black cab. They settled in and it sped along, past expensive shops and then up Marylebone Road. Sera watched the signs flash by, but she didn't recognize the other streets, and she felt a bit lost.

Once in Highgate, they entered the front hallway and came face to face with a young Indian woman, her dark hair drawn back from her face, dressed in a police uniform. She smiled at them as she hurried out the door. Marc called as Joan unlocked the door to the flat. Sera fished her phone from her purse as she stepped over the sill. The heels of her sandals clicked on the pale hardwood floor.

"Are you still at the hotel?" Marc asked.

"We just arrived at the flat," Sera said. "Is your meeting over?"

"It was quicker than I anticipated. I'll be there shortly."

Sera slid her phone back into her purse. Joan had laid out the paperwork on the small square table in the kitchen. Sera glanced at the top sheet of the lease, but aside from her name and Marc's, and a few other words, the words might as well have been written in Greek.

"All the paperwork is in English," Joan remarked with an apologetic smile.

"That's all right. Marc will be here shortly."

"That will give us enough time to do the walkthrough," Joan said, picking up a stapled packet from the table. She clicked her pen. "Let's start in here, shall we?"

Joan was thorough. She inspected every cupboard, every appliance, and even the floor for dings and scrapes. Then she made notes on her papers. She did the same in the bathroom, noting a chip on the side of the bathtub, and a small crack at the edge of the mirror. The slight imperfections didn't really matter to Sera. She liked the blue and white patterned tiles, similar to the ones in her tiny flat back in Paris. They were a bit of home away from home.

Her phone buzzed as she and Joan went into the large living room.

"I'm just about there," Marc said. "Can you let me in?"

Sera went to the bay window and peered down into the street. A black cab had just pulled up outside. "I'll be right down," she said.

Joan held out the keys. "We'll program the door code for you before I leave."

Sera smiled and took the keys, and hurried down the stairs and pulled open the front door just as Marc came up the steps. He grinned at her.

"You're all flushed," he said, bending to kiss her, cupping her cheek, his thumb stroking over her cheekbone.

"I ran down the stairs," she said when they broke apart.

"It's more than that," Marc replied. He studied her and she stood still under his inspection, wondering what he saw. "There's a sparkle in your eyes. It's been a long time since I've seen that."

Without warning, he scooped her up, sweeping her off her feet and carrying her over the threshold. She gasped and clutched at his neck. "Marc!"

"I couldn't resist," he said, kissing her again. Sera glanced up the stairs.

"Are you going to carry me all the way up?" she asked sweetly.

"Are you saying that I couldn't manage it?" he asked, pretending to drop her. She giggled.

"It is a long way."

Marc started up the steps, moving purposefully and easily. He paused in front of the door on the first floor landing.

"Are you sure you want to go further?" she asked.

"It's tradition," he said, barely sounding winded.

"But we're not married," she replied. Marc chuckled.

"We aren't," he allowed, "but it is still our new place," and he emphasized the word 'our', "and the tradition stands."

When they reached the top, Marc stepped into the apartment and let her down. Sera wished he could have held her longer. She leaned against him, her arm around his waist, her head resting against his chest. His heart beat under her ear, a sound that soothed her.

"Bienvenue chez nous," she said. She'd never thought any of this could happen, that they would be together, or even that she was alive. An image of Jeremy Gordon, bloodied and coming for her, swam across her vision. She shivered. Marc tightened his arm around her.

"You're safe, I promise you."

"Ah, monsieur, you've arrived."

Sera raised her head. Joan had emerged from the bedroom, her list in hand. She made a few notes, then stopped, giving them a once over.

"My apologies. I didn't realize I was interrupting something."

"Quite all right," Marc said, loosening his embrace. Sera

wished he had kept his arm around her, but she felt reassured that their fingers remained twined together. "I understand there are some papers to sign?"

"In the kitchen," Joan replied. "I'll just finish up in here and then we can take care of the lease. Overall, the flat is in very good condition." She walked the perimeter of the living room and made a notation on her pages, then ushered them into the small kitchen. Marc picked up the lease and read through it, then took a pen from the inner pocket of his suit jacket. He marked a section of one page, crossing out a few words and writing in new.

"We'll do six months at first," he explained, "then we'll renegotiate." He looked at Sera. "By then we'll know if we'll stay, in which case, I'd rather buy a flat."

"Understandable," Joan remarked. She glanced at Marc's addition. "If you would sign please, monsieur."

Marc signed on the line indicated and then gave his pen to Sera. She signed beside his name and then Joan signed and dated the lease. She took a second set of keys from her pocket and laid them on the table.

"If you have any questions, please do call. The information for the management company is in the folder, and they'll take care of any repairs and such, if required." Smiling widely, she shook their hands and then left them alone in the flat.

"Our apartment," Sera whispered, almost in awe. Now it was done, and they were truly staying in London. Marc squeezed her fingers.

"And this calls for a bit of a celebration. A nice dinner, a little surprise…" He winked at her.

"Where are we going?"

"It's a surprise," he repeated. "And then we'll go back to Claridge's and have one last night in ridiculous luxury."

Sera laughed. "It will be perfect."

They took the tube from Archway Station and transferred onto the Piccadilly line at King's Cross.

"We need to stop at Leicester Square," Marc told her. "Then we'll walk to Charing Cross Road from there."

They didn't walk far, and Sera wasn't quite sure where they were when they stopped walking, and she wasn't sure why.

"Where are we, exactly?" she asked. Marc led her through a glass door and she found herself in a huge bookshop.

"There are four floors, but there's one section in particular I think you'll like." He took her upstairs and though she wouldn't have minded looking at some of the books they passed, even if they were in English, he didn't give her time to stop. They came to a section of floor to ceiling shelves, and at first, Sera couldn't understand why he'd brought her here, but then the titles seemed to leap out at her from the shelves.

French titles.

It was like seeing old friends again, the ones you thought you might not ever see again. Sera stepped forward and pulled a book from the shelf, Colette's 'Gigi', and flipped through it. She turned to Marc.

"There are translations just across there," he said, looking pleased with himself.

"You know just how to make me happy." She moved into his embrace once more and he bent to kiss her, though it was a chaste kiss.

"Now you won't feel so homesick," he replied.

"May I help you?"

Sera turned in Marc's embrace. A young woman dressed in a shop uniform stood nearby with her red hair pulled back into a braid. A look of hurt flashed over her features and her eyes widened in surprise. Sera felt Marc tense beside her, and she glanced up at him. He'd become almost expressionless. It all came together. Sera remembered the receipt that had fallen from one of his books in his flat. It had been signed 'Madelaine', and Sera would bet the contents of her bank account that the book receipt's Madelaine and this girl were one and the same.

CHAPTER 5

"Marc, won't you introduce me to your friend?" Sera could tell the girl didn't understand her, so she said it again in her halting English. "Madelaine, isn't it? Enchantée." She held out her hand to the girl, stealing a glance at Marc, who couldn't hide his surprise this time.

Madelaine shook her hand politely, but with obvious reluctance. "Pleased to meet you," she said, though she was anything but pleased. "And you are?"

"Seraphina, Marc's…" she didn't know which word to use, and she glanced at Marc again in confusion. His hand rested on the small of her back, a purposefully possessive gesture.

"She's my heart, mon amour," Marc said. At his words, Madelaine's professional veneer crumbled. Sera heard Marc talking, explaining, but he spoke too fast in English for her to follow. Whatever he said to the girl didn't soften the blow. Madelaine's expression faltered further, then slid into a neutral mask, but her eyes were bright. She brushed a lock of hair behind her ear and a silver cufflink glinted at her wrist. Sera's brows rose. So it was like that.

"Let me know if you need any help," Madelaine said tightly before retreating.

Sera turned to Marc. "What did you say to her?"

"That we were together, and not to make a scene."

Sera grimaced. "That wasn't very kind. She's the one you were seeing, wasn't she?"

"Was." His tone told her that he didn't want to talk about it.

"But you're fond of her and she's in love with you. Why else would you give her a set of your cufflinks?" Sera tamped down the jealousy that rose inside her, knowing that he'd been intimate with the girl. In spite of her liaison with Marc, she envied Madelaine's youth, her slender form and pale freckled skin, and the slight air of innocence about her. Aside from her complexion, Sera could have reflected a younger image of Madelaine, five or six years ago.

"It was easy to indulge her, and it's not like those cufflinks were my favourite pair."

"She's pretty," Sera said, "but you never broke things off with her, did you?"

"What for?" Marc was irritated now. "I promised her nothing, no commitment; she knew that."

"I don't know that she did. Marc, you need to go talk to her— you can't leave it like this." She nudged him in the direction Madelaine had gone. "I'll wait here."

"It's too late, Sera. What's done is done."

"Either you talk to her or I will," she said. If she had to, she'd do her best to soften the blow. When Marc still hadn't moved, she added, "I felt like that when you slept with Xavière back then. You at least owe her an explanation."

Marc frowned. "Xavière was a mistake," he said, "A horrible mistake."

"I know."

"You know I love you, Seraphina."

"I know." She turned her attention to the books. "I'll be here when you're done."

Marc searched almost the entire shop before he found her, hidden away behind a shelf of military history. Madelaine held a small stack of books and she shelved them methodically. She didn't look at him, though she knew he was there.

"I'm sorry, Madelaine," he said, keeping his voice low so they wouldn't be overheard. She didn't speak to him, didn't even give him a glance. He waited, and when she'd shelved the last book, she turned to him.

"That was really low," she said, her hands clenched at her sides. "Did the two of you laugh and gossip about me, about how young and gullible I was?"

"I never spoke about you to her," he said. It was mostly true.

He'd never mentioned Madelaine by name.

"If you didn't speak about me, then how did she know my name?" Madelaine retorted.

"I don't know."

"You could have called, and told me you'd found someone new. Even that would have been kinder."

"Sera isn't new."

"Then you cheated on her when you were with me?" Madelaine was incredulous.

"When I met you, we weren't together," Marc replied, "but Sera and I have a long history."

Madelaine drew in a sharp breath. "Did you care for me at all?"

"If I didn't care, I wouldn't have come back," he said. "And I certainly wouldn't be here, speaking to you now. I'm sorry I hurt you."

"After the first time, I doubted you'd be back," she said. "After the second time, I thought maybe—and the third time, I really thought our relationship might have been something more than fucking."

Marc didn't know what to say to that. To him it had been more than fucking—she was smart and beautiful, and every man's dream—but she wasn't Sera, and he hadn't been able to keep himself from thinking of Sera, even when he'd been with Madelaine.

"A great deal has happened since I last saw you," he said finally.

"In a couple of months? How much could happen in so short a time?" She crossed her arms and shifted her weight, her brow rising.

"In a matter of hours, everything changed," he said, "And the situation wasn't pretty, or fun, but circumstances brought Sera back to me and I won't lose her again." His voice had thickened over his last few words and he cleared his throat. "I will not come here again, if that will make it easier for you."

Madelaine sighed, her skeptical posture relaxing. She looked at him with sympathy now, though the hurt still shone in her eyes.

"I don't think I've ever seen you like this," she remarked, her words holding no insult, no scorn. "I suppose I have Sera to thank for that, for making you seem more human, and less…" she paused, pondering, searching for a word. "Cocksure."

Marc chuckled dryly. "She'd be delighted to hear that."

Madelaine glanced away, looking down the aisle. "I need to get back to work," she said. "Don't stop coming here on my account, but don't expect me to come talk to you, at least not for awhile."

"Je comprends. We may be here more often—we have moved to London for the time being."

Madelaine looked startled. "What brought that on?" she asked. "I thought you would never leave Paris."

"It's a long story."

"Maybe one day you'll tell me. Over drinks, perhaps." Madelaine started away. "Goodbye, Marc."

Sera spotted Marc when he walked around the corner, his expression grim. She itched to know what they had shared, but didn't want to pry. When he reached her side, she took his hand.

"Ça va?"

He shrugged. "Pas mal. Have you found anything to read?"

"Just a few things." She indicated at the pile of books at her feet. "You know you shouldn't let me loose in a bookshop." Aside from two novels in translation, one of the staff had helped her find a couple of books on learning English, and a French-English dictionary. She let go of his hand and bent to pick up the stack. For a moment, her grasp slipped and Marc steadied the pile.

"This isn't too bad. I expected more."

"Next time," she assured him.

Once outside, Marc directed her down Charing Cross Road, back the way they'd come. When she went to cross the street to the Tube station, he stopped her, grasping her hand.

"Hungry yet?" he asked.

Sera's stomach answered before she could, giving a loud gurgle. "I guess that says it all."

Marc chuckled. "I know just the place, a little home away from home. Did you notice where we're standing?"

Sera shrugged. "What am I missing?" She felt like she'd spent every moment so far gawking like a tourist. Her neck ached from craning it to take in her new surroundings, and her eyes were starting to feel scratchy.

Marc gestured to the restaurant on their right, an eatery with large plate glass windows set in red-painted wood, and gilt lettering that read 'Café Rouge'. Sera's throat tightened and she tamped down a wave of homesickness. Marc opened the door; the curved glass glinted in the late day sun.

Inside, the café did feel like home, with a dark wood floor, walls painted a cheery yellow, with a small bar off to one side. It wasn't very busy yet and a hostess came to greet them. She spoke in English, somewhat ruining the effect of the decor, but Sera didn't mind. She led them to a table and gave them their menus. Again, in English, but the variety of dishes were just like home. Sera relaxed in her chair.

"It is a bit like home," she said. "How did you find this place?"

"By chance," Marc replied. "The café belongs to a chain, but I like the French flair. I was famished one day and it was nearby. And it doesn't serve English food."

"English food?"

"The usual restaurant fare—lots of breads and fried food. Pizza, sandwiches, fish and chips." He glanced at his menu. "Their liquor selection here is good—you won't ever have to explain how to make a kir royale."

"I wonder if they have music here in the evenings," Sera said, looking around. There didn't seem to be a spot for a stage. A pity. She would have liked singing here.

"I don't know. Are you making a list?"

"I will be, once we have moved in, but I dread auditioning again."

"Just go in for a drink and start singing," Marc suggested, giving her a wink. "It worked well the last time."

"It did," Sera acknowledged. "One of our better wagers. Do you think I should choose '*La Vie en Rose*'?"

"It's familiar, people like it. I know once you audition, you'll be getting lots of offers."

"A shame your cello is so big, Marc—it won't be as easy for you to audition."

Marc shifted in his chair. "About that—I will need to leave the city next week to catalogue Mrs. Lancaster's late husband's collection. You'll have to start on your own."

Alone? Sera's hands went cold and she tried to suppress a nervous shudder. The server arrived and they ordered, and when she left, Sera found her hands were shaking.

When they returned to the hotel, Sera was quiet—too quiet. Marc spoke to Edwards and arranged for their things to be moved into the flat at Highgate Hill in the morning, then bid the butler goodnight. He found Sera in their bedroom. She stood at the open closet door, perusing the dresses she'd brought with her from Paris.

"You look lovely in all of them," he said, and she smiled, but the joy was short-lived. "Don't be nervous. You'll charm your audience so much, that they'll demand encores."

"I hope so." Sera came into his arms, relaxing against him with a sigh.

"Don't worry so much," Marc said. He knew how to take her mind off things. As he'd done earlier that day, he scooped her up in his arms, except this time there wasn't far to go. He dropped her into the centre of the bed, and Sera rose onto her knees before him, catching his tie in her hand. Using it as a lead, she tugged him towards her and he let her. She undid the knot and slid the silk away from his neck, letting it dangle in her grasp as she held it out to him.

"You didn't bring your handcuffs, did you?"

He took the tie from her hand and she pulled her shirt over her head, dropping it to the floor, soon her bra followed. She unzipped her skirt and let it fall, pushing the lace of her underwear over her hips and off. He hesitated.

"You're doing it again," she said. "Remember our wager?"

"Are you sure?" He had to ask. Since that night with Jeremy, their lovemaking had become tame in comparison to the time before. At first, she'd seemed unwilling for more between them, but as they became comfortable with each other again, Marc held back for fear of hurting her or going too far.

"Oui." She knelt on the bed, her hands on her knees, waiting for him. Her dark gaze smouldered, her lips parted in anticipation.

Marc stepped forward, cupping her cheek with his free hand before sliding it down her neck and into her hair. He twisted her hair in his grasp, tight, forcing her head back, exposing her throat. He kissed her hard, his tongue pressing past her lips, tasting her, devouring her. She yielded, then responded, battling with him for dominance until he broke off the kiss.

"On your stomach," he said, and she complied. He braided her hair, pulling it away from her face, and then grasped her wrists, tying them behind her back. Her legs dangled over the edge of the bed and Sera shifted until her hips aligned with the edge.

The desire rose in him so sharp, he nearly took her right then. He breathed in, tamping down the urgent need, Pausing to get himself under control, he shrugged out of his suit jacket and hung it over the chair. When he returned to the bed, he parted her thighs, sliding two fingers into her wetness. She tightened around him, tilting her hips back, trying to make him go deeper.

He gave her buttock a sharp smack, and heard her gasp. Redness bloomed on her skin, forming the shape of his handprint. So delicate. He withdrew his fingers and slapped the other cheek, pairing the handprints.

Stepping back again, he unbuttoned his shirt and draped it over the chair with his jacket. Then he returned, delivering two sharp slaps, and then a third set. Her intake of breath made him smile and he caressed her over the reddened skin, then down between her legs again. Two fingers slid inside her easily; she was slick with arousal.

"Oh, ma chère." He pressed a third finger into her, curving his fingers into her g-spot. She moaned, squirming on the bed. He withdrew and she sobbed out a plea. "Not yet."

Marc lowered himself to one knee, letting his breath ghost over her thighs. He had to taste her desperate arousal. Holding her legs apart, he flicked his tongue over her clit and though she tried, she couldn't move away. Her breathing grew ragged as he tasted her, bringing her close to orgasm, but he pulled back before she could let go. They weren't even close to finishing yet. He loved bringing her to the brink again and again. It was a torturous pleasure for both of them.

He sat back on his heels. The wetness dripped down Sera's thighs and she had twined her spread fingers together, her knuckles white and resting on the small of her back. Light as a feather, he ran a finger down the back of her thigh. She was so beautiful. He stood. They both needed more. He shucked his trousers and briefs and bent over her, laying a kiss on the back of her neck, covering her with his body, his cock teasing between her thighs.

"Marc, s'il te plaît," Sera begged hoarsely, pressing her thighs together, drenching him in her wetness.

Marc took a deep breath, parting her thighs with his hands, and thrust home. She took him in to the very hilt and that tight heat was nearly his undoing; her whimper of pleasure had him teetering on the edge. He held himself there, deep within. She quivered around him and his grasp tightened on her hips hard, even as she rose on her toes to get closer to him, arching her back, doing everything she could to get him to move.

Marc withdrew almost completely and she struggled against his grip, though her position left her with little leverage. He thrust deep and she spasmed around him, her eyes closing, her mouth in a silent scream, her entire body rigid with her orgasm. He withdrew again, slowly, tormenting himself as much as he tormented her, drawing the sensations to a fine point, where his breath stuttered in his chest.

He saw stars.

"Now that was like our first few times," Sera said, tucking herself next to Marc under the covers of the big bed. He could hear the faint traffic noise from outside, and the glow of the streetlights came through a crack in the drapes, but it was otherwise peaceful.

"So, I won't have to sleep on the sofa tonight?" Marc asked, giving her arm a gentle pinch.

"Not tonight," she quipped. He chuckled.

"Wager or not, you know I won't let anything happen to you," he said, his voice surprisingly gruff. His hand covered hers where it lay on his chest.

"I know."

CHAPTER 6

In the morning, they packed their suitcases, preparing to check out. Sera lingered in the door to the suite, taking everything in for one last time.

"You'll miss this place, won't you?" Marc said. "As will I, but we can always come back when you need a little pampering."

"Or when I get tired of cooking," she replied. Marc chuckled.

"That's why there's takeaway."

A porter helped them with their luggage, supervised by Edwards.

"Your things will arrive at the flat in a couple of hours," he said. "We have it all arranged."

"Much appreciated." Marc shook Edwards' hand and Sera noticed he'd given the man a substantial tip. Edwards accompanied them to the door of the hotel and helped the porter load their bags into the black cab that sat waiting.

Sera smiled at the butler and held out her hand. "Thank you, Edwards," she said in English. He took her hand and bent over it like a knight of old might have done. "My pleasure, madam. I hope we shall see you again soon."

The journey to the flat seemed more familiar now. Sera recognized some of the street names and signs as they passed, and when the cab began its ascent of Highgate Hill, she sat forward in her seat.

"Almost there," Marc said, resting his hand on her thigh.

When they arrived, it took them several trips to get all their bags upstairs and Sera wished for a porter as she struggled to carry each one. Finally, she dropped her bag to the floor and wiped her forehead. Marc came in behind her with the last suitcase.

"We'll have half an hour before the rest of our things arrive," he said.

"Just enough time for a coffee," she replied, "if there is any." She went into the kitchen, and searched through the cupboards. Though they had a full complement of dishes and pots, there was no coffee, or any other food. Sera sighed. "Do you think we have time to go out for a coffee?"

Marc leaned against the door frame. "I'll wait for the movers if you want to get the coffee." He winked, and she rolled her eyes.

"But I'll have to speak English," she said dryly.

"Every little bit helps," he said, "but espresso is much the same anywhere."

Sera nudged him with her elbow as she passed him, and picked up her purse from where she'd left it on the sofa. "Do you just want an espresso, or something more?"

"A latte, s'il te plaît," he said, coming up behind her. "And a croissant, if they have any."

"All right." She rose on her toes to kiss him. "I'll be back soon. Have fun with the movers."

Sera skipped down the stairs and ran outside onto the sidewalk, soon heading down the hill toward High Street. She couldn't remember if there had been a coffee shop, but there had to be. Her vague memory of the High Street served her well and she found a coffee shop next to an Indian takeaway. Inside, there was a short queue at the till. She joined the end, looking up at the menu chalked onto the wall. She repeated her order to herself, dreading not being understood by the clerk, a harried young woman in a rumpled shirt and apron.

Someone bumped her from behind and she glanced back. A thin-faced man with a two-day shadow, wearing a dark suit that hung on his lean frame, typed furiously into his phone, and compulsively shifted his weight from one foot to the other. When he realized she was staring, he looked up, and scowled at her before dropping his attention back to his phone.

"Next," the clerk said, and Sera realized it was her turn. She stepped up to the counter and gave her order.

"Two lattes and two croissants," she said carefully.

"Large or extra-large on the lattes?" the clerk asked, snapping the gum in her mouth.

"Large?" Sera wasn't sure.

The clerk leaned over to check the bakery case. "No croissants. You want something else?" When Sera didn't reply straight away, the girl signed and gestured to the case, repeating in a slow, loud voice, "Something else?"

Sera studied the bakery items, trying to decipher the handwritten cards. Finally, she pointed to something that looked edible, a sort of scone with fruit. "Two, please."

The clerk rang in the order and Sera found a £10 note in her wallet. The girl snapped her gum again and made change, handing her the coins.

"Merci," Sera said out of habit, then blushed. "Thank you."

"Have a nice day," the clerk said, her gaze already moving past Sera. "Next."

Sera waited for her order and when it came, she stuffed the scones into her purse, and carried one cup in each hand. Even though the cups had plastic lids, she tried not to jostle them as she walked carefully back up the High Street. At the front door to their building, she paused. Before she had to decide whether to put the cups down or stack one on top of the other while she dug for her keys, the door opened. The young woman from the other day stood there, wearing the same uniform as before, but with a bowler cap covering her hair. She smiled and held the door wide.

"Come in," she said. Her English was accented, but she spoke clearly and Sera could at least understand her words. Sera passed into the hallway.

"Mer—thank you." She corrected herself as she spoke.

"You're new here, aren't you?" the young woman said. "I'm Pari Kumar; I live on the first floor just below you."

It took Sera a moment to process what she'd said. "Nice to meet you. I'm Sera Durand." Sera glanced at the coffees she held.

"Vous êtes française?" Pari asked. Sera was startled.

"Oui."

"I went on an exchange," Pari said, answering the question Sera was about to ask. "Comes in handy sometimes for my job."

"You're a"—Sera studied the uniform—"police officer?"

"PCSO," Pari said, "but it's almost a police officer. I'd like to be a proper WPC eventually."

The acronyms left Sera puzzled. Pari translated them into French for her.

"Police Community Support Officer," she explained. "And a police constable. Will you be living here long?"

"Six months or more," Sera replied.

"Knock on my door sometime," Pari said. "We can go for coffee. You can practice your English, and I can practice my French. D'accord?"

"Oui." Sera smiled and Pari headed out the door with a jaunty wave.

Marc was directing the movers when the phone rang. They had arrived shortly before the call and were gamely hauling cases, including his cello, up the stairs to the flat. He followed them up as he answered.

"Oui?"

"When can I expect the Monet?" Royale inquired.

"I said I'd call when I had something," Marc replied.

"You didn't mention you'd gone away," Royale said, his tone conversational. "London's lovely this time of year, and Mademoiselle Durand, even in her typical Parisienne black, looks as if she's settling in. One wouldn't even know she'd been with Jeremy Gordon."

A chill ran down Marc's spine.

"Nothing to say? I know your petite femme will be back soon, so I won't linger."

Marc interrupted him. "What the hell are you playing at?"

"Just making a point," Royale said, still amiable. "Don't try to fob me off. I might be in Paris, but that doesn't mean you're home free." He coughed, a wet, thick sound that made Marc grimace and hold the phone away from his ear.

"I have a line on something," he said, though it was a complete fabrication, "but I need time."

"Keep me apprised," Royale commanded. "Françoise will take messages." He rang off.

"Sir, where would you like these?" One of the movers held two cardboard boxes—neither exceptionally large, but they were heavy. He shifted under the strain. Books.

"In the reception room," Marc said. "Anywhere."

Where was Sera? He thought she'd be back by now. Someone knew where they were, someone who worked for Royale. He looked out the bay window and down the street, but he couldn't see her. Crossing the room to the door, he pulled it open and was about to start down the stairs when she came around the corner to the last flight, carrying two takeaway cups, and a paper bag that poked out from her purse.

Marc had never been so glad to see her. He met her on the stair, taking the cups from her. "I was beginning to worry," he said.

"I wasn't gone that long, was I?" she asked, kissing his cheek before she moved past him and into the flat. "There was a line in the shop and only one clerk making coffee."

He took a deep draught of his latte. "You know how I am about my coffee."

"Of course." She set the paper bag on the coffee table atop one of the smaller boxes. "No croissants though."

The movers came to the door. "That's all of it, Mr. Perron," the one man said. When he saw Sera standing there, he nodded and added politely, "Madam."

Marc pulled out his wallet and handed each man a tip, however, neither would take the money. "The hotel's already paid us," the one man explained, "so no worries." They departed and Marc closed the door behind them, making sure it locked.

"Where shall we start?" Sera asked, turning in a slow circle to take in the boxes and general clutter. Marc went to the bay window again, and glanced down into the street, his gaze sweeping the road, the sidewalks, the cars—but if anyone observed them, he was well hidden.

"Most of the unpacking is in the bedroom," Marc said. Sera's clothes and his waited in cardboard wardrobes. Sera smiled to herself as she stepped into the bedroom and Marc followed.

Inside there wasn't much space thanks to the two wardrobes. Sera had placed her cup on the nightstand by the bed, a queen-sized affair in a dark wood frame with a fluffy white duvet. She picked at the tape on the box, finally tearing it away and folding down the top to expose the hanging rail of her clothes. Marc opened the doors of the built-in wardrobe that ran the length of the wall facing the bed.

"My side, your side?" Sera asked, gesturing.

"Fine with me." He watched her unpack, hanging dresses and trousers, neatly folding her shirts and underwear before placing them on the lower set of shelves that divided the wardrobe into two. She bent over the box, reaching down to grab something from the bottom. Marc set down his coffee and came over. "Need help?" Sera's fingers scrabbled on the cardboard as she straightened. Her face was flushed and her hair in disarray, falling over her eyes.

"It's too deep," she said. Marc pushed the hair away from her eyes and tucked it behind her ear before she could do it.

"Or you're just too small," he said. She jabbed him in the stomach and he bent over, pretending he'd been winded. She laughed and as he rose, Marc scooped her up, throwing her over his shoulder.

Sera squirmed in his arms, her legs flailing, her hands pummelling his back, but he held her tight, taking the two steps to the bed. "Put me down," she demanded, though she was giggling too hard for it to be much of a demand.

Marc lowered her to the bed and she sprawled on the duvet, her hair a dark wave. He sat beside her and bent over her, lowering his mouth to hers, his hand at her waist. At first he was gentle, barely touching her lips, his tongue darting out to tease her, but she wrapped her arms around his neck, pulling him down to her.

"We'll never get anything done," she murmured against his lips, "but right now, I don't care."

"We have all the time in the world," he said, remembering her words in the cathedral in Saint-Germain-des-Prés. If he didn't find a Monet for Royale, their time would be cut short.

CHAPTER 7

Sera double-checked her list of London jazz clubs as Marc set down his small suitcase by the door. He came over and sat beside her on the sofa.

"I'll be back sometime tomorrow. Are you sure you don't want to wait another few days to start looking for work?"

Sera felt the warmth when he placed his arm over her shoulder; she leaned into his strength. "I'm better off starting the job search now, at the beginning of the week when it's slower," she reasoned. Though she saw his frown, she continued on. "I can't sit around doing nothing, Marc. I haven't performed in months. I'm rusty."

"Where will you try first?" He studied her list.

"There are lots of clubs in Soho," she replied, tapping the paper. "I can hit several this evening and not have to travel too far."

"Be careful," he said, "and take a black cab home. Don't go on the Tube."

"You're just about to lose our wager," she chided him, but his serious expression didn't ease. "Marc, I'm a grown woman. I'll be fine. Jeremy Gordon isn't out there lurking."

"Yes, you are a grown woman, and no, he isn't lurking," Marc replied, "but still—"

"I'll be careful," Sera said. "Jeremy told me where he used to hang out—the Dalston—and I have no plans to go anywhere near there."

"Call me when you get back to the flat," Marc said, rising from the sofa. He held her hand and she rose with him. "I don't care if it's two in the morning."

"I promise I'll call," Sera said, standing on her toes to kiss him goodbye, circling his neck with her arms, and pulling him down to her lips. He returned her kiss with the same ardour, tasting like the espresso he had drank over breakfast. She wished he could stay. The door's buzzer beeped and they broke apart.

"That's my cab," Marc said. "I'll see you tomorrow."

"And I'll talk to you later."

They kissed once more and she walked him to the door. He lifted his suitcase.

"Lock up after me," Marc said as he opened the door.

"That's a comment that will have you sleeping on the sofa," Sera said. She tugged on his tie, a conservative dark blue that matched his eyes. He smiled at her and she let go, smoothing down the silk. Then he was gone, off to Mrs. Lancaster's estate, and work.

Sera closed the door and locked it as he'd asked, and as she would have done anyway. Sometimes his concern was endearing, and she loved him for it, but gone was the daredevil man she'd known, the man who took risks, who pushed her outside her comfort zone. She wanted that man back. Damn Jeremy Gordon—and damn Royale. She rubbed her neck, remembering where Jeremy's blade had rested that last day. A shiver ran up her spine.

He was dead.

She went into the bedroom and pulled open the wardrobe door, her dresses hung in a neat row. A strappy black dress with an uneven hem caught her eye. When she reached for it and pulled it out, the cloth shimmered lightly from the sun shining in through the window. It was tailored to hint at her curves without being glaringly sexual, the cleavage low enough to be feminine, but high enough to be modest. She laid the dress on the bed and stripped off her clothes, walking through the flat to the bathroom. After her shower, she would rest, and then be ready for her night. She didn't know what the clubs here expected. Thinking about the possibilities caused her nerves to flutter and made her stomach roil. She took a deep breath. She could do this; she would do this.

In Soho, walking from the station at Leicester Square, Sera found the first club on Frith Street with no problems. Nearly empty when she entered, she lingered just inside the door, marshalling her courage.

"Can I help you?" A waitress in a low-cut black mini dress and very high heels strolled over, her blonde hair loose down her back. Sera felt frumpy and small, like someone's poor relation, in her modest black dress.

"I'd like to see the manager, please," she said, the line sliding off her tongue with some ease. She'd spent time practicing.

"What for?" The woman's brow furrowed.

"I'm looking for work," Sera explained.

"We're not hiring," she replied. "Try again later."

"As a singer," Sera added, but the woman still shook her head.

"We get people in all the time; we have more singers than we know what to do with. You'll have to try somewhere else." The woman turned her back and walked away, moving to the bar to speak to the bartender. They glanced at her and Sera was sure she was the topic of their conversation, and disdain.

Head held high, she left the club, but on the street, she paused. What if they were all like this? At the next club a street over, the answer was the same, but an older man delivered the bad news.

"I could put in a good word for you," he said, reaching for her arm with his pale, fleshy hand. "If you have something else to offer." His gaze devoured her, so she backed away. She knew that sleazy look all too well, and though he was considerably less repulsive than Royale, she couldn't suppress a shudder of disgust.

"No, thank you." She walked to the door and pushed it open.

"Go on then." The man shooed her out. She slipped by a group of people on their way in.

Each club was the same, and her spirits sank further. On the street again, she kept walking. There were more people about now, hanging out on street corners, waiting in queues at the small, exclusive restaurants. Sera's pace slowed. Had she come too far? She walked a bit further, until she came to a crossroads. None of the street names were familiar, and she turned back. Or at least, she thought she'd gone back the same way she'd come. The sun had set and the street lamps flickered on, and the street seemed different than it had appeared before.

A neon sign flickered above a shadowed doorway, showing a grand piano and the words 'Jazz Bar' in red, with cursive writing above the words. Below the piano, in plain white, was the word 'Sanctuary'. She fumbled for her list of clubs in her purse, squinting in the low light. This club wasn't on her list, not that she could tell. She stuffed the paper back into her bag. It couldn't hurt to try.

Sera opened the heavy metal door. Illuminated by a bare bulb, a set of stairs stretched downward, through a tunnel of plain grey concrete with a metal rail. Tattered gig posters covered the walls, and the ones she glanced at were for dates long past, for musicians she'd never heard of. But the sound of a piano wafted up. Sinatra. She waited, but though the cue came and went, there was no singer. She took hold of the rail, cold under her palm, and headed downstairs.

When she reached the bottom, she pushed through a pair of dark curtains and found herself in a small yet luxurious club. The spare, rough look of the stairwell had been deceptive. To her left was a bar in dark shining wood, lit by recessed track lights. A bartender polished glassware, dressed in a smart waistcoat and tie. Gold cufflinks glinted at his wrists. He gave her a welcoming nod, and she returned it with a hesitant smile. Her gaze swept over the club.

The low-ceilinged space held numerous tables, which were laid out with white table linens and set with glasses. Candles in silver holders glowed. A couple sat at a table near the stage, but the place otherwise seemed empty. The pianist, with his dark blond hair slicked back and dressed in a simple tuxedo, effortlessly played the old jazz standards. He too gave her a polite nod.

Sera went to the bar and slid onto a stool. The bartender was instantly attentive, his blue-eyed gaze keen. She felt as if he'd taken in every detail about her in the space of a couple of seconds.

"Good evening, madam. Welcome to the Sanctuary," he said smoothly. "What may I pour for you tonight?" When Sera paused, he continued. "I have a very nice French white from Sancerre, or I could mix you a cocktail."

"The wine sounds lovely," Sera replied. She'd have one glass to fortify herself, and then continue with her search. "Merci."

When the bartender smiled at her, she noticed the slight wrinkles around his eyes, and the light freckles across his tanned nose and cheeks. Not a fake tan, but a real, honest-to-goodness exposure from the sun tan. He was broad shouldered in his shirt and waistcoat and she watched his long tapered fingers as he expertly opened a bottle of wine.

"De rien," he said, placing a goblet in front of her on a leather coaster, then pouring. The wine sparkled in the glass and she lifted it for a tasting sip, recognizing the slight mineral quality to its bouquet, particular to the region.

"Bien?" He asked, and she nodded, replacing the glass on the bar. He poured again, giving her a generous amount.

"Merci beaucoup," she said, giving him a soft, brief smile.

"What brings you to our city?" he asked, in accented but skilful French. "A visit?"

Sera took a bracing drink of the wine. "I live here now," she said. "And I must look for a job."

The bartender replaced the bottle of wine in a fridge under the bar and asked, "What do you do, madame?"

"Je suis chanteuse," she replied glumly, thinking of the clubs she'd been to and the many more she had yet to visit. Would she be able to find work? She couldn't work in an office, not here. Her English wasn't close to good enough, even if she spent time practicing with Pari, as the woman had offered. She frowned, staring into her glass.

"No luck yet?" The bartender sounded sympathetic and she lifted her gaze. His eyes were on her and he seemed kindly encouraging. "Are you any good?" The corner of his mouth twitched. The question was an obvious one and they both knew it. Sera gave him an amused smile.

"No one in this city has given me a chance to prove it," she said.

"Is that so?" His gaze moved beyond her and he made a beckoning gesture with his hand, just once. The sound of the piano tapered off and in the ensuing quiet, Sera heard footsteps.

"What is it, Julian?"

Sera glanced to her right. The pianist stood there, looking between her and the bartender. Julian, she amended mentally.

"Mayson wanted you to find a new singer, didn't he?" Julian gestured to her. "Voila."

The pianist looked her over, sizing her up, but she returned his frank gaze, standing her ground while her heart beat thrummed in double-time at this surprise opportunity.

"What do you sing?" he asked, his dark eyes fixed on her.

"Piaf. Dietrich. Dalida—" she listed off several more names.

"You can't get away with only singing '*La Vie En Rose*'," he remarked.

"I prefer '*Hymne d'amour*'," Sera replied. She wasn't an untried youth. "'*La Vie En Rose*' is too…" she searched for the correct word in English, but couldn't find the term.

"Predictable?" the pianist suggested.

Sera nodded. "Oui."

The pianist smiled, though his gaze wasn't as friendly as she'd hoped. "I'm David Santiano," he said.

"Sera Durand. Enchantée."

They shook hands. "And you've already met Julian, of course."

"Not formally," Julian said, extending his hand. Sera took it and he bent to kiss the back, his lips a feather light touch on her skin.

"Enchantée, madame." He reluctantly released her hand when it became obvious David was waiting for them to finish.

"Leave your jacket and purse," David said. "Julian will keep them while you come down to the piano. Let's see how you do."

"All right." Her mouth felt dry and her stomach fluttered with nerves. She shed her jacket and Julian took it and her purse, tucking them behind the bar.

"Break a leg," he said.

She followed David to the stage and he settled behind the piano. "What do you want me to sing?" she asked, moving towards the microphone. David raised a hand to forestall her.

"Just you and me for the first one," he said. "You'll need to warm up. How about '*Dans le bleu du ciel bleu*'?"

Sera nodded and licked her lips, taking a few deep, long breaths, letting her body relax. David played the first few chords and she heard her cue. It was a soft song, easy on her voice, and she was glad of the French lyrics. She could concentrate on her skill instead of having to remember English.

David seemed to track every breath she took and every note she sang of the song, his keen gaze missing nothing. When she finished the last verse, she felt exhausted, yet exhilarated. It had been two months since she'd last performed and she missed communing with the music, the appreciation of the crowd, and hearing her own voice rise and fall with the melodic line.

David's dark eyes gleamed, and a slow, almost calculating smile spread across his face. "Now you can go to the microphone," he said. Sera stepped away from the piano and crossed the few steps to the centre of the stage. She reached for an older style mic with its chrome casing gleaming in the spotlight. She glanced back at David and he winked at her as he played the first few chords. She recognized the music straightaway.

'*Hymne d'amour*'.

Sera stepped back from the microphone, feeling almost light-headed as the small crowd applauded. David came out from behind the piano and gestured towards her with an outstretched arm, before taking a short bow and leaving the stage.

"You need to meet the owner," he said. "I suspect he'll offer you a job. Speak English though. He'll appreciate that more than French."

She'd sung an entire set of songs, slipping easily into her role of performer, her voice dancing effortlessly with David's music, and she'd lost a greater awareness of the club, her world having shrunk to the stage and his piano.

"D'accord—right." She stumbled on the word.

"Magnifique," he said. Sera felt her cheeks grow warm.

"Thank you."

"Mayson's in his office," Julian said to David, and partly to her. "He said to come see him when you were done."

"What did he think?"

Julian shrugged. "I would hope he liked it. He didn't seem unhappy, at least."

"Mayson wears a dour expression most of the time," David said to her in an aside, leading her past the bar to a heavy door. "But he's a lovely man. Very fair. Just…English. No French." David knocked and Sera heard a click. He turned the knob and pulled open the door, gesturing for Sera to precede him. She took a slow, measured step inside.

The owner sat behind a dark mahogany desk, wearing a dark suit, shirt, and tie that seemed to match the club decor. His bald head gleamed, and when he looked up from the invoices on the desk blotter, she realized he was far younger than she'd first thought, perhaps in his late forties.

"You have a beautiful voice," he said, his own voice a pleasing baritone with almost no discernible accent. "Welcome to the Sanctuary. Please, have a seat."

Sera took the chair he indicated. David lingered behind her until Mayson gestured at him to sit too. "You'll make my neck hurt if I have to look up at you."

"Sorry, boss," David said, lowering himself into the other chair, comfortably crossing an ankle over the opposite knee. Something unspoken seemed to pass between them.

"Julian tells me you're new to the city," Mayson said, his grey eyes focusing on her.

"Very new."

"And you've had experience singing, it's apparent," he remarked, more to himself than to her. "My experience with singers is that they are flighty."

"Not me," Sera said, the words slipping out before she could stop them. But, unlike Royale, who would have slapped her for such an interruption, Mayson chuckled.

"So you say." His mood darkened abruptly. "But less French songs. I can't stand them."

"Of course," she stammered.

He gave her a closer inspection. "David, you know what I told you." He glanced over at David, who sat forward in his chair.

"I know, but you heard her. She's fabulous. Give her a chance, Jack."

"I don't give chances. Not for Frogs like her. Not since…"

"I know you miss him." David's tone softened, becoming conciliatory, comforting. "But don't let that make you turn away the best singer we've had walk through our doors in years."

Sera sat motionless, her hands in her lap, wondering at the turn of conversation.

"For me, Jack?"

Mayson sighed, and sat back in his chair.

"Show me you're dedicated, and reliable, and I'll hire you on permanently," he replied, speaking directly to her. "We're open every evening from seven-thirty until three. You'll work tomorrow through Sunday, with Monday and Tuesday off. If your attendance doesn't falter, and if David thinks you have the skill to maintain the sort of performance you gave tonight, then you're in."

Sera could hardly believe it. Mayson gave her a hint of an amiable smile, showing slightly crooked teeth, and she felt a weight lift from her shoulders.

"Do we have a deal?" He rose from his chair, coming around the desk and stopping in front of her. He held out his hand. Sera took it and he gave her a firm handshake.

"Deal," she said, "but only once I know my pay."

"Of course. £100 a night, and if the business picks up, or the club makes more, then it'll only go up from there."

"I accept."

"Good." He squeezed her fingers gently, and then let go. "Go see Julian. He'll tell you how to get in before we open, show you around, all that. I need to speak to David."

Sera rose and left the office. Mayson closed the door behind her and she floated rather than walked to the bar. Julian grinned at her, a wide smile that made her feel warm inside. He knew she'd gotten the job, even before she said anything.

"We'll be seeing you again," he said as she slid onto the stool she'd occupied earlier that evening. "You've made my night, Sera." He poured her another glass of wine and set it before her on the coaster.

"One glass was enough, really." She was giddy from the knowledge that she had a job; she didn't need alcohol.

"Enjoy it while you can," Julian advised. "Mayson works us all hard." He winked and she smiled in relief to realize he'd been joking.

"All right. What time is it?" She realized she hadn't checked her phone in some time. Marc would be worried.

Marc.

"It's about midnight," Julian said.

Sera's heart sank. Marc would be worried, but worse, they were supposed to have found work together. "Can I have my purse, please?"

"The wine's on the house," Julian said as he passed her bag over the bar. "Or rather, on me."

"Merci beaucoup." He held her gaze for a long moment, but then she glanced down to her bag, digging into it for her phone. What would she tell Marc? She had no idea if the club was looking for other musicians; she hadn't even thought about inquiring when she'd spoken to Mayson.

There was a text from Marc, a short 'Ça va?' She replied with another text just as short. 'Bien.' She set the phone on the bar and took a sip of her wine.

"You're not late for something, are you?" Julian asked, indicating her phone. "You have somewhere to be?"

Sera knew she could go home, but the flat would be empty without Marc. She'd finish her wine, and then get a cab.

"Not yet."

CHAPTER 8

Marc called it a night just before midnight, hours after Mrs. Lancaster's dinner and gossipy conversation. Her late husband's estate was a shambles, with no rhyme or reason to his methods of organization. Now, Marc wished he'd handed off the cataloguing of the estate to Dawson and his assistants rather than take on the work himself. Too late now.

He left the binder of catalogued works on a side table in the library, itself a dusty repository of books with several landscape paintings of varying age and value. The hall outside the library was quiet, the lights dim. Mrs. Lancaster was likely already in bed. At dinner, she'd mentioned that she "kept early hours."

"Early to bed and early to rise, that's the way it's always been," she'd said, her good cheer never wavering. "But work as long as you like, Mr. Perron."

Marc found his way to a back reception room with floor to ceiling French doors that led outside onto a stone patio. He stepped outside to view a quaint, but small formal garden beyond. The chill night air refreshed him, and washed away some of the fatigue brought on by the close, warm quarters inside. He checked his phone, but there were no messages from Sera. Before he put the phone away, he sent her a brief message.

He should be there with her, because Royale knew they were in London. What if someone had seen them together, or worse, had observed Sera alone? Marc pulled out his silver cigarette case and lit one, pacing to the stone railing at the edge of the patio, looking out over the dark garden and at the circular pool in the centre glimmering in the moonlight. He checked the time. Too late to call Fournier, but he left a message anyway, reminding Fournier to send him the month's reports. Aurore, Perron et fils' competent receptionist, would send the reports, but he needed to know that Fournier wasn't making a mess of things. He was good at his job, but Marc still wondered whether his talent at the auction house and with clients extended to the duller parts of the business.

Marc took a deep drag of his cigarette, letting out the smoke in a slow stream. The habitual movements were reassuring, calming. He ground out the cigarette and turned to go back inside. He'd get an early night and hopefully things would be better tomorrow. He didn't relish having to sleep in a cold, empty bed in a little-used guest room. He wanted Sera beside him, her dark hair spread over the pillow, with the sound of her peaceful breathing, and her warm body against him.

His phone buzzed and he checked the message, thankfully from Sera. *Bien.* Well, that was something, but little comfort in his empty bed.

Home? he replied.

Soon. xx By the time he'd reached the bedroom, she'd texted him back.

Once inside his room, he put his phone on the bedside table and changed into pyjama pants and a black t-shirt to ward off the chill of the old manor house. When he returned to the bedside table, he had another message from Sera.

In the cab.

Marc stretched out on the bed under the flower-patterned duvet and closed his eyes, though for a time, he didn't sleep. About half an hour later his phone vibrated insistently.

"Bonsoir, ma chère."

"Bonsoir, Marc." She sounded cheerful for such a late hour.

"Did you succeed?" he asked, anticipating the answer.

"I thought I wouldn't," she confessed, relaying her evening incidents. Marc wanted to throttle the man who had propositioned her. "And then I saw this tiny club, called the Sanctuary, and a conversation with the bartender led to an audition, and then a job."

"I knew it wouldn't take you long," Marc said. If he was there, he'd open a bottle of champagne and they could toast to her success.

"But we haven't gotten a gig performing together," Sera replied, her voice a whisper.

No, they hadn't, even though they'd pictured performing as a pas de deux. "I'll make special appearances," he said, trying to lighten her mood.

"You're not angry?"

"Not at all, ma chére. If I were with you, I'd show you exactly how pleased I am."

That brought a throaty laugh from her and the desire rose in him. He wanted to slide up behind her in bed, part her thighs and thrust home, tease her clit until she begged him for release. "Is that so?

"I would tie you to the bedpost and make you beg me for release." He heard her intake of breath.

"How long are you away?"

"I won't be back tomorrow as I had first thought," Marc said. "This estate is a mess."

"Oh." The single word was enough for him to hear her disappointment. "What about Wednesday?"

"J'espere."

"Moi aussi. But tell me more—what would you do to me if I were tied up at your mercy?"

Marc chuckled. "You're going to torture me since I'm not with you?"

"Bien sûr. Perhaps I should be the one tying you up. Catch you by surprise."

"And what would you do?" His hand slipped into his pyjama

pants.

"You'd be tied spread-eagle on the bed so you couldn't touch yourself," she said, her voice low, almost husky. "Because knowing you, you're already hard—aren't you?"

"Of course." He kept his strokes long and slow, not wanting to end the sensations too soon.

"I'd start by nibbling your ear, letting the goose bumps rise on your skin, not touching you anywhere else."

Marc's breath hitched.

"But then, I'd follow the line of your neck, bite into the muscle, leave the first mark on your skin. And when your focus is on that pain, that's when I would pinch your nipples hard, one after the other. If you weren't hard already—"

"I am."

"—You would be after that. And though I'd take note of your hunger, I would ignore your begging cock, and continue to tease your nipples instead, biting and sucking until you're writhing under me."

Marc drew in a deep breath. He was painfully hard and he wished Sera were here to take him into her mouth and bring him to completion.

"I'd listen to you beg as I ran my nails over your belly, so close to where you want me to be." She chuckled.

"Dieu," Marc breathed. His strokes quickened and he closed

his eyes tight, picturing the vivid scene.

"And just when you think you can't take anymore," Sera said, her voice a seductive whisper in his ear, "I'd straddle you and let my sex brush along your cock so you could see how wet I am, how ready."

"Seraphina." Marc's entire body thrummed with need.

"And when you've about given up, that's when I'd take you, engulf you, ride you—but you can't come yet, mon coeur…"

Marc groaned and eased off, moving back from the brink.

"Not until I do," Sera said. She broke off and he could hear her breathing quicken, hear the little noises she made when she was close. "But when I do, I want to hear you." Her little whimpers became a low cry, almost a sob, and Marc shuddered with his own release, gasping and groaning as he came over his hand. He could hear her breathing, and knew she could hear his.

"Mon Dieu," he said again, opening his eyes, seeing the faint shape of the bed's canopy above him in the dark.

"I miss you," came Sera's quiet voice.

"I'll be home as soon as I can, ma chére."

"Remember when we used to do this all the time?"

"When you were still a nanny for that couple who lived in the 16th arrondissement? I used to show up for work on two hours sleep." Marc remembered his uncle's annoyance when he'd stumble in late, rumpled and ill prepared.

"I never got any sleep."

"Neither did I, but it was worth it, ma chére."

He heard her yawn. "I have to work every night this week," she said.

"Then you'd best get some sleep. I'll call you tomorrow when I know how much longer this job will take me."

"If you're not back by this time next week, I'll come rescue you," she quipped.

"It will be sooner than that, I promise. Bonne nuit, ma chére."

Marc rolled up his sleeves and lifted the dust cover from a mis-shapen pile in the corner of the attic. Although he tried to disturb as little as possible, when he lifted the cover, dust motes floated in the air, lit by the sunlight from the gabled window nearby. He found over a dozen framed canvases that were bracketed between the wall and a wooden side table in need of varnish. He grasped the closest painting, enclosed within a gilt-painted frame. The canvas was dull and dark, and when he set the frame down, propping it against the table, his hands came away black with grime. Whatever the image had been, it would take immense restoration work to bring it back to its proper state.

The next frame, somewhat sheltered by the first, was in better shape—only the frame needed cleaning or replacement. It was a pastoral scene, a field with haystacks. When he peered closer at the canvas, the brush strokes seemed hurried, almost careless. He

looked for a signature, but there was none to be seen. Yet, the subject matter was familiar, reminding him of a Monet. He set the
canvas aside. The chances of finding a Monet among the pile was
close to none, and he knew it was wishful thinking. Perhaps later
he'd remove the frame and see if there was an artist's mark somewhere. The frame covered a significant portion of the canvas
edges, a poor choice by the framer.

The next three paintings were also pastoral scenes, though each
was done in a different hand, and the artist's signatures were ob-
scure. Marc retreated to the binder he'd left on a table under the
single bare bulb in this section of the attic. He flipped through the
pages, but none of the works were listed that he could tell. His fingers left black smudges on the pages and he wiped his hands on his
jeans.

"Mr. Perron?"

Marc retraced his steps to the attic door. Mrs. Lancaster stood
on the stair below and she smiled when she saw him.

"Lunch will be ready shortly," she said.

"Just what I wanted to hear," he replied, even though he wasn't
ready to stop. He should be done by now; he knew he'd spend the
rest of today and possibly even tomorrow completing the cataloguing.

Mrs. Lancaster frowned, eyeing his dirty jeans and hands, and
the grey smudges on his t-shirt. "You'd best come down and tidy
up before we eat," she said, gesturing to his clothes.

Marc started down the stairs towards her. "I didn't expect so much dust," he replied. "When did you say your husband purchased the house?"

"About ten years ago," Mrs. Lancaster said, preceding him down the stairs, "but we never got round to cleaning out the attics. So much work. The previous owner left a great deal of clutter and it took long enough just to get the rest of the house up to my standards." On the first floor, she paused by the door to Marc's guest room. "Lunch will be on the terrace in the back," she said. "It's such a lovely day for dining al fresco."

"I'll be there shortly," Marc said. In his room, he walked through to the ensuite and caught a glimpse of himself in the mirror. He was filthy, but until he finished, there was little he could do about the worst of the dust covering him. He washed his hands and arms up to the elbow, washing his face as well. The hand towels Mrs. Lancaster had laid out were obviously new, almost crisply white, and he hated to soil them, but it couldn't be helped.

On the terrace, Mrs. Lancaster sipped tea from a dainty cup, its fine bone china painted with roses. A small platter of sandwiches sat atop the wrought iron table with its glass top, along with a tureen of tomato soup. Marc sat in the chair across from her and she waved her hand at the food.

"Please, help yourself." A bowl of soup sat on a charger in front of her, but it looked untouched. Marc served himself a full bowl of soup and placed two sandwich halves—one egg salad, one chicken—on his plate. He poured a glass of water from a pitcher in the centre of the table.

Mrs. Lancaster let him finish his soup before she started her questions. "Do you think the estate will make some money?" Her hands trembled as she held her teacup.

"It should, just by sheer volume alone," Marc replied, "but a definitive answer will come from the auction." She seemed to wilt at his answer. "Some of the paintings will need cleaning before they're sold—they were poorly stored in the attic. Hence the grime." He gestured to his dusty clothes.

His phone buzzed and he pulled it out, rising from his chair. It was Dawson. Giving Mrs. Lancaster an apologetic smile, he walked to the other side of the terrace, down wind and out of earshot.

"Back in London yet?" Dawson asked.

"Still at the Lancaster estate. The attic is a mess of paintings and junk, with a good portion belonging to the previous owner. You'll love the furniture when you see it, aside from the pieces recovered in hideous upholstery."

Dawson chuckled. "Isn't that always the way. As planned, I'll be out tomorrow to look things over."

"I'll likely still be here," Marc said, "up to my elbows in dust. By the way, you wouldn't happen to know how many haystack paintings Monet did, would you?"

"The haystacks? Twenty-five in the official series, from 1890 to 1891, but there are several more outside that range, and really, who knows how many others he might have done. Why, do you think Lancaster bought one?"

"Could be, but it's not in Lancaster's lists, so it might be from the previous owner. And it might not be a Monet at all. I doubt a valuable painting would be forgotten up in an attic."

"Stranger things have happened," Dawson said. "I'll send you a list of the known ones."

"Appreciated." Marc barely heard Dawson's reply as the line cut out. He turned slightly and Dawson's voice came in clearer.

"Set it aside and I'll take a look at it tomorrow."

"Will do, unless I can find a signature that proves it's definitively not a Monet."

"I bet it's some hobbyist with a fancy for hay," Dawson replied. They said their goodbyes and Marc returned to the table.

"That was Mr. Dawson; he'll be here tomorrow to evaluate the furniture," he told Mrs. Lancaster. He took a bite of his sandwich, eating quickly. He wanted to get back upstairs to examine the canvas and take it out of its frame for a proper look.

"How long do you think it will take him to evaluate the furniture?" Mrs. Lancaster asked. Marc finished his sandwich before replying.

"He'll bring an assistant and will have it done in a day."

"I'll have to tell Martin to fill the larder," she said, "and make up another room, just in case."

Marc finished his meal and rose to his feet. "Merci pour le déjeuner," he said, giving her a polite smile. Her cheeks flushed a pale pink and she returned his smile.

"My pleasure entirely," she said, sounding a bit flustered.

"I'll be upstairs until supper," he said, "if you need me."

"I always have a cocktail at five, if you'd like to join me." Her cheeks went a bit pinker still.

"I'd be delighted."

He left her sitting on the terrace, and returned to the attic. The painting lay where he'd left it against the table. He picked it up. No artist's signature could be seen on the canvas, but the framing covered a full inch of the painting's edges. He turned it over. The paper backing crackled with age against his hands, and a half-rusted wire had been strung across it to hang. At the bottom left corner, the paper had a tear two inches in length, and he took up his penlight, inspecting what he could see of the back of the canvas. Would Mrs. Lancaster notice—or even care—if he took it apart? If this was indeed from the previous owner, she hadn't even seen it.

To hell with it. He'd have it re-framed—properly—if she made a fuss. He ran a finger through the tear, along the edge of the frame, tearing it further. Little puffs of dust rose in the air and he sneezed. With a final yank, he tore the paper off, revealing the plain back and the crossbars of wood that braced the tension of the canvas's rectangular frame.

He used his keys to bend back the small nails that held the canvas in place on the frame, then let the frame fall free. He flipped the painting around, his gaze going to the lower corners, the most likely place for an artist's mark.

Nothing.

Marc bit back a curse. He was about to place the bared canvas back in the pile of paintings, but he paused, and instead laid it out flat on the small table. On his phone, he looked up Monet's haystacks and compared one to the piece he had before him.

There was an uncanny similarity, and he wondered if this could be the work of a student of Monet's, or perhaps an unsigned study for the series. He put his phone away. How likely would it be that Royale would know enough about art to discern the truth? If this was presented as a Monet, the thrill alone might be enough to blind him to its lack of provenance. Add in a good story about bilking an ignorant widow, and Royale would lap it up like the greedy man he was.

Marc set the painting carefully aside. He would offer Mrs. Lancaster £500 for it, and make the attempt. At the very least, it would keep Royale at bay a while longer.

CHAPTER 9

In the early afternoon, and long before she had to be at the club, Sera went walking. She bought a coffee from a nearby shop and crossed over Highgate Hill to the Catholic church of St. Joseph's. She thought about going inside, but the greenery of the park called strongly and the stonework of the church seemed gloomy and almost grim in the day's sunlight.

Once past the gate, the path into the park was wide, paved in smooth asphalt, and she followed it along, down a gentle hill. As she came over the rise, she looked down onto a pond, perhaps even a stream. A bridge crossed over the water to her left, but she headed towards several benches scattered nearby, taking up a seat on an unoccupied one. A light breeze played over the water, creating tiny ripples. She took a deep breath. She could hardly hear the traffic from the road; only the breeze and the birdsong sounded here. She sipped her coffee, watching a pair of ducks foraging at the edge of the pond, submerging themselves beneath the water.

The smell of cigarette smoke wafted in the air and she glanced over her shoulder towards the acrid odour. A man stood on the bridge, a cigarette in hand, looking down at his mobile phone. He seemed familiar somehow, but was far enough away that she couldn't make out his features. After a short time, he walked on, and the air cleared. When Marc returned from the country, she should bring him here, Sera thought. This was why she'd chosen the flat on Highgate Hill. In Paris, she hadn't lived close to any parks and had rarely seen such an expanse of trees and grass, or heard such quiet. She could grow to love it here.

A man jogged along the path with white ear buds in his ears, his long legs eating up the distance. He passed her bench with some speed, his t-shirt sticking to his sweat-soaked torso. She turned her attention back to the pond. A gull of some sort alighted on the bank, flapping its wings. It plucked at a stale crust left in the grass, seeming to chortle over its find, then seized the crust in its beak and flew off.

Sera heard footsteps on the path, first at a quick pace, but they slowed, and she could hear laboured breathing. Pari, clad in snug black nylon tights and a baggy pink shirt, sank down next to her on the bench.

"You have a much better idea," she said in French to Sera.

"Do you always run along here?" Sera asked, her English hesitant.

"Mostly. It's nicer than inhaling traffic fumes along the road. I need to stay in shape to catch all those little blighters when they shoplift." Pari laughed, taking the tie from her hair and smoothing out the windblown strands before putting it up again.

"Are there many?"

"More than you'd think." Pari shook her head. "What do you do? I hope something more glamorous than policing."

"I sing," Sera replied.

"Utterly glamorous."

"No, not really. It's…" She tried to think of the words in English, but failed. "It can be hard." She told Pari of the man who had propositioned her.

"They're not all like that, are they?"

"Not all," Sera said, reverting back to English. "Some men are nice." Julian, for one. And David. Even Mayson, though he didn't like the French. She was lucky this time. Sanctuary was nothing like Le Chat Rouge.

Sera squeezed onto the Tube, clinging to a bar near the door. People seemed to press in on all sides, including a very pregnant woman who wore a blue and white 'Baby on Board' pin on the lapel of her jacket. No seats were available, so she clung to the pole, her gaze averted. At Piccadilly Circus, Sera edged between the other commuters and out onto the platform, her face flushed from the stale warmth of the car. On the street, it took her a few moments to orient herself. The club was a few minutes walk.

At the street door, Sera rang the buzzer. After a moment's pause, she heard the click of the lock disengaging. The stairway was as grim and gloomy as it had been the night before. When she pushed through the curtain, Julian was behind the bar setting up. The club was otherwise empty, and David's piano sat silent on the darkened stage.

"Bonsoir, Sera."

"Bonsoir, Julian. Am I so early that I'm the first here?"

Julian took clean glasses from the dishwasher and wiped off water droplets with a soft cloth, before placing them in neat rows. He worked methodically, but quickly. "David's here, but he's with Mayson, so you have a few minutes to relax. Is there anything I can get for my favourite chanteuse?"

"Just water, thank you. And I can't possibly be your favourite." Sera perched on a stool, glancing around at the sumptuous club. She'd worn one of her nicest gowns, a clingy black dress embellished with sequins that would glitter under the spotlight.

"Why can't you be my favourite?" Julian placed the glass of water before her.

"Why is the stairway so grim when this place is so expensively decorated?"

Julian raised a brow. "Mayson said once that it reminded him of where he'd come from and helps to keep his mind on business so he won't end up there again, but personally, I think he just likes to keep people on their toes and discourage all but the most curious."

"Strange."

"He has his quirks," Julian agreed. He took out a cutting board and knife, and reached into the fridge under the bar for a box of lemons and limes. She watched him slice up the fruit into precise wedges, the knife flashing. It didn't take him long.

The door to Mayson's office opened and David emerged. His tie was askew and he straightened it as he walked to the bar, stopping beside her.

"So, you came back after all."

"Why wouldn't I?"

David shrugged. "Some do, some don't. He glanced at his watch, a gold Rolex. Sera's eyes widened. "A gift from an admirer," he said, noticing her interest. "Let's go down to the piano; we need to talk about tonight's setlist."

Sera left her empty glass on the bar and Julian picked it up and put it in the dishwasher as she slid off the stool and followed David to the stage. He pulled out the piano bench and sat, lifting the fallboard.

"Come, sit down," he said, patting the space beside him. Sera sat on the edge, but he shifted over, giving her more space. "I don't bite."

"Good to know." Sera re-settled herself next to him.

"Can you play?" he asked, his hands resting on the keys, feeling out a quiet melody as he talked. It sounded a bit like a Hoagy Carmichael composition, but with more flourishes. He let the notes meander from the original tune, ending up with something more blues than swing.

"Not at all." She reached out, her fingers ghosting over the shiny keys. "I've always wished I could." She had learned a bit from Marc, but that was years ago and she'd forgotten the lesson.

"Do you always perform alone, or are there other musicians sometimes?" she asked, remembering that she'd never mentioned Marc.

"Usually just me. Why? Do you know someone?"

"My,"—and here she hesitated over the word as she'd done before, not sure it conveyed all Marc was to her—"copain—boyfriend—is a cellist, and a good one."

"You have a boyfriend." David chuckled and she frowned. "Julian will be disappointed," he explained. "He's taken a fancy to you."

Sera glanced up at the bar, and Julian must have felt her gaze, for he lifted his head from what he'd focused on and met her scrutiny. Her cheeks burned and she looked away, back to the keys. "I should have said something."

"He's a big boy, he'll get over it. So your boyfriend is a cellist. Jazz or classical?"

"Both," Sera said, "he composes too."

"I'll see what the boss thinks. It would be up to him, but even if he likes the idea, your boyfriend would have to come in for an audition." David took a small pad of paper from his jacket pocket. The top page held a list of songs. "This is tonight's setlist."

Sera looked at the titles, and was relieved she knew all of the songs. David had curated a mix of ballads to offset the faster songs and had stuck to a classic, mid-century range. When she pointed this out, he said, "We'll start working other material into the set-lists when you're permanent. And we'll stay away from the Piaf. Boss's orders. I have a few compositions of my own that I think would suit you well too."

"Play me one," Sera said. She glanced around the club. Still empty. "How about now?"

"You're awfully demanding," David replied, but he looked amused rather than annoyed, a smile lingered on his lips. "I've been working on this song for the past few weeks. Give me your honest opinion."

It started out softly and she watched his fingers on the keys, moving unerringly over the ivories. The sleeve of his tuxedo jacket brushed her bare arm as he reached for a lower chord and she wasn't sure if it was the tone or his touch that raised goose bumps, but then he began to sing, his low tenor seeming to be just for her. He sang a song of unrequited love, its lyrics so poignant that tears pricked at her eyes.

When he finished, she wiped the moisture away.

"That bad?"

"It was beautiful," she corrected, "but so sad. Is it…?" She broke off.

"About me?" David finished for her. His expression seemed weary, though the night had just begun. "Happy people don't write music, do they?"

"Sometimes they can," Sera replied, thinking of the songs Marc had written for her, "but it isn't usual."

David glanced beyond her and she followed his gaze to the bar. A man had come in, thin and not especially tall, his dark hair cut short. He shook Mayson's hand. David sighed. "That song's not ready for the public—I don't know if it ever will be." His attention went back to the piano and he picked up some sheet music, shuffling through the pages until he found what he was looking for.

The title wasn't familiar to Sera. She read over the staffs, hearing the notes in her head. David began to play, and it was cheerier than the last tune, a jaunty swing-style jazz song, with little flourishes and phrases that were entirely modern.

"Another of yours?" she asked. There were no lyrics with the music and she listened to the song in its entirety.

"I wrote that when I was younger," David said. "I was happier then, before I worked here."

"Is it that bad?"

"No, only sometimes." David glanced at his watch. "Go put your stuff behind the curtain. At the break, I'll unlock the dressing room for you. It's tiny, but at least there is one."

Sera rose from the bench. "Who's the girl who made you so sad?"

David's mouth turned up at the corners just slightly. "Get me drunk one night and I might tell you."

"She'd be silly to turn you down," Sera said before she ducked behind the curtain. She heard David snort as she set her things in a small pile by the dressing room's plain black door. When she returned to the stage, David was composed, professional and poised. He laid the set list on the piano.

"Ready?"

It was as if he'd never sung that song, never admitted to his sadness. Sera didn't know what to make of it.

Marc shook Dawson's hand before he left Mrs. Lancaster's estate. He'd said his goodbyes to the dowager earlier and he itched to return to the city, and to Sera.

"Have a safe trip back," Dawson said. "I hope we're not stuck here as long as you were."

"There's far less furniture than there is art and clutter," Marc replied.

"And that haystacks work you found?"

"Not a Monet." Marc forced a chuckle. "Wishful thinking. Still, a good work, though worth little." He picked up the canvas resting against the wall. "But it's something Sera would like, so I bought it from Mrs. Lancaster."

"How much?" Dawson looked the painting over critically, his gaze missing nothing. "No signature, not the best brush work, but it is charming. A nice souvenir."

"I gave her £500," Marc said. Dawson nodded.

"Just right. Will you arrange the estate sale through our house?"

"That would be best. I'll have the listings over to you when I can."

"Excellent. We'll pencil in a date for next month. It should give us enough time to get it all packed up and arranged."

Marc returned to the city later than he'd planned, having been stuck in traffic due to an overturned lorry on the M1. He reached the flat just before eleven. It was quiet and dark and once he'd showered and changed, he didn't want to sit around waiting for Sera. He pulled on a blazer over his t-shirt and dark jeans, and caught a cab to Soho. The streets were busy with people and he almost missed the sign for Sanctuary. The red cursive neon letters 'Jazz Bar' flickered erratically. He pulled open the heavy door and descended the stairs. If he hadn't known what he'd find, he might have wondered if he was in the right place. The cement stairs re-minded him of a disused bunker. He pushed through the curtain and into a dim, candlelit space.

Marc's gaze went to the stage, the brightest point of the club. Sera's voice filled the room with a rich rendition of '*Moon River.*' He paused to watch her, the shimmer of her gown, her dark hair swept up off her shoulders in a chignon, diamonds glittering in her ears and around her neck. He remembered the first time he'd seen her on a stage, half a decade ago, at a small club in the fourth ar-rondissement. Back then, she had trembled from her nervousness, but now, she was confident and assured as she performed, wearing her talent and sex appeal like a second skin. When the song ended, he went to the bar, and waited for the bartender to finish serving the couple in front of him. They retreated with their drinks to a table near the stage, the last free table in the place. Marc took a seat at the bar.

"Welcome to Sanctuary," the bartender said, placing a coaster in front of him. "What can I pour for you?"

Marc scanned the bottles on the shelf behind the bar. "Scotch, the Macallan."

"An excellent choice." The bartender turned to fetch the bottle. Marc chuckled.

"You would say that even if it wasn't." He craved a cigarette, but London's bars had gone non-smoking.

"Possibly, I would," the bartender allowed. "But I saw you admiring our new addition and I knew you had to be a man of taste."

"She is lovely, and quite talented," Marc agreed. "I have seen her perform before."

The bartender's brow rose along with the level of scotch in the glass. "Really?" He set the glass in front of Marc. "£15."

Marc took out his wallet and laid the money on the bar, along with a tip. "I have followed her career for years. You might consider me her first fan."

The bartender gave him an amused smile, the sort one would give to someone a bit delusional. "Should I inform security?"

"She'd be disappointed if you did." Marc took a slow sip of the scotch, savouring the taste. The bartender looked like he was about to reply, but was interrupted by a man coming up to the bar. He was broad about the shoulders, in a plain dark suit, his fingernails bitten to the quick on his hand where he rested it on the wood.

"The boss in?" the man asked. The bartender jerked a thumb towards a heavy metal door close to the bar. "Go on through, mate."

There was a break in the music and Marc turned to the stage.

"After the break, we'll return for one more set," the pianist announced, playing a dramatic trill on the keys. A few people laughed. "You won't want to miss it." Applause filled the club and Sera and the pianist left the stage, heading towards the bar.

When she spotted him, she rushed forward, and he rose from his stool to embrace her, feeling her warmth through the thin satin of her dress. She lifted her face up and he accepted her invitation, kissing her soundly. It felt like he'd been away for weeks instead of days.

"I didn't know you were going to be here," she said, breathless and smiling.

"I didn't want to wait any longer to see you."

The pianist watched them with an amused smile, and then addressed Sera. "Is this your cellist boyfriend you were telling me about earlier?" He held out his hand to Marc. "David Santiano."

"Marc Perron." They shook hands.

"We'll arrange a time for you to audition," David said. "Julian, could I get some water? I'm parched."

The bartender—Julian—poured two glasses, handing one to David and setting the second one on the bar, catching Sera's eye.

"Merci, Julian." He gave her a nod and went to serve another customer.

Marc kept his arm around Sera and she leaned into him as she sipped her water. David still looked amused as he observed them.

"You have disappointed Julian," he said. "He's pouting."

"Should I be worried?" Marc kept his tone light, but he watched Julian at his work—the man seemed to be purposely avoiding them now.

"I wouldn't worry, he'll get over it," David said.

"I hope so," Sera said.

"If he doesn't, I'll talk to him." David smiled and changed topics. "What brings you and Sera to London? She mentioned that the two of you were new to the city."

"Work, mostly," Marc replied. "And the change of scenery is pleasant."

"What do you do?"

"Antiques, and estates."

"One of our regular customers is into antiques," David replied. "Aaron has a shop, though I've never been. I don't much care for antiques myself. Modern and new is more my taste."

"As is mine."

David seemed surprised. "Really? That's rather odd, given your profession."

"Minimalist lines are my preference, but with a feature piece. However, I'm not about to decorate an entire flat in 18th century brocade and gilt."

"Or like some old matron's front parlour," David added. "I'm glad Mayson put his foot down with the club's design. When he bought it, the designer suggested turning it into a pub."

"I can't imagine it," Sera said, finishing her glass of water and setting it on the bar. She slid out from under Marc's arm and rose on her toes to kiss his cheek. "Time to go to work."

"Five more minutes," David said.

"I just need the powder room."

"I'll be here when you're done," Marc said. She flashed him a smile, then headed to an alcove near the stage.

"After the show, I'll introduce you to the boss," David said. "I think we could use a cellist, but Mayson makes all the decisions. He's not one for music appreciation when it costs him money."

"Mayson? His name is familiar." Too familiar. Marc remembered Gordon's mention of his boss while at the cemetery in Montparnasse. He'd compared Royale to Mayson, saying: "He's a lowlife compared to Mayson. Not even fit to clean my boots."

"He owns several clubs in town," David said.

"That must be why. If he's not keen on paying full rates, I can do occasional appearances. It's more of a sideline for me."

"That's expected. I'm sure antiques are more lucrative. I'll propose Saturdays to Mayson and we'll go from there. At least your accent's not as obvious as Sera's." David held out his hand and they shook again. "See you after the set." He grinned and headed down to the stage.

Mayson. It had to be the same man. What were the chances? And what did David mean about his accent? Strange. Marc frowned as he watched Sera step up to the microphone. Her gaze found him and she smiled, a slow, sultry smile that promised him everything. He blew her a kiss and her smile widened. He barely heard the song, only registered that she began to sing, her gaze still fixed on him. At the bridge between the chorus and the second verse, she winked at him before her gaze shifted away, becoming the coquette, targeting one man after another, and skilfully playing the crowd.

Marc finished his scotch and turned back to the bar. Julian stood watching the performance, drying long-stemmed champagne flutes as he took them from the dishwasher. The heavy metal door just past the bar opened and a middle-aged man in a dark suit emerged, the low light gleaming on his bald head. He stood about six feet tall with broad-shoulders, and his hands were thick like a butcher's as he adjusted his jacket. Julian came to attention immediately and sidled over, inclining his head towards the man as he spoke. Marc supposed this must be the boss—Mayson.

Mayson glanced at him, a quick, calculating look, taking his measure. He said something to Julian, and then came round the bar, moving confidently through the crowd until he stood beside Marc.

"Jack Mayson," he said, holding out his hand. Marc took it.

"Marc Perron." Mayson's handshake was firm, polite, with none of the jockeying that some men did, trying to prove their prowess. He held Marc's hand a beat too long.

"I've heard of you," he said in the same measured tone with which he'd introduced himself. "We have a mutual friend."

"A business associate," Marc corrected. He had never considered Royale a friend.

Mayson let go of Marc's hand. "Noted. Royale has few friends."

"And he counts you among his friends?" Best to ask the question when they were in the open, surrounded by unsuspecting members of the public. He had phrased his question carefully, allowing for Royale's friendship with Mayson to be assumed, lessening the chance of violence.

Mayson snorted. "When it suits me." He waved Julian over. "My usual, and give him another shot of whatever he's drinking. On the house."

"Yes, sir." Julian poured another scotch for Marc, and then mixed a martini for Mayson, measuring each ingredient precisely, and placing two olives on a pick, resting it on the edge of the glass.

"We should talk," Mayson said, "in private." Marc considered his options, but before he could say anything, Mayson chuckled. "I don't murder people on my own premises."

"It wouldn't be sensible." Marc lifted his glass.

"If you need reassurance, I give you my word," Mayson said. "I know how Royale handles his affairs and I don't blame you for your caution. Come with me."

Mayson led Marc to his office, opening the door with a heavy key. Inside, he gestured to a seat in front of his desk as he sat in his own chair, leaning back. "Make yourself comfortable."

Marc took the seat offered, waiting for Mayson to begin, sipping his scotch. Mayson took a leisurely drink, seeming to savour the liquor.

"How long have you known Royale?" Mayson asked, setting his glass on the desk.

"Too long," Marc said. "Years." Since his uncle had run the firm, when Marc was a young man.

"I want answers."

CHAPTER 10

"Jeremy Gordon—he was like a son to me," Mayson said, though there was no emotion to his words, only the simple statement of facts. "I want to know what happened. The truth—nothing less."

"What did Royale tell you?" Marc stalled. The truth, the full truth, would end in bloodshed if Mayson was anything like Royale.

Mayson's expression grew grim. "Only that Jeremy had been killed, his body burnt beyond recognition—an ugly way to go. And that he'd been seeing some singer at Le Chat Rouge."

Marc shrugged. "I met him there, but I didn't know him. And there were several singers at the club. I can't say who he might have been seeing." His tone matched Mayson's calm, giving nothing away.

"You didn't know him? He did some work for you."

"He did, but we didn't spend any time together beyond a few short meetings. Hardly enough time spent to get to know the man.

What else did Royale tell you?"

"Are you calling him a liar?"

"I wouldn't put it past him," Marc said simply. "Gordon did speak of you to me during our one meeting—he said you were far better than Royale, stronger, more powerful. Royale was a peon in comparison."

Mayson's grim expression broke into a grin. "He had a way with words." He had a strange fondness for Gordon; his smile had become almost wistful. Marc had no such feelings for the man.

"You knew him well?"

"I raised him up." Mayson's voice filled with pride. "Took him off the streets, under my wing."

"Then why send him to Royale?"

Mayson's nostalgia vanished. "I had my reasons." He tossed back his martini, then reached for a packet of cigarettes on the desk. Marc rose and extended his lighter when it appeared Mayson had misplaced his own. "Obliged." He offered the pack to Marc, who withdrew the silver cigarette case from his pocket. Marc sat back in his chair, watching Mayson with caution as he smoked.

There was a knock at the door and Mayson pressed a button on a panel on his desk. Julian poked his head in.

"Alan is here to see you," Julian said. "Should I send him in?"

"In a moment," Mayson said. He rose and came around his desk, and Marc came to his feet. Mayson held out an ashtray. "No smoking in the club itself. Bloody laws."

Marc stubbed out his cigarette. "It's become similar in Paris."

"Tomorrow, we'll talk further. Bring your cello and you can play a set with David and Sera."

"Of course."

"We'll see if you're any good."

As he walked back into the club, Marc was sure Mayson didn't just mean his musical ability.

Sera sank back against the seat of the cab, boneless with exhaustion. Marc put his arm over her shoulders and she leaned into his warmth. Soon they would be home and she wanted nothing more than to have a hot shower and crawl into bed.

"Did Mayson like you?" she asked, not managing to stifle a yawn. She closed her eyes. "You were in his office awhile."

"He invited me to play tomorrow evening," Marc replied. "We'll go from there."

"Good. He's a strange one. I don't know why he doesn't like the French." It seemed that everything was coming together as she'd hoped. She rested her hand on his thigh, the denim warm against her skin. He put his hand over hers.

"I'm sure he has his reasons. You did well tonight," he said, "and you reminded me of earlier days when you first started performing; you seduced the entire audience."

"I only needed to seduce you." She squeezed his thigh. His answering chuckle rumbled in his chest, and in her ear.

"You succeeded, ma chère." His fingers traced delicate circles on her upper arm and Sera found her exhaustion fading. She kept herself from squirming under his touch, but only just. Still, he knew the effect he had on her.

"We're almost home."

In response, she shifted her hand higher on his thigh. "Not soon enough."

The cab pulled up outside their flat and Marc paid the driver. Sera went ahead of him, walking softly up the stairs. Marc caught up with her halfway to the top and she was hyperaware of his presence behind her. At their door, her hand shook and she barely managed to get the key in the lock. Marc pressed up against her, the heat emanating from his body as he slid his arm around her waist. His warm breath teased the nape of her neck and his lips brushed the sensitive skin, making her shudder.

"Do you need help with the door?" he asked, his voice a low whisper. He covered her hand with his own and they turned the key together.

The door swung open and they step-shuffled inside into the darkened hallway. She turned in Marc's embrace and he pinned her against the wall, his hand sliding under the hem of her dress, lifting her leg so she could hook it about his waist. He hoisted her up, her dress hiking up around her hips, her core pressed to him, grazing the buckle of his belt. She clung to him, her arms tight around his neck, rocking her hips against him.

In the dark, she sought his lips and they melded together until it seemed they were one. Her head swam and when they broke apart, she slumped forward against him. Marc shifted her in his arms and carried her into the bedroom.

The mid-morning sun streamed through the bay window of the reception room when Marc roused himself from sleep. They had finally gone to bed early that morning, but he couldn't sleep any longer. There was too much he had to do. He pulled on last night's jeans and moved to the kitchen to make an espresso. While it brewed, he dug out his phone from his jacket pocket and checked his messages. There was one call from an hour ago. He checked his voice mail.

Aurore's panic-stricken voice played in his ear.

"Monsieur, please call me right away." She choked back a sob. "There's been a pile-up on the Périphérique and Guillaume's been taken to l'Hôpital Pitié-Salpêtrière." She did sob then and Marc didn't bother listening to the rest of the message. He called Perron et fils. Aurore picked up on the first ring.

"Merci de Dieu," she said, her voice trembling in his ear. He heard her take a breath to try to calm herself.

"Aurore, what happened?"

Between sobs, she told him that while on his way to meet a client, Fournier, his second-in-command and the man he'd left to run the firm in his absence, had been involved in a serious car crash on the boulevard Périphérique.

"Will he be all right? What did the hospital say?" What he wanted to ask was, who did this? He wouldn't put it past Royale. He shook his head. They couldn't create a pile-up.

"I don't know, monsieur. He had to be cut from his car. They found his card and called here."

"Lock up the office and take the rest of the day off," Marc said, thinking rapidly. He needed to finish with the catalogue of the Lancaster estate before he left London, and have the work sent over to Dawson. Then he could pack and take the Eurostar back to Paris.

"But what about the clients, and the work?"

"I'll come back later today—no, tomorrow," he amended. He'd promised Sera that he would perform with her tonight. "Our clients will understand, Aurore."

"D'accord, monsieur. I'll close up and go to the hospital. Do you need me to book you a ticket?"

"I'll do it, Aurore, don't worry. Send me word when you get to the hospital."

Marc hung up and went to pour his espresso. He drank it standing up, looking out the bay window towards the park. He wouldn't need to courier the painting to Royale now. He could deliver it in person. Royale would be satisfied with the painting in his possession, but Marc didn't trust him.

Retracing his steps into the kitchen, he poured another espresso from the moka pot on the stove. He'd have to stay in Paris while

Fournier recovered; Aurore couldn't run the firm on her own.

But he hated leaving Sera alone in London.

A door clicked closed and he heard water running in the bathroom. Sera was awake already. Maybe she would want to come back to Paris with him. By his side, Royale couldn't get to her. He stepped back out into the reception room as Sera came out of the bathroom, her face damp and her hair brushed. They embraced and she leaned into him, resting her cheek on his chest, over his heart.

She pushed back and looked up at him, her brow furrowed. "Is something wrong?" She knew him too well. He told her about Fournier. "Mon Dieu. When will you know more?"

"Aurore will let me know when she gets to the hospital," he said. "But this means I have to go back to Paris."

Sera leaned into him once more. "Will you be gone long?"

"Until Fournier is better. I can't leave Aurore to handle everything on her own. Will you come with me?"

He heard her sigh, and then she lifted her head to look at him. "I can't. I don't want to lose this job."

"There will be other jobs. I would worry about you here on your own."

"I'll be fine," she said. "You don't have to worry. I'm getting used to living here, and I can manage. I can always call Pari if I have any trouble you know."

"She's not a real police officer," Marc said.

"She is so. Marc, I'll have people to go to if something happens, you don't have to worry. But you won't be that far away. You're only a few hours by train. Will you come back to see me on the weekends?"

"I'll come as often as I can," he vowed. "I could never stay away from you for long, ma chère."

"One day is too long," Sera said. "It will be strange sleeping in an empty bed. Must you go today?"

"Tomorrow morning. The firm can wait until then. We'll perform tonight at Sanctuary and show them how good we are. I'll talk to Mayson about performing regularly when I'm back. We'll make this work somehow."

The taxi dropped them at Sanctuary and Sera held the door open for Marc; he preceded her down the stairs with his cello. David was already seated at the piano when they entered and he waved them over.

"Good, you're early." He pulled back the curtain. "We can store your case back here for tonight. I have a setlist on the piano."

Sera let Marc and David figure things out, while she picked up the setlist and skimmed it. She knew all the songs, though she wasn't sure if Marc did. The piano had been moved to accommodate a straight-backed chair and a music stand on the far side. Marc came up behind her.

"What are we playing?" He glanced over her shoulder and

down at the list. "Not bad." He walked across the stage and settled onto the chair, having taken his jacket off. He wore a black shirt with silver cufflinks that suited the tone of the club. Positioning the cello between his thighs, he tightened the bowstring. The first draw of the bow produced a discordant sound, so he adjusted the pegs, then drew the bow across the strings again.

David resumed his seat at the piano and Sera removed her jacket and placed her things in the dressing room beside Marc's blazer. She checked her makeup in the mirror, reapplying her lipstick. When she returned to the stage, Marc and David were talking.

"She mentioned something about you being a composer as well," she caught David saying.

"I've written a few things," Marc replied. He played the first few notes of '*Ma Chanteuse*', her favourite of all his compositions. The notes made her breath catch in her throat—the piece always brought back memories. "Unless you want to sing something else." The song tapered off. Sera stepped up to the microphone.

"Je suis prête," she said. He began again and the words came to her as they always did, with memories of when he'd first sung them to her, as a surprise one romantic afternoon. Her voice rose and fell with the melody and it didn't matter that it was only the three of them in the club; she sang as if there was a full house.

"If it were entirely up to me, I'd hire you on the spot," David said to Marc when they finished. "And you, Sera—there's a certain something, a richness to your voice, when you sing…" He grinned. "C'est l'amour, n'est pas?"

Marc chuckled. "C'est vrai."

The first few customers began to trickle in and David glanced at the setlist. "Were there any you didn't know?"

"No, but I may be a little rusty," Marc admitted. "I've stuck more to classical in the last while."

"We'll see how you do," David said, "and afterwards we'll talk with Mayson."

Sera glanced up to the bar. Mayson stood there talking to Julian and to a thin, shorter man in a dark suit. The man seemed familiar, but she could only see the back of his head.

David played the first few notes of '*Baltimore Oriole*' and she heard Marc join in, his cello giving the song a greater, almost mournful, depth.

There was her cue.

After the last set, Marc put his cello back in its case, then joined David and Sera at the bar. Sera sipped a glass of cranberry and soda and David cupped his hand around a tumbler of whiskey.

"What can I get you?" Julian asked, polite but cool.

"Scotch, on the rocks. Glenfiddich," Marc requested. "And one for yourself." The bartender's coolness thawed somewhat and Marc bit back an amused smile. He'd noticed Julian's coolness on his last visit and seen his indulgent fawning over Sera. It would be hard to miss.

Marc glanced around the club. Mayson was nowhere to be seen.

"He's in his office," David said, noticing the look. "Go on in."

Marc bent to kiss Sera's cheek. "I'll be back shortly." She turned to him and he kissed her again, brushing her soft lips with a gentle touch of his own.

"I'll be here," she murmured.

Marc took his scotch and went to the office door. It felt strange being a supplicant, after so many years of being his own boss. He didn't particularly care for it, though it was a little thing he could do for Sera. He knocked and heard the click as the lock disengaged. He pushed the door open and went inside.

"That's quite the security system you have," he said as he took a seat in front of Mayson's expansive desk, placing his scotch on the arm of the leather chair.

Mayson chuckled. "Better to be safe than sorry around these parts," he said. "Too many gangs and thieves." He lit a cigarette and held out the pack to Marc. "Help yourself."

Marc pulled out his cigarette case. "Thank you, but I still have some of my own."

"You're a talented musician," Mayson said, getting right to the point. He loosened his tie and leaned back in his chair. "But yet you went into business. Why is that?"

"Money," Marc replied. And family obligations, but Mayson didn't need to know his background.

"Isn't it always? Speaking of which, I don't want to pay you to play for a full five nights a week." His gaze fixed on Marc, as if he was waiting for Marc to complain.

"That's for the best," Marc said. "I've been called back to Paris tomorrow due to an emergency at the firm, so I couldn't commit to that many nights."

"Saturdays only then?" Mayson suggested. "David can make up a name and we'll advertise your trio to the punters."

"And the wage?"

"£100 a night. I'm not a rich man." Mayson took a deep drag of his cigarette, blowing smoke rings towards the ceiling.

"I doubt that," Marc replied. Mayson guffawed.

"That's classified." His mobile phone, resting on the desk, buzzed. He reached for it, and Marc sat back. "Mayson." His jaw clenched. "The fuck he did." Mayson fiercely stubbed out his cigarette in the ashtray. "You find that little bastard and bring him to me. That gear was mine and he knew it." He listened a moment. "Call me when you have him." He set the phone back on the desk, and lit another cigarette.

"Trouble?" Marc leaned forward and stubbed out his cigarette in the ashtray on Mayson's desk.

"Just business."

Marc raised a brow at that, but said nothing.

"Keep it to yourself, what you heard," Mayson warned.

"D'accord." The French words slipped out and Mayson's hand clenched where it rested on the blotter.

"Fucking French," he muttered.

"My apologies," Marc said smoothly. "Habit." He observed as Mayson relaxed a fraction. "Why hire Sera if you hate the French?"

"She's talented." Mayson looked at him squarely. "But you, I'm not so sure. Too convenient."

Marc stiffened, then forced himself to relax. "You can trust me."

Mayson snorted, the sound uncouth in a well-dressed man. "The last man who said that to me was an undercover cop."

"And what happened to him?"

"Sent him back to his masters. Stupid git."

"I'm not a cop."

"Obviously. You don't have a stick up your arse."

Marc let out a choked laugh.

"And you dress better," Mayson observed.

"Thank you."

"We'll stick to our deal for now. Saturdays." Mayson abruptly changed the subject.

"Agreed."

"Give my regards to Royale if you see him," Mayson said, lighting a second cigarette, his mouth quirking up at the corner. "Tell him I'll be in touch."

"Of course." Sensing he was being dismissed, Marc rose. "I'll see you next Saturday."

CHAPTER 11

"Call me when you get home from the club," Marc said, bending to kiss Sera. She entwined her fingers with his and their hands brushed against the silky peignoir she'd slipped on when she got out of bed. Fashioned of ivory silk and lace, it was as pale as her skin. He wanted to strip it off her, but he was already close to being late for his train.

"I will," Sera said, her arm slipping around his waist, and under his suit jacket. Her hand was warm against his back and her soft form fired a delicious torture. "I'll be fine. My English is getting better, and there's always Pari to help."

He debated telling her of Royale's threat, and of Mayson, but the truth would do no good now. The painting was in his luggage and soon Royale would have no reason to complain.

"If you were staying home, you'd be sleeping on the sofa," she said, giving his tie a gentle tug.

"Sleeping alone, I might as well be."

"I'll see you on Friday night," Sera said. "Or earlier if you can get away. Give my best to Fournier when you see him."

"D'accord. À bientôt, ma chère." Marc kissed her once more, and then reluctantly let her go. She stood in the doorway as he went down the stairs. He glanced back just once and she blew him a kiss.

St. Pancras bustled with commuters at this time of day. The noise was amplified by the glass inside the terminal, and the long stretches of bare tile floor. Marc joined the queue for the self-serve tickets and then another queue to go through security. The agent glanced at his ticket and passport and then waved him through the scanner. French immigration barely looked at his passport, giving him only a brief, "Bonjour, monsieur," before stamping the page and sending him onward.

Passengers milled about the lounge and he walked its length before he found a seat on a leather-covered bench next to a young man who didn't even look up from his phone. Across the cluttered aisle, under a screen listing departures and arrivals, a young woman sat rocking her infant daughter while a toddler-aged boy slept hard beside her, his head on her leg. Her husband came to sit beside her, holding two bottles of water. He handed one to his wife and took the infant from her, rocking the child gently. They kissed, briefly and tenderly. He wondered what having a family might be like, but pushed the thought aside. Sera and him with kids had never been a consideration before.

Marc unzipped his bag and took out his laptop. There was a message from Aurore, and he read it quickly, hearing the first announcement for boarding. She detailed Fournier's condition and it was apparent that he would be out of commission for a long while yet, with a broken leg, two broken ribs, and various other injuries. Marc sent her a reply letting her know his schedule, and then logged off. He got to his feet, gathered up his bags, and followed the crowd to the moving walkway. The ramp moved at a discernable angle leading upward to the platform. He propped his luggage at his feet and kept tight hold of the handle of his rolling suitcase.

A young woman in front of him tried to place her suitcase upright and it rolled backward. He caught it with his free hand, almost unbalancing himself.

"Oh. I'm so sorry!" The girl's cheeks flamed in embarrassment and she grabbed the handle, brushing his hand. He ceded the suitcase to her and she struggled to position it until he reached forward to help. "Thank you." She gave him a shy smile, looking utterly charming in her dark skinny jeans and leather jacket, with a red scarf wrapped haphazardly around her neck. Her hair was dark brown, a riotous mass of curls that spilled over her forehead.

"De rien."

She was pretty, barely out of her teens by the looks of it, and he felt only the barest stir of desire. She turned forward again, looking up to their destination, and he frowned. His feelings shouldn't surprise him, but they did. A few months ago, he would have considered her ripe for the picking, but now? Only Sera would do.

At the top of the escalator, he lifted his bags and strolled down the platform to carriage number eight. He'd managed to book the last solo seat in the quiet car. He lifted his bags up the steps and then went up himself, stowing the suitcases in the luggage compartment before going through into the main cabin, He placed his laptop bag under the seat, and then sat down. The car filled quickly and he checked his watch. They'd be off any minute now.

Marc relaxed in his seat as the train pulled out of the station. Just over two hours from now, he'd be back in Paris. He hadn't expected it to happen this soon, and without Sera. His phone buzzed in his pocket and he took it out, hoping it would be her.

If only he could be so lucky.

Marc rose from his seat and went into the connector between cars before he answered. "Oui?"

"Bonjour, monsieur. My employer wishes for an update." It was Françoise, Royale's secretary.

"Impatient, isn't he?"

"I would say he has cause to be," Françoise replied in a prim tone.

Although Marc had a painting in his possession, it wasn't ready to be passed on to Royale. He needed to make certain it would pass as a Monet. "He'll get his wish," he said tersely. "At the moment, I have other issues to deal with."

"Yes, the accident of your associate. Poor man." Françoise clucked her tongue and Marc felt a surge of anger, and he wondered irrationally if she'd had anything to do with the accident.

"Did the crash make the papers?"

"Pile-ups like that always do," Françoise said. "Royale happened to mention it to me. He also mentioned that I should tell you that what he said last time still stands."

"I'd expect no less." If he could go back in time, he'd have kept his uncle from getting involved with gangsters, and risking the firm for easy money.

"We'll be in touch," Françoise said. "Don't take too long. By the way, it seems that prior events haven't hurt votre petite amie much—she still sings as lovely as ever at Sanctuary."

The line clicked and went dead. Marc glowered at his phone, fighting the impulse to throw it through a window. Blind fury wouldn't help him. Instead, he scrolled through his list of contacts, stopping at a familiar name.

Perfect.

Sera tried to go back to sleep after Marc left, and lay in her bed for over an hour before boredom and frustration drove her out. She showered and dressed, pulling on a pair of dark trousers and a simple blouse, and then made herself breakfast and coffee. She opened one of the books she'd bought recently, but it wasn't to her taste, not today. She was too aware of the slow passage of time, and the days remaining until Marc returned.

She hated feeling this way. When she'd broken off her relationship with Marc years ago, saying goodbye had felt like severing a piece of her heart, and she'd been at loose ends for months. It frightened her that she'd gotten so quickly used to having him there to take care of her. It made her vulnerable.

Sera put her book aside. She'd go get another one, something that would keep her mind off things. If she left early for work, she could stop by the bookstore on her way. For now, she'd take a walk into the park.

Instead of sitting by the pond as she'd done the day before, she strolled across the bridge and followed the path further along until she came to a set of black, wrought iron gates. She continued through them and found herself on a small road. The sign said 'Swains Lane' and the road was barely wide enough for two cars to pass abreast. A stone building much like a chapel, stood on one side of the road, a small brown hut nestled closer on the other side. A wide, winding path blocked by a guardrail stretched between rows of graves and she realized she must be at the entrance to Highgate cemetery. She went into the hut; a tiny gift shop that seemed to also serve as passage through to the cemetery itself.

Black and white postcards sat in small neat packets on a rack on the wall and in a box on the desk. A young woman with dirty blonde hair tied back in a bun looked up from her book.

"Did you want to see the cemetery?" she asked, setting her book aside. "It's £4 to see the East side only, which is where we are now. I would recommend the West side too, but today's tour has sold out."

Sera dug in her purse for her wallet. "Just the East side then." The girl gave her a pound coin in change and a brochure.

"Enjoy."

Sera stepped out onto the path. The sun beat down on her as she unfolded the brochure. Most of the names of famous burials were unfamiliar to her, but one caught her eye. George Eliot. She'd read 'Middlemarch' at school, but in translation. Still, the grave would be a good starting point.

Smaller unpaved paths and trails wound amongst the gravestones, half-shrouded by bushes and undergrowth. An odd mix of graves emerged closer to the main path. They seemed more recent and were in good condition, their text easily readable, but further back, some of the gravestones were overrun with ivy, the stone and the text eroded away with the passing of time. She had to backtrack to find the path that led to George Eliot's grave, after going as far as the gaudy monument to Karl Marx. The path led up a gentle slope and a grey, simple plinth was set back from the trail. A pair of birds twittered in the trees above her and she realized she couldn't hear any of the traffic noise.

Retracing her steps, she returned to the main path and walked past Marx's monument. To her right, a thin dirt track meandered deep into the mass of trees and greenery. She glanced at the map. Only faint lines marked the paths in this part of the cemetery. She pushed aside a dangling branch and forged forward.

Grass and wildflowers brushed at her legs and she heard the buzz of a bumblebee as it whizzed past. Most graves were smaller in this section; some held urns and a few were topped by weeping widows. The path grew smaller still as she walked, until she had to edge between two stone slabs. When Sera glanced back, she couldn't see the paved path, even though she could trace the way she had come.

A cool breeze blew through the trees, carrying with it a chill and the scent of cigarette smoke. Looking in the direction the scent came from, Sera could see nothing but trees and graves. She kept walking as the sunlight faded and the clouds rolled in. She quickened her pace, found another path, and followed it uphill, hoping to return to where she'd started. A giant raindrop splattered against her cheek and she hurried along. Unlike a Paris cemetery, there were no mausoleums where she could take shelter and she didn't want to get caught in a flash rainstorm. There was a crackle of leaves and brush behind her, but she didn't stop to look back.

Sera burst out onto the main path. The scattered raindrops she'd felt were heavier now and she bent her head, wishing she'd thought to bring her umbrella. The breeze picked up, its cold fingers sliding through her sweater, raising goose bumps. When she finally made it back to the hut, she was chilled through, her hair lank and damp down her back.

The girl looked at her sympathetically. "No brolly? You're not the only one." She gestured to a man coming up the path, his head bent, his hands shoved in his trouser pockets. He didn't come through the hut, but flashed them a glare as he squeezed around the guardrail and continued on. Watching him go, Sera thought she'd seen him before, in the park. It was too late to check for sure; he was gone, having walked down Swains Lane and out of sight.

Sera hugged herself, suppressing a shiver. The rain beat down on the roof and she wondered if it would ever let up. She said as much to the girl.

"There's blue sky coming," the girl said, pointing to a spot just beyond the trees. "It won't last long. Do you have far to go?"

"Not far." Sera browsed through the postcards while she waited.

"The packets are £2 each," the girl said helpfully. The sound of rain on the roof lessened and Sera glanced out the window. Within a few minutes, the rain had stopped completely, though the leaves on the trees still fluttered in the breeze. "You should be all right now."

"Thank you. It's a lovely cemetery."

"Come again, if you'd like. We're open every day."

Sera gave the girl a wave as she left, hurrying through the park, glancing around, trying to spot the man who'd been following her. Out in the open, the wind hadn't settled and she wrapped her arms about herself again as she crossed over the pond and went up the hill. Never was she so glad to be home as when she opened the front door of her building and slipped inside, pausing by the hallway radiator. Once in the flat, she pulled off her sweater and draped it over a chair to dry before she stripped off her shoes and wet socks.

The clock on the microwave over the stove said two p.m. and she hadn't realized she'd been gone so long. She hurried into the bathroom to warm herself with a hot shower. Once under the spray, her shivers ceased.

Before he went to the office, Marc took a taxi from Gare du Nord to the hospital. Aurore's text had been precise in its directions and he found the firm's receptionist in a sterile waiting room. Her usually spotless clothes were rumpled, and dark smudges lay underneath her eyes. A weariness had settled about her that made her seem older than twenty-five. He dropped his bags to the ground and gently kissed her cheeks, one brief touch on each side. She clung to him and he embraced her. She felt fragile in his arms, almost too delicate to be real.

"Ça va, Aurore?" She gave a minute shake of her head. "And Fournier? Have you heard anything more?"

Aurore lifted her head from his shoulder. "He's alive," she replied. "His leg is broken, badly, and a couple of ribs, as I said. But his head hit the window—the air bag didn't deploy—and he was unconscious when they found him…" She pressed her lips together and her chin trembled.

"Unconscious?"

Aurore nodded and sank back against him once more. Marc closed his eyes and sighed. Paris would be a long-term stay, longer than he'd expected. "Will they allow visitors?"

"Only for a minute. He's in intensive care."

"I'll go talk to a nurse." He'd see Fournier, and then there was work to do. "Have you slept, Aurore? Or eaten?"

Aurore wiped her eyes and stepped back. "Un peu."

"Go home then," he said. "Get a cab—the firm can pay—and get some rest. I'll see you at the office tomorrow and we'll figure things out."

"Oui, monsieur." She managed a shaky, tentative smile. "À

demain."

At the nurse's station, a young woman answered his query. "Leave your bags here, then come with me. Your visit will have to be brief. The young lady said she wasn't sure if Monsieur Fournier had any family. We really need to contact them."

"His father lives in Lyon," Marc replied, "but I don't think they've spoken in years. Something to do with him not approving of his son's choices." A familiar refrain.

"No siblings?" the nurse pressed.

"Not that I'm aware of."

They came to a large, glassed-in room, which held several beds arrayed in a semi-circle around a nurse's station.

Marc almost didn't recognize Fournier, with his forehead swollen and bruised, a bandage half-obscuring his hair, tubes snaking his arms, and draped in a blue gown. A chuckle bubbled up from his chest and he stifled it, sure the nurse wouldn't approve. If Fournier were awake, he'd have complained to anyone within earshot about how hideously he was dressed. Seeing him out of his signature-striped waistcoat was sobering.

"What have the doctors said about his recovery?" Marc asked, standing at the foot of the bed.

"He'll live," the nurse said, "but until he wakes, we won't know the extent of his head injury. The scans can only tell us so much."

"How did the accident happen?"

The nurse shrugged. "The paramedics who brought him in said he had to be cut from his vehicle, caught as it was in the centre of the pile-up. They're not sure how the accident happened."

Marc took one of his business cards from his wallet and wrote his mobile number on the back. "I'm his friend, and his employer," he said. "Please, if you could call me if anything changes, or if he gets worse. I'll try to contact his father if I can, even if they are estranged."

She took the card and tucked it into her pocket as she led him back to where he'd left his bags. "We'll keep you informed as best we can, monsieur."

Only the slow blink of the light from Aurore's computer, and the flashing red from the phone at reception, greeted Marc when he unlocked the door to Perron et fils. He flicked on the light, illuminating the receptionist's desk and the leather chairs in the stark, modern room. He bent to pick up the bundle of mail that had been dropped through the door slot and locked the door behind him before he walked through to his own office.

The tapestry behind his desk hung as it always did, its muted colours in startling contrast to the sleek dark lines of the room. Leaving his suitcases by the door, he tossed the mail onto his desk and took his laptop from its bag. His leather chair creaked when he sat. He checked his email but there was only a message from Dawson, letting him know he'd finished the cataloguing of the furniture and acknowledging the receipt of the list Marc had sent yesterday.

Marc took up the packet of letters and removed the elastic

band. Sales circulars and obvious advertisements went in one pile, leaving him with a far more manageable selection of mail. Using a pewter letter opener, he sliced open each envelope in turn, setting invoices and payments to one side. There was a letter from the care home where Sera's mother resided, which provided a regular up-date. He read it and sighed. Sera's mother—practically his mother-in-law—was doing well, other than her regular demands to go to the casino. He put the letter aside, knowing he'd have to talk to Sera, but not today. It would keep until he went back to London.

He double-checked the number of the reproduction artist he knew, a man that charged only thousands for nearly identical re-productions of paintings that cost millions. For a small fee, a signature ought not to be so hard.

CHAPTER 12

The bookshop on Charing Cross Road buzzed with customers. Sera edged round a couple in the middle of an aisle who were discussing—debating, more like—the possibilities for best crime writer. After a wrong turn, she found the stairs and went up a level. She must have chosen the wrong direction because she seemed to wander the entire floor. Maybe she'd picked the wrong floor and the books in translation were on another?

She spotted a uniformed staff member at the end of an aisle, a girl with tautly braided auburn hair. Sera approached her.

"Excuse me, do you know where I—" Her words dropped off as the girl turned. It was Madelaine. Sera stuttered through the rest of her question, feeling uncharacteristically awkward.

"Just over there." Madelaine pointed and Sera turned. She must have walked past it.

"Thank you."

"Can I ask you a question?"

Sera paused, then turned back to face her.

"Bien sûr. Of course."

"Is it true what he said, that you were together before he met me?"

"Over five years ago," Sera replied. "And then a few months ago we got back together."

"A few months?" Madelaine's eyes narrowed and she pressed her lips together. "It was you he was talking to on the phone, wasn't it?"

On the phone? Sera couldn't think of what the girl was talking about.

"About two months ago, one night, talking dirty. That was you he was talking to, wasn't it? I don't know much French, but it wasn't hard to figure out what he meant."

Sera forgot to breathe. She remembered that phone call—alone in her dressing room, and Marc alone in his hotel room in London—no, not alone.

Madelaine leaned close, her face inches from Sera's, her grey eyes snapping. "So, he lied to you too. While you thought he was thinking of you, he came in my mouth."

Sera stumbled back a step, feeling queasy.

"Even what he told me last week was a lie," Madelaine hissed. "I never had a chance; he was with you already. That bastard. I loved him, and better than you."

"Je ne savais pas." She hadn't known, though she should have.

"How many women does he have on a string? Do you know? God, he played me. He must have laughed, thinking how I had loved him."

Madelaine put her hand to her mouth as if to hold in her fury, or her sorrow. Looking at her, Sera knew Madelaine was in love with Marc. And the truth hurt, squeezing her heart like a vise. Jealousy and bitterness soured her happiness. He'd had affairs before, with Xavière, so why not again? That it was two months ago didn't matter. Their intimate moment, their sharing, had been experienced by an intruder, and she hadn't known. He'd lied to her, and used her to spice up his playtime with another woman.

Madelaine glanced at her then, noticing the stares they were getting, and turned on her heel and walked away.

Sera's eyes burned and she took a deep breath, and then another, but she felt stifled, like the bookshop was a cave and not an airy, bright building. She made her way to the staircase and rushed down, pushing through the glass doors and out onto the sidewalk. If she could, she'd go back to the flat and curl up in bed, but if she did, she'd miss work and lose her job. Reluctantly, she headed towards Sanctuary. The passers-by studiously ignored the tears she couldn't hold in, while she swallowed back the sobs that threatened.

When she reached the club, she paused at the top of the stairs, wiping her face with her sleeve. She took the concrete stairs slowly, clinging to the cold metal rail, pushing through the curtain.

The house lights were up and it was as bright as she'd ever

seen it. Julian stood by the bar, shrugging into his shirt. He glanced over his shoulder and by his expression she knew she hadn't done enough to hide her distress. Julian didn't even bother to button his shirt; it fluttered open as he came to her, showing the white singlet underneath.

"Ça va, Sera?"

It was the concern in his tone that undid her. She shook her head, her hand over her mouth, turning away from him.

"Sera?" His hand rested on her shoulder, gently turning her back towards him. Tears blurred her gaze.

"Rien. It's nothing," she managed to rasp out.

"Are you hurt?" Julian examined her face as if she might have an injury. Sera wiped her eyes again, drying the tears that threatened to fall.

"I'm fine," she said, but he didn't drop his hand from her shoulder.

"You can trust me, Sera," he assured her, his brow furrowed with concern. He held his arms wide. "If nothing else, I give good hugs."

Sera hesitated, feeling as if she'd be cheating if she accepted his compassion, but then she reminded herself why she'd been crying in the first place. And Julian was a friend, albeit a new one. She moved into his embrace and he wrapped his arms around her snugly, resting his chin on the top of her head. His warmth surrounded her, seeping into her body, and the subtle scent of his cologne was soothing in itself. His heart beat steadily under her ear.

"Better?" he asked when she stepped back.

"Oui." Sera tried for a smile, but it wouldn't come.

"Who has upset you? I'll have a word." Julian looked determined. "Is it your boyfriend? I'll set him straight."

"Sort of. Not exactly." She didn't want to talk about it. "I'll just go get ready before David gets here." She headed towards the dressing room.

"Sera?" Julian called. She glanced back. "Drink after work?"

"D'accord."

Julian grinned. "Tres bien."

The evening's performance, usually a euphoric experience, couldn't banish Sera's low mood or the betrayal she felt. It shouldn't have mattered—she'd known Marc had had other women—but she had trusted him and he'd used her as a part of his intimacy with Madelaine.

Madelaine. She looked like a younger version of herself, but with red hair, as if Marc was stuck on a certain look, a certain age. She felt queasy at the thought as she stepped out of her dress and changed back into her street clothes. Looking into the mirror hanging on the back of the door, she studied herself. Benoît, the pianist at Le Chat Rouge, had always said she didn't look her age, but she felt old and tired suddenly. She wanted a cup of tea and her bed, even if it would be cold and empty. Except, she had promised Julian a drink.

There was a knock at the door and she shoved her folded dress into her bag. Julian popped his head round the door.

"You decent?"

"If I wasn't, it would be too late now, wouldn't it?" she replied. He chuckled.

"True. But you've been in here so long I thought you must be."

"And you weren't just trying to sneak a look?"

"I would never." He pushed the door open further. "Coming for a drink? My treat."

"I should go home," Sera said. "I'm not fit company."

Julian held out his hand. "Of course you are. There's nothing better than a drink after a long night. Even if it's only one." Reluctantly, she took his hand, gathering up her bag and jacket.

"Just one," she said as he tugged her out of the dressing room. His hand was firm around hers, and warm; the cuff of his leather jacket brushed her wrist, the dangling zipper cool on her skin. He pushed through the stage curtain, holding it aside so she could pass through. The lights in the club were up and already a team of cleaners had arrived.

"Where's everyone else?" she asked as they moved towards the door.

"David went to see Mayson. They are meeting with people

from the other clubs Mayson owns. Why he likes to do business so late, I'll never know." Julian let go of her hand. "Let me help you with your coat. It's cold out tonight."

Julian held her jacket for her as she slid her arms into the sleeves and his hands rested on her shoulders for a beat too long before he smoothed out a non-existent wrinkle.

"Merci beaucoup." Sera settled the strap of her bag over her shoulder. "Where are we going?"

"Just a little place," Julian said. "Good drinks, good service. The bartender's a friend of mine and he'll see us right."

On the street, she didn't object when he took her hand again. It was cold; a fierce wind had picked up and it chilled her fingers to the bone and whipped her hair around her face. Fortunately, they didn't go far. They walked a few blocks to a bar deeper than it was wide, with a sleek bar that ran almost the entire length of one wall. A few high tables with stools were scattered throughout. It was busy, but not oppressively loud, and Julian nodded to the doorman, who let them pass. He found her a spot at the far end of the bar, on the remaining free stool.

"Don't you want to sit?" she asked, leaning in so he could hear her without her having to raise her voice.

"I'm fine," he said, though he shuffled a bit closer to give the couple next to them some space. "What would you like to drink?" He waved the bartender over and they exchanged greetings.

"Julian, who's your friend?" The man held out his hand, giving Sera's hand a friendly shake. He grinned, his eyes dark in the low light. He wore a snug black t-shirt that emphasized his broad shoulders, and his dark hair was cut almost military-short.

"Tony, meet Sera, the new singer at Sanctuary. Sera, this is Tony, the best bartender in the business."

"I taught Julian all I know," Tony said.

"Nice to meet you."

Tony whistled. "A French bird. Enchantée, madame. What can I get for you?"

"Anything you want," Julian said. "My treat."

"In that case"—Tony winked—"I'd recommend a bottle of Veuve or Cristal."

Sera laughed when Julian looked horrified. "Just a gin fizz. Nothing fancy."

"Not fancy?" Tony chuckled. "You're getting off easy, mate. Your usual?" At Julian's nod, Tony pulled out a pint of Smithwick's and then set about making her a gin fizz. He cracked an egg over the cocktail shaker and let the white pool at the bottom, then added the gin, lemon juice and orange blossom water, and a splash of cream. After filling the shaker with ice, he put the top on securely, mixing the ingredients. Then he poured them over a tumbler full of ice and added soda water from the gun at the bar. After placing a curled slice of lemon on the edge of the glass, he presented it to her.

"Your drink, madame."

"Merci beaucoup."

Tony waved away Julian's money. "I'll start you a tab."

Julian lifted his beer. "Santé." Sera echoed the toast and took a sip of her gin fizz. The mixture was tart on her tongue and it took a couple of sips before she became used to the taste.

"I haven't had a gin fizz this good since I was last at La Coupole," Sera remarked, remembering the last time, some years prior, when she'd gone with Marc for an intimate dinner. She frowned.

"That's not the face of a woman who likes her drink," Julian commented. "You can order something else if you'd like. Even Veuve."

"I'm fine with this," Sera replied. "My mind's on other things. Tell me something about yourself, Julian. I feel like I hardly know you."

"You've asked for it now," Julian quipped. "Born in Yorkshire, hence my accent." She hadn't noticed, but then, most Englishmen sounded the same to her. "And I was a bit of a troublemaker as a kid. Wanted to be an actor but failed to get into RADA. Still, I stayed in London, and here I am, fifteen years later."

"Any brothers or sisters?" she asked, wanting to keep him talking. It would keep her mind off of Marc.

"One of each. I'm the baby," he replied. "The family despairs that I'll ever make much of myself."

"They don't approve?"

"It's not a respectable job, my father says. He reckons I should have gone into business with him and my brother, building homes." Julian grimaced. "No thank you. But what about you? Any siblings?"

"None." Sera took another sip of her gin fizz, stirring the ice. "Maman had me, then Papa left, and…" She shrugged. "C'est tout."

"How'd you become a performer?"

"I didn't set out to be. I was an au pair, at least until I was sacked. Then I didn't want to go back home, so I started waitressing. My boss heard me sing."

"I bet he was utterly taken with you," Julian said, draining his glass. He caught Tony's eye.

"Maybe. But it got me out of waitressing, and it was a better job. Mostly." Except for Royale. She shivered. Julian put his arm around her.

"You cold?"

Sera shifted closer to him. Not cold, but the weight of his arm was comforting, reassuring.

"And you came to London to get famous?"

Sera glanced up at him and he winked at her, making her realize he was only teasing.

"If I'm lucky," she replied, giving him a nudge. "But I won't forget you when I am."

"Good." Julian leaned close, his mouth hovering by her ear. "I'd miss you if you did."

Tony interrupted their moment. "Another gin fizz?" he asked as he placed a fresh pint of Smithwick's in front of Julian.

"Please." She sucked the last of the gin up her straw and pushed the glass aside.

"Take me with you if you do get famous," Julian murmured in her ear. She patted his hand, trying not to giggle.

"It'll be a rider in all my contracts," she replied. Julian clasped her hand, bringing it to his lips, his blue-eyed gaze fixed upon her.

"Promise?" He held her hand even after he'd kissed it again, and she let him, though it seemed strange to be holding the hand of a man other than Marc. Not that he was here to complain. Her amused smile faded and she took a sip of her drink.

Moving to London hadn't gone at all like she'd intended—she was here, alone, while Marc dealt with business, a business he'd promised her he'd give up. They were supposed to be performing together, writing new songs, leaving their old lives behind. Except he hadn't left his life behind, not by a long shot. The only thing they'd really managed to leave behind was Le Chat Rouge—and Royale.

"Ça va?" Julian asked, giving her fingers a gentle squeeze. His concern for her was touching. Marc had been that way once, back when they'd first dated. He had been on the Eurostar as well, but that felt almost like another life.

"I'm fine," she said, trying to keep from sounding morose, but the words came out sharper than she'd intended and she winced. "Sorry. I really ought to go home. I'm not much fun tonight." She shifted on her chair.

"Don't go," Julian said, still holding her hand. "Finish your drink and then we'll go downstairs to the dance floor."

"Dance floor?"

"You'll like it. Drink up, then we'll have a dance before we go. It's still early yet."

Sera sipped her gin fizz, the lemon sour on her tongue, even with the added sugar water. The glass was half full when she put it down and pushed it away. "That's all I can manage." When she got to her feet, the room swam along the edges of her vision and she realized the gin had affected her more than she thought it would. "One dance."

Julian led her to the back of the bar, zigzagging through the crowd to a wide staircase. Flashing lights glimmered on the stone and she could hear the beat of the bass over the conversation. At the bottom of the staircase, Julian led her down a short hallway that opened up into a wide, dark room, lit by moving spotlights and a glittering mirror ball. She hesitated and Julian hooked his arm about her waist, pulling her forward into the heat of the crowd, their bodies writhing to the rhythm.

He found them an empty place near the middle of the crowd, and he began to move to the music. Sera felt overwhelmed by the noise and the crowd that pressed in on them and when he drew her in, protecting her from the flailing dance moves of a man nearby, she was relieved. His thighs brushed against hers; they were practically skin-to-skin. She followed his lead and found herself moving to the harried beat of the bass. A strobe light flickered, illuminating his features and he grinned at her, lifting her arms about his neck. She lost herself in the heat, in the rhythm, in the press of his muscled body against her own softer form, moulding herself to him. They moved as one.

And when she felt his lips on hers in the darkness, seeking her out, she didn't pull back.

CHAPTER 13

Marc took the painting to Didier Laval's studio in the Marais, a third floor apartment on the rue Payenne, in a plain-faced Haussmann-era building that looked like it had seen better decades. Although he could afford better, Laval preferred his old studio. The elevator clanked its way lethargically down from the top floor and Marc decided to take the stairs. The studio door was open a fraction and he knocked as he came in.

"Didier?" Marc called, and received a response almost immediately.

"Come through to the studio," Didier called back.

Marc walked through a cluttered hallway and living room set up like a studio apartment, and into what used to be the bedroom. Didier stood with his back to the open door, working on a small canvas. Other canvases leaned against the walls: a Cezanne, a Manet—Olympia, of course—and several of the Mona Lisa.

"Ah, Marc." Didier turned, paintbrush in his left hand. He was barefoot in tattered jeans and his once-white smock was splattered with paint. He held out his right hand and they shook. "It's been awhile. Still running Perron et fils? I've had several clients from Fournier in the last while when they lost out on original works."

"Fournier's mostly taken over for me," Marc replied, "but he's laid up after an automobile accident, so I'm handling the business for now."

"Give him my best. Now, what have you brought me?" Didier laid down his paintbrush and Marc unwrapped the painting, setting it on Didier's second, currently empty easel. He inspected it closely, his nose almost touching the brushstrokes, before he glanced at Marc.

"This isn't new," he said. "Where'd you get it?"

"Car boot sale," Marc said. "I liked the look of it."

"Reminds me of Monet's haystacks," Didier remarked. "I can see why you wanted the signature put on—but what I don't get is why you need to fake it. This isn't just some reproduction." He gave Marc a reproving look. "This doesn't seem above-board."

"I have a client who fancies it but would like to impress his wife," Marc replied. "He's the one that suggested the signature be Claude Monet's. Can you do it?"

"Oh, I can do it," Didier said, "but it's not..." He broke off, turning back to the painting he'd been working on, a Manet, dabbing at a smudge. "What if the wife wants to pass it off as a real Monet at auction a few years down the line? Then we're all in trouble."

"It'll be in the contract," Marc replied easily. "And I'll keep its provenance on record so there's no question of it later."

"I don't know. It's one hell of a risk. At least with my original paintings, it's obvious. This…" Didier fished a crumpled pack of cigarettes from the pocket of his smock, and a lighter. He lit one, then offered the packet to Marc.

"Non, merci. I'm trying to cut back."

Didier took a deep drag as he put the packet back. "This painting, and what you want me to do…there's something off."

"My client's not some fly-by-night huckster," Marc said. "My uncle knew him. It's been years."

Didier rubbed the side of his nose, looking as if he was weighing his options. He paced to a desktop computer set up in the far corner, and brought up a scan of an early Monet painting: *Impression, Sunrise,* and zoomed into the signature. He studied the landscape intently, and then glanced back at Marc.

"If this blows up in your face, I had no part in it," he said firmly. "None."

"D'accord. Can you do it now?"

"Leave it here; the paint will need to dry overnight."

"I'll come back for it tomorrow, then."

"Tres bien. If you have cash, I'll take the €500 now, but if not, you can pay me tomorrow."

Marc took out his wallet and handed over ten crisp €50 notes.

"Much appreciated." Didier tucked the money in his smock. "I'll see you tomorrow."

Marc called Royale's secretary when he returned home from Didier's studio. He had work to do yet, but the sooner he got this over with, the better.

"Monsieur Royale has been waiting for your call," Françoise said.

"I have a business to run," Marc reminded her, "and he's not my only client." He heard her tsk before she transferred him through.

"Perron. Good news?" Royale coughed.

"I have a Monet for you."

"Bring it over tonight," Royale commanded. "I'll tell Jean you're expected."

"Tomorrow," Marc countered. "Before the bar opens. I don't want a club full of observers."

Royale grumbled, but to Marc's surprise, acquiesced. "Tomorrow then. The wife will be pleased."

"And you can call off your watchdog, whoever it is."

"Not yet. Not until we complete our transaction. À demain."

Marc set his phone aside and went into the kitchen, making himself an espresso. He lit a cigarette and cracked open the kitchen window. He'd call Sera later and check in to make sure she was safe. He didn't trust Royale, and he didn't trust whomever Royale had paid to keep tabs on them. If only he'd been able to spot their observer.

Marc stubbed out his cigarette. Time to get back to work.

Julian had insisted on seeing Sera home, though she'd assured him she would be fine. The cab idled by the curb as he walked her to the outer door, coming up the stairs behind her. She pulled out her key and turned to him.

"I'll be all right from here."

"Are you sure? It's no trouble."

"I'm sure. Good night, Julian."

He bent his head to kiss her, but she took a half step back. In the late night chill, she'd come to her senses, and he hadn't pressed her until now.

"I can't. I'm sorry, Julian. I shouldn't even have kissed you before." He moved forward again and she laid a hand on his chest. He covered her hand with his before bringing it to his lips.

"D'accord." He held her hand when she went to pull back. "But remember, if you need anything at all, or if he treats you poorly, I'm here for you. I promise."

Promises.

Marc had given her promises, more than a few, but Julian

seemed so earnest, and kind.

"Thank you. I'll remember. Bonne nuit, Julian."

He let go of her and stepped back, retreating to the sidewalk and opening the door of the cab. When she glanced back after unlocking the door, he stood there still. She gave him a little wave and he nodded, getting into the cab. Before she closed the door behind her, she saw the cab drive off, up Highgate Hill.

Once inside the flat, she stripped her shoes from her tired, sore feet and let her coat drop to the sofa as she passed it on her way to the bedroom. She left her purse on the floor, pulling out her phone to send a quick text to Marc. He would be reassured she was home, but she didn't really want to talk to him. The scene with Madelaine still stung and her lips were swollen from Julian's kisses. What she wanted was a shower and bed.

Sera gathered her peignoir from where it lay on the duvet. On the nightstand, her phone vibrated insistently.

"Bonsoir, Marc."

"Bonsoir, ma chère. I've missed you."

"Moi aussi." She wanted to confront him about Madelaine, ask him what he'd really told her that day in the bookshop, but it wasn't a conversation for the phone, for this late at night.

"Off to bed?" he asked, his voice low, its tone sending a shiver down her spine. If he were here, they'd be going to bed, but not to sleep.

"Shower, then sleep," she said, yawning. "It's been a long

night." A lethargy spread through her limbs and her eyes burned. Before she could sink down on the bed, she went through the flat to the bathroom.

"I'd be there if I could."

"I know." Sera set her peignoir on the vanity beside the sink. "But you'll be back. Bonne nuit, Marc."

"Bonne nuit, ma chère. Je t'aime."

"Je t'aime," she whispered back before she ended the call. The tightness in her chest from earlier in the night returned and she took a deep breath, setting the phone down and stripping off her clothes. She wouldn't cry. She'd cried enough already today.

Once under the hot water, she thought she would be fine, but she wasn't. Sera squeezed her eyes shut. The tears spilled out from under her lashes, mingling with the damp heat of the shower spray. A wave of homesickness overtook her. She wanted to be back in her small garret apartment, with its homey, mismatched furniture and its view of the rooftops. In her own bed, her own kitchen, tiny as it was, with her own friends.

From her savings, she'd paid six months of the rent in advance, but if she went back to Paris, she wouldn't have a job. Could she even get one now, or would Royale have spread word of her disloyalty and made her an anathema to other clubs? She wiped her face, though her hands were as wet as her cheeks. It wasn't all bad here. She had Pari, and Julian, and a job in a club she liked. She didn't have to face Royale, or Jean. And she had Marc.

Except, she wasn't sure if that was enough, and there was

Madelaine, too.

Marc had inspected the canvas before Didier had wrapped it for him. To all but the most educated, the work was a Monet. Now he strode purposefully along the boulevard St. Germain, and turned into the side street approaching Le Chat Rouge. This afternoon, the area was thronged with people, tourists mostly, but the club itself was shuttered and dark. He rang the buzzer, unbuttoning his summer-weight suit jacket. It was nearly La Rentrée, and the late summer sun was hot on his back.

The tall wooden door swung inward and he stepped inside, taking off his sunglasses and letting his eyes adjust to the gloom. Jean shut the door behind him and locked it once more.

"Royale's waiting for you," Jean said. "I didn't think you'd be back so soon." He laughed softly to himself and led Marc past the bar and into the back hallway to Royale's office. The air was cool, but smelled stale, like cigarettes and spilled beer. Jean knocked on the door and they heard the imperious reply.

"Entrez!"

Royale sat behind his desk, engrossed in something on his laptop, occasionally tapping the track pad. He glanced up. "Ah, you're here. Bien."

Jean departed, closing the door.

"I went to a lot of trouble for this, Marc said, lifting the wrapped canvas. "You'll have to keep it hush for awhile."

Royale chuckled as he lit a cigarette. "Quick fingers, eh? No matter. Unwrap it."

Marc undid the brown paper wrapping carefully, reminding himself to act as if he had a priceless masterpiece in his hands. He held the canvas gingerly, displaying it to Royale.

"A Monet," Royale said, sounding awed, the first time Marc had heard him be anything but demanding. He stared at the painting; his eyes roamed over every detail before settling on the signature in the bottom corner. "Where did you get it?"

Marc propped the painting on one of the two straight-backed chairs facing Royale's desk, and lowered himself into the other. He took a cigarette from the silver case in his inner suit jacket pocket and lit it before answering.

"A certain widow of my recent acquaintance didn't know what she had," he said. "Thus why it must be kept hush. I don't want the truth to come out."

Royale frowned. "For how long? My wife will want to show it off."

"Several months at least," Marc said, "but you really should keep it quiet anyway—it'll make you less of a target for thieves."

"As if a thief would have the balls to try and rob me." Royale guffawed, but his laugh turned into a cough. He dabbed at his watering eyes with a handkerchief. "Still, I see your meaning."

"Tres bien. And in return, call off your little spy."

Royale pulled out his phone, scrolling through his messages.

"Must I? You might find this interesting, Perron." He chuckled when he found the message he was searching for. "Your lovely lady went dancing with another man last night. Do you know what she gets up to when you're not around? She must have a thing for Englishmen." Royale licked his lips, the motion lewd. It turned Marc's stomach.

"I'm not worried about her."

"As you will." He seemed disappointed that Marc hadn't risen to his bait. "I do miss seeing her around the bar. Delectable. It's all men in here now—a real pity."

"No new chanteuse?"

"Their talents have been lacking, but the new man has improved business."

Marc rose, not bothering to wait for Royale to dismiss him. They were quits. "À bientôt."

"Take a look at this before you go," Royale said. He'd been fiddling with his phone and he flipped it around so Marc could see the screen. The image seemed a blur of people under a strobe light.

"What am I looking at, exactly?" With some reluctance, he moved closer.

"In the centre, just there." Royale zoomed in on a couple in a passionate embrace. "That's the thanks you get for being too permissive with women."

"That could be anyone." Sera wasn't the only woman with dark hair like that.

Royale shrugged. "Not the best photo, I admit." He fiddled with his phone again and brought up another photo of the same couple, except this time they weren't kissing. It was Sera and she was with Julian, the bartender from Sanctuary. "This one is clearer, I'm sure you'll agree. I'm just looking out for you, like your uncle would have if he'd been alive. It would be better to find a woman you can trust, after all."

Marc kept his expression carefully neutral. His uncle had kept a series of mistresses—hardly a man to take advice from regarding women—and he doubted Royale had any real paternal interest.

"C'est rien," Marc said with an insouciant shrug. He went to the door. "We're even now." He considered telling Royale about Mayson, but decided against it. The less Royale knew, the better.

Royale scrutinized the painting. "Yes, we are."

CHAPTER 14

Sera sat by the pond in Waterslow Park, watching the ducks frolic, her arms wrapped around her knees. A book rested on the bench beside her, but she wasn't in the mood for reading. It was several hours yet before she had to go to work, but the time seemed to drag. She smelled cigarette smoke before a shadow fell over her, and for a moment, she hoped it would be Marc.

It wasn't Marc.

A man in an ill-fitting suit stood beside the bench, looking a bit worn, his thin face reminding her of a rodent. He gestured toward her with his hand while holding the cigarette, his fingers yellowed.

"May I? All the rest are taken."

She glanced about and saw that her bench was the only one with space. Nodding, she shifted over to give him room, keeping her book between them.

"Ta," he said, settling onto the bench's far end. Close, but not too close. She thought he looked familiar somehow, but she couldn't quite place him.

"You new 'round here?" he asked, taking a drag on his cigarette before he stubbed it out on the side of the bench, dropping the butt to the ground. "I've been seeing you about lately."

"Yes, new." Sera glanced away, hoping to discourage him. She hadn't come here to talk to anyone.

"Pretty here, ain't it? Wish my shop was 'round these parts."

"Your shop?" she couldn't help asking.

"Antiques and fine art," the man said. He held out his hand. "I'm Bates. You should come see it. I have lots of lovely things for a lady. I'd even give you a discount if you found something you fancied."

Sera shook his hand, but only briefly. He grinned, showing crooked teeth, one with a chip missing.

"What ya reckon?" he asked, his gaze fixed on her.

"No, pas pour moi," she said. He reminded her of the insistent beggars and souvenir sellers in Paris as he continued on.

"No? I've some lovely items for an elegant madame such as yourself," he said. "Hair combs, clasps, necklaces, all that."

"Non, merci." Sera rose, hastily scooping up her book.

"Don't go on my account." The man rose with her, and it seemed to her that he tracked her every movement, casually cutting off her escape routes. She backed away from him as he smiled, his expression rapacious. "Come on, sit down."

Sera shook her head. With another few steps she was away from the bench and had a clear path back to the trail, and home.

Home. She didn't want to lead him there, where he could lie in wait for her, especially as Marc wasn't there. Was Pari around? She couldn't remember her schedule, though Pari had told her the last time they'd spoken. She hurried away, up the hill, glancing back every so often. The man—Bates—followed her, but he kept his pace to a meandering stroll. For a second, she doubted he was following her at all, but when she glanced back, she saw him smirk. She picked up her pace, reaching the park entrance and Highgate Hill in record time.

Instead of going home, she darted into a pharmacy and pulled out her phone, dialling Pari's number. It rang twice and then Pari picked up.

"Pari here," she said, sounding cheerful as always. Sera let out a relieved breath.

"Pari, it's Sera. Are you at home?"

"For a little while yet. Do you want to come over for tea?"

"I think someone's following me," Sera blurted out. She went to the back of the shop, away from the windows, tucking herself out of view behind a shelf.

"Where are you?" Pari was all business. "Are you somewhere public?"

"The pharmacy on the High Street. I haven't seen him go by," she said, peering around the shelf.

"Stay there. I'm coming over."

"All right."

"And keep your phone handy. I'll be right there." Pari rang off and Sera clasped her phone to her chest. Peering outside again, she stepped back in alarm when she thought she saw Bates walk by on the street. The bell over the door jangled and her heart skipped a beat.

"Hello, Mr. Chatterjee," she heard Pari say, greeting the older man who ran the shop.

Sera stepped out from around the shelf and Pari caught sight of her, hurrying over. She was dressed in jeans and a flowing blouse of dark crimson. Sera had never seen a more welcoming sight.

"You're so pale," Pari said, drawing Sera into a gentle hug before urging her towards the front of the shop. She said something to Mr. Chatterjee in a language Sera didn't understand. "We'll go back to my flat and have some tea. All right?"

"D'accord. But what about…?"

"We'll be fine. If we're hassled, we'll call the Old Bill."

They left the shop arm in arm. Sera snuck cautious glances around as they walked, but she didn't see Bates anywhere. Once in Pari's flat, Sera sank down on the low sofa while Pari went into the kitchen and put the kettle on. She came back with two steaming cups of tea and set one in front of Sera.

"Tell me more about this man," she said. "And if you want to, we can make a report."

Sera told her all she could remember. "And I think I've seen him in the park before." She paused, thinking. "And once in the coffee shop."

"Anywhere else?" Pari's brow furrowed and she frowned. "I don't want to call him a stalker just yet, but he's around an awful lot." She nudged Sera. "Have some tea. It'll make you feel better."

Sera took up the cup and sipped. "I wish Marc were here. I'd feel safer."

"How long is he gone?"

"He said he'd be back this weekend. I wish it were sooner."

"Would he come back early if you asked him?"

Sera fidgeted, tracing the blue stripes on the white porcelain cup. What she'd found out the day before didn't bear thinking about, and she didn't want to say a word to Pari. "He's been so busy, he might not be able to. And even if he could, it wouldn't be tonight." She shuddered. "What if I go to work and Bates is there?" It reminded her too much of Jeremy.

"Beg off sick?"

"I can't. I need this job."

Pari pursed her lips, staring down into her tea. Then she glanced up. "I'm not working tonight or tomorrow. If you'd like, I could come with you."

"Would you?" Relief washed over her. Having Pari accompany her to the Sanctuary would give her a sense of security, even though Julian and David would surely intervene if anything happened.

Julian. She had almost forgotten about last night. He had accepted her rebuff, but she wondered if he'd have changed his mind and would pursue her anyway. It would be best if Pari were there.

"You don't have to stay all night," Sera said. "I don't finish until three in the morning."

Pari shrugged. "I'll have a couple of drinks, maybe flirt a bit, talk to you during breaks—the night will fly by."

"Are you sure?"

"Of course I'm sure. I wouldn't offer otherwise, silly." Pari patted Sera's knee. "Better call your boyfriend. I know he'll come back if you're worried."

Marc unlocked the heavy door at Perron et fils while balancing a coffee and two croissants in his free hand. The lights were out so he flicked the switch, illuminating the reception area. Behind the glass partition, Aurore's desk was stacked with files and the message light flashed on her phone. He was early, but from the looks of it, his day would be long. He left one of the croissants on her desk and continued back to his office.

In contrast to Aurore's workspace, Marc's desk was neat as a pin, though that wouldn't last for long. He took a deep draught of his coffee and shed his jacket, hanging it over the back of his chair. Leaving the croissant on the desk for later, he retraced his steps into the hall and pushed open the door to Fournier's office.

The furniture, though beautifully restored and upholstered was old. Two brocaded armchairs with carved wooden feet and arms sat opposite a large mahogany desk. Fournier's only nod to modern style and comfort was a fancy leather office chair. Marc settled himself behind the desk, and reached for the leather-bound day-planner set to one side. Fournier loved his phone with an almost unholy passion, but he always wrote down his appointments in the day-planner.

"My boyfriend dropped his phone in the toilet at Le Dôme, and lost his entire life," Fournier had said once. "I don't plan to do the same."

Marc opened the book, and flipped through the entries until he came to this week's appointments. He noted that only half the appointments from the day of the accident had been crossed off. Between that horrible day and now, Marc counted another half-dozen appointments that had not been kept. He sighed and pinched the bridge of his nose.

When someone knocked on the open door, Marc glanced up. Aurore stood at the entrance looking ethereally pale, and tired. She came forward and took a seat in one of the brocade chairs, the green fabric making her choice of clothes—a pale blue A-line dress—seem washed out.

"Bonjour, monsieur. There's a lot to do."

"There is. I will need Fournier's appointments rescheduled, and will also require the details of all coordinating files. I am available to start filling appointments this afternoon, if you're able to arrange it."

"Oui, monsieur. Fournier was trying to bring together a full collection of Byron first editions for a new client, a Monsieur Thompson. The last few days, he's been calling some of the book dealers he knows."

Marc read off names from the day-planner.

"Those are the ones," Aurore confirmed. "Then we have an American couple who just inherited the flat of their great-grandfather, a second-floor apartment in the seventh. They want the pieces appraised before they decide whether to sell or pay the inheritance tax." Aurore took a breath, but Marc suspected she was nowhere near done. She rattled off information on another three files.

"We'll manage somehow," Marc said, though he wasn't sure how he'd do everything, familiarizing himself with the files and still making every appointment.

"Monsieur," Aurore said, interrupting his musing. "That man, Monsieur Royale, the client who wanted the Monet—will he be back?" She seemed ill at ease; he'd never seen her that way before.

"No, he's been dealt with. Did he threaten you in any way?" He watched her carefully, noting how she tensed, her gaze cutting away to the floor.

"He's an awful man."

Marc rose and came around the desk. "I'm sorry, Aurore, that you and Fournier had to deal with him at all."

Aurore looked up at him, her grey eyes troubled. "He said he was a client, but I couldn't find him in the files. He had such a temper."

"He was my uncle's client, before—well, before your time. Don't worry about him any longer."

Aurore took the day planner, glancing over the entries from the past week. "Let me grab you these files and then I'll start calling." She walked towards the door, and then pivoted, looking back. "We'll get this done."

"Merci beaucoup, Aurore. I don't know what I'd do without you." Marc stepped forward. "If you can arrange appointments for this afternoon, please do. The sooner we get caught up, the better."

Back in his own office, he downed the rest of his coffee and threw the paper cup into the bin. Aurore came in with three binders and laid them on the desk. "Monsieur Thompson is willing to meet this afternoon. He called while I was getting this together. You'll find his information in the top binder."

Marc pulled it towards him. "Send the meeting information to my phone when you have a moment, s'il vous plaît." He opened the binder. "Hopefully, I can be up to speed by this afternoon."

"Oui, monsieur." Aurore retreated and he heard her high heels on the parquet floor.

Fournier had made extensive notes on Thompson's file, including a detailed list of the books he wanted to purchase, each listed by year of publication. Another page held possible sources: antique booksellers, upcoming auctions, and a few of the firm's other clients who might be willing to part with some of their collectables.

There were several antique book fairs coming up and Fournier had put a star beside two in Berlin and Florence. The fairs would each last a week, and he knew already that he'd have to break the bad news to Sera. He might still be able to make it back to London for the weekend, but he'd be away more than either of them had ever planned for.

His phone vibrated and he saw the information he needed. The man lived in the 16th, not far from the Place Victor Hugo. Aurore had set down the hours for their meeting. A second vibration announced another appointment; this was one with a Monsieur Sand at an office in La Defense. He considered his options and decided he'd have to pick up the Peugeot from its spot in the garage near his apartment off Avenue Wagram.

The second binder held Sand's information. He not only collected modern art, but also had a passion for early Expressionist works. On his wish list, Fournier had outlined several main pieces, each with their auction information, and then a larger list of smaller, and dare he say cheaper works, including sketches and lithographs.

Marc pulled his desk calendar in front of him. The book fair in Berlin neatly coincided with an art auction, where he might find one of Sand's desired pieces, but the other auctions would mean he'd have to cut his time short in Florence in order to make it to Amsterdam and Oslo. He marked out the days on the desk calendar, and then into his phone. The schedule would be tight, but if all went well, he'd be back in London every weekend for Sera. It wouldn't leave them much time to practice for their performances, but they'd make it work.

Pari came back from the kitchen, carrying two plates with sandwiches and cookies.

"Nothing fancy, I'm afraid, but at least it's edible."

Sera got as far as taking her phone out of her bag, but she didn't call Marc. Although Bates had scared her, she hadn't been hurt. And Pari would be with her tonight, so she wouldn't have to worry. If she called, she'd add to Marc's worries, and he was already overprotective.

Sera put her phone back in her bag. "It looks delicious."

"Did you call him?" Pari handed her a plate.

"No, he has too much to do. Besides, I have a police officer on my side."

Pari grinned. "You do. I'll be an undercover police-woman to-night. What should I wear? I don't want to stand out."

Sera thought Pari would stand out no matter where she went or what she wore; her confidence and beauty would be alluring to many men. "A little black dress would fit in. And some black pumps to match."

"That's easy enough." Pari bit into her sandwich.

"You don't have to stay all night if you don't want to," Sera said. "I'm sure David or Julian would see me home if I asked."

"All those men." Pari nudged her. "Lucky you."

"It's not like that," Sera replied, "Though Julian would like it to be. He wasn't very happy to meet Marc."

"I'll make sure to flirt with him. I like a challenge."

Marc squeezed the Peugeot into a parking space on a side street near Avenue Foch. It had been a quick drive from his apartment near Place des Ternes, just through the roundabout at the Étoile. He strode up the street. Monsieur Thompson lived in an expensive mansion, likely worth close to seven million euros. He wondered where Fournier had met the man, as there had been no mention in the file.

A housekeeper let him in, her plain and rather dowdy uniform was slightly rumpled, and she showed him to 'la bibliothèque', a word the woman used with reverence. She knocked and at an acknowledgment, opened the door. "Entrez, monsieur."

Marc stepped inside and realized exactly why she'd been so reverent. The room was large, with high ceilings and wall-to-wall bookshelves in dark mahogany, broken only by the gilded fireplace with the requisite painting above, and a second door at the other side of the room. Heavy green velvet curtains obscured the windows.

A similar pair of velvet armchairs flanked the fireplace, and a desk and chair occupied one corner of the room. The rest of the room was full of books, and Marc took in the extensive collection.

"Bonjour, Monsieur Perron." Thompson rose from one of the armchairs where he had been sitting, carefully setting aside the book he'd been reading on a small, round end-table.

"Bonjour." Marc moved forward and they shook hands amiably. "You have an impressive collection, monsieur."

Thompson chuckled. "And no doubt you could stay here for days without protest. My collection is the work of a lifetime, Monsieur Perron."

Up close, Marc noticed that the man was older than he had seemed; the dim light had softened the crow's feet at the corners of his eyes, and obscured the slight hunch to his form in his proper suit. Thompson's hair was still dark, but grey highlighted his temples.

"I think I'd be happy browsing here for at least a month," Marc replied.

"A man after my own heart. Come, sit, and we can discuss what I'm looking for. Your lovely assistant tells me that Monsieur Fournier is unwell."

Marc settled into the armchair Thompson indicated, setting the binder on his lap. "An accident on the Périphérique is to blame," he said, "but I've reviewed the files Fournier left." He opened the binder, flipping forward to the list of works.

"I usually attend these auctions and fairs," Thompson said, "but this year my granddaughter is getting married—in Cannes—and she'd be crushed if I wasn't there."

"Understandably."

"If only she'd chosen a date a few weeks later," Thompson lamented, though he still wore a slight smile. "It can't be helped. A friend of mine told me that an almost complete set of Byron's first editions would be auctioned off for charity, and I can't pass them up."

Marc ran his finger down the page. "It's quite an extensive collection."

"And expensive," Thompson added, "but still, the money doesn't really matter. Of course, the cheaper you can get them, the better."

"Bien sûr. Do you have a maximum range?"

"No more than a quarter of a million over their listed value," Thompson said. "I'd pay double if I had to"—and Marc raised a brow at that—"but I hope I won't have to. Perhaps it will be useful to have you there in my stead, then my enemies won't bid it up through spite."

"They'll know eventually, but it might throw them off the scent for awhile."

Thompson chuckled. "I'll miss having the opportunity to gloat, but it'll be worth it. Now, let's go over the rest of the list and I'll tell you my priorities."

Pari walked Sera to Sanctuary's door. "I'll go wander for awhile," she said. "Have a bite to eat before I come back."

"The club opens officially at eight."

"I'll be back by then," Pari said, giving Sera a hug.

Sera descended the concrete stairs, barely paying them any attention. Julian winked at her when she pushed through the curtain. She smiled, though hesitantly, not wanting to encourage him after last night. She'd made herself clear, but she had kissed him, after all.

Actions spoke louder than words.

Instead of going to the bar, she went straight to the dressing room. Her cheeks felt hot and she knew she was postponing the inevitable. Setting her bag on the floor beside the small vanity, she took the seat in front of the mirror, and pulled out her makeup case. After eating this afternoon, she'd run out of time and hadn't been able to do her makeup before she and Pari had to leave. She had changed, however, and she wore a dress that looked modest from the front with a neckline that cut straight across her collarbone, but when she turned, an expanse of her pale back showed.

Sera dusted her face with loose powder, then picked through her case. Smoky eyes tonight, and dark crimson lips. Sultry, to balance the modesty of the dress.

There was a knock at the door.

"Come in," she called, applying her lipstick.

David entered, closing the door behind him. "Lovely dress," he said, tracing a finger briefly along the edge. Him too? He smiled at her in the mirror. "Don't worry. I'll leave the pining and sulking to

Julian. You're not really my type."

Sera hadn't realized her expression had said so much. "I hadn't
—"

"Yes, you thought it."

"What is your type then?"

"You haven't figured it out? Fortyish, bald, dresses well, gives
nice gifts…" He flashed his Rolex at her again. "Owns a few
clubs; I'm sure you know the type."

Sera couldn't believe she hadn't seen it. "Well, don't I feel
foolish."

"Don't worry about it. We keep things pretty hush, easier that
way. But Julian is sulking out there. What did you do to him?"

Sera pressed her lips together.

"Ah." David nodded sagely. "Drinks, was it? Did he take you
back to his place afterwards?"

"He saw me home," Sera said, her voice sharp. "To the front
step."

"No wonder he's sulking," David replied. "Usually his flirta-
tions come to more than that—if he's to be believed. Do you want
me to talk to him?"

"No, I'll manage. A friend of mine's coming tonight and maybe
he'll shift his attentions."

"As long as your boyfriend won't be beating him bloody later."

"He won't. He's away, working."

"But when he comes back?"

"He won't," she said again. She hadn't planned to tell him, especially not after Madelaine's revelations. In comparison to those acts, her own transgressions paled.

David shrugged, pulling a folded page from the pocket of his suit. "Here's the setlist I drew up for tonight. I've added a few new tunes." He passed it over and she scanned the list.

"It shouldn't be a problem."

"Très bien. If you're ready we'll go warm up. And hopefully the music will turn Julian's frown upside down." He passed his hand over his face, reminding Sera of a mime as he grimaced and smiled.

"You've missed your calling," she quipped. "You should have been an actor."

"Maybe I am, in my other life," David replied.

"You have time for that?"

He laughed. "Let's go."

Marc went to the hospital in between appointments, but Fournier was much the same. He stopped back at the office. Aurore glanced up from her work when he pushed open the heavy door. She gathered up a stack of mail.

"This is all yours," she said. "I've done up the deposits, but you'll need to endorse the cheques since Guillaume isn't here."

Marc took the mail from her. "No rest for me tonight then." Aurore rubbed her eyes. She looked exhausted. Marc glanced at his watch. Six. "Go home, Aurore. Get some rest."

"Merci, monsieur." She gave him a wan smile. "I'll go visit Guillaume."

"I was just there," Marc said as she gathered up her purse and laid her coat over her arm. "He's had no improvement." Her shoulders slumped and he could tell she was trying not to cry.

"Go home," he said again, gently, putting a hand to the small of her back and leading her towards the door.

In the doorway, she turned to him. "What if—" she began, pressing her lips together.

"He'll recover," Marc said, though after seeing Fournier today, the words felt like a lie. But Aurore seemed reassured.

"À demain."

He watched her leave, and then went back into the office, locking the door behind him. On his desk was a stack of paid invoices and cheques, and he set the mail aside. Although he hadn't smoked in his office for some time, he went to the window and lit a cigarette, perching on the sill. It overlooked a small, winding street, and he watched the workers heading home from nearby offices. He wished he could join them, but he had several hours work ahead of him yet. When his day was complete, he wouldn't even have the pleasure of seeing Sera afterward.

Marc took a deep drag on his cigarette. She'd danced with Julian, kissed Julian. She hadn't spent the night with him—unless she'd lied. He wanted another look at the photos Royale had shown him, but he wasn't about to call and ask. Instead, he pulled out his phone and sent her a text. Stubbing out his cigarette in the ashtray that sat in the corner between the wrought-iron rail and the wall, he went back to his desk, and placed his phone beside him, hoping it would buzz.

While he waited for her reply, he went through the paperwork, signing cheques and double-checking Aurore's work out of habit, though she had never made an error that he could recall. When he next checked the time, it was past seven, and still he'd heard nothing from Sera. She'd be starting work soon, and though he could look up Sanctuary's number, he held back. The photograph could have been faked, altered, but he doubted Royale would have bothered to go to such trouble.

The week in Paris stretched out before him—appointments, paperwork, Aurore, Fournier. What he really wanted was Sera.

CHAPTER 15

Two songs into their first set, Sera spotted Pari at the bar in front of Julian's station, and Sera wanted to laugh. Pari hadn't bothered with subtlety. At the break between songs, Sera glanced at David, whose gaze had slid over to the bar, noticing the turn of events. He flashed her an amused smile, then leisurely intoned the first chords of *'How Little We Know'*, though that song wasn't the next on the set. She did giggle then, as David segued into the next song. Sera couldn't help the smile that lingered at the corner of her mouth as she sang.

At the break between sets, she went straight to the bar to see Pari, who had engaged Julian in a debate over which chain store's coffee was the best.

"Starbucks is all burnt," she countered.

"But Pret is just as bad, as is Costa," he replied.

"Sera!" Pari gave her a hug. "Goodness, you were wonderful. I wish I'd come to see you sing before now." She gave Sera a nudge in the ribs. "And you didn't tell me about the cute bartender." Though it was a stage whisper, Sera heard David's chortle behind them.

"We only hire the best-looking men here," he quipped. "If I may say so myself."

"Not all men have heads as big as David's," Julian replied with a straight face.

Pari giggled, a girlish sound, her eyes sparkled and she fixed them on Julian. "I like small-headed blonds."

"Pari, this is Julian," Sera said, though Pari had likely introduced herself already. Pari held out a hand and Julian accepted it, acting similar to the first time they had met. Pari seemed charmed by the attention, and Sera didn't think it was an act on her part. Maybe, Julian's affections could be distracted.

David reached over the bar top and snagged two glasses, taking the bar gun and filling them with water. "Don't mind me—I know she's much prettier than I am." David handed one of the glasses to Sera.

Pari laughed and patted David's arm. " Sorry, guess he likes women."

"I'm used to that with men. Mostly."

"You've lucked out, Sera. Julian and David are charming."

"Don't I know it," Sera replied. Some of the tension she'd felt earlier eased as Julian paid more attention to Pari.

"Now if your man was here," Pari said, "then we'd really be set."

"Saturday," Sera replied.

"You'll have to come again," David remarked, beating Julian to the invitation. "Marc will be playing with us. I still can't decide how to advertise it. A jazz trio, perhaps?"

"You need a band name," Pari said, taking a sip of the vodka and cranberry Julian had poured for her.

Sera and David looked at each other. Her mind was blank—a band name hadn't even occurred to her and David seemed to be in the same position. He shrugged.

"If you think of one, let us know."

"I shall," Pari said. "Julian can help me consider the possibilities."

Sera stifled a laugh. She hadn't expected Pari to play up her flirtation this much. She didn't feel so guilty now about leading him on, and Marc would never have to know.

David touched her elbow. "Time for the next set."

Alone in his apartment off Avenue Wagram, Marc paced. If he'd had his cello, he would have played it, ridding himself of his tension, but the instrument was in London. As was Sera, and it was still too early in the evening for her to call. She'd be on stage now, of course. He lit a cigarette, but even that didn't help. As it grew later, he went to bed, but set his phone beside him, where he'd hear it ring when she called. He fell asleep waiting.

The phone woke him early in the early morning. It vibrated noisily on the wood nightstand, and he was still groggy as he answered.

"I thought you'd be awake already." Sera's tired voice came over the line. He glanced at the clock, its glowing numerals showing 5:59.

"In a moment, yes," he said, sitting up in bed. He turned the alarm off before it could ring. "Are you home?"

"Just arrived." He heard her yawn. "It was a longer night than expected. Pari has so much energy. She wanted to go out afterwards and we went to this bar Julian knows."

"The three of you?"

"And David too, but he only stayed for one drink. Pari and I shared a cab back, so I hung around until she was ready." She yawned again. "If I'd known I would be home this late, I'd have left her and Julian to dance until dawn."

"Julian and Pari, is it?" Maybe Royale had been mistaken. Pari had hair as dark as Sera's.

"Seems to be." Sera sounded amused, but her next words were solemn. "How is Fournier? And the firm?"

"Not well." Marc rubbed his eyes. He wished he could have had another hour's sleep. "I think I may have to be here—a long time."

"But you'll be back this weekend, won't you?" A hint of anxiety crept into her voice.

"Friday night," he said, "Even if I'm on the last train out of Gare du Nord."

"Good." Her next words were a whisper. "I miss you."

"I'll be back in London in a couple more days," Marc said. "I'll even come straight to the club."

"I'll look for you. Oh, and Marc…"

"Oui?" he asked, when the pause stretched more than a moment.

"I'll talk to you tomorrow."

"Tonight, you mean?"

"After work." She yawned again. "Bonne nuit, Marc."

"Bon matin, ma chère." He set the phone aside. Had she meant to say something more? It wasn't like Sera to be uncertain, but then it also wasn't like her to be out so late either. She sounded exhausted. Two late nights, if Royale's photos were to be believed.

He didn't want to believe.

CHAPTER 16

It was nearing midnight when Marc arrived in London, but he almost didn't make it back at all, and had come close to missing the last Eurostar out of Gare du Nord. Sweet-talking the gate attendant had gotten him through. As he descended the stairs into Sanctuary, Sera's musical voice greeted him.

He stopped in the dim privacy of the stairwell to listen to Sera, free of any distraction as she sang of love and loss, *'Mon Légion-naire'*. The old gig posters on the wall crackled when he leaned on them, his hands in the pockets of his leather jacket. The haunting tone of her voice enveloped him, and he lingered there until she'd finished, the applause rising to take the place of the music.

The opening bars of the next song, a more upbeat tune, began as he pushed through the curtain. He paused in the entry, his gaze fixed on the stage, on Sera. Her dark hair shone under the spot-light, flowing over her shoulders in a dark wave, blending with the black satin gown that fell to her knees in a handkerchief hem. When she noticed him, she winked, the movement carefully timed to a flourish in the song. He blew her a kiss and went to the bar, taking a free stool.

Julian greeted him with a nod as he fixed a tray of drinks for one of the waitresses, then he came over.

"Back from Paris? What's your poison?" His coolness seemed to have mellowed, which surprised Marc. He'd been expecting Julian's usual chill, and he wondered if he had Pari to thank.

"Finally. I'll have a cognac."

Julian poured him a measured snifter. "You made it just in time for the last set."

"I came close to not being here at all," Marc said.

"Sera's friend Pari is sitting down near the stage," Julian remarked. Marc half-turned, glancing over his shoulder and spotted Pari sitting alone with a glass of wine in front of her, her expression rapt. She reminded him of Sophie when he'd first met her, watching every performance with an awe usually reserved for relics like the Sancta Camisia in Chartres cathedral. He wouldn't join her and interrupt.

"Sera mentioned she might be here, after joining her at the club the other night."

Julian cracked a smile before he was called away to fill another drink order. Marc turned his attention back to the stage.

After her set, Sera went to Pari's table, catching Marc's eye as she went. He left his stool and made his way towards them.

"I wish I didn't have to work tomorrow night," Pari said mournfully, her fingers playing with the stem of her glass. "You'll miss Marc and I performing," Sera said, "but there will be other Saturday nights."

"Not for a few months at least," Pari replied. "Not until the next rota change."

"Call in sick?" Sera suggested, knowing the idea was a cheeky one.

"If only!"

"Bonsoir." Marc set down a snifter and took the free chair, leaning over to kiss her. It was a brief touch, but he stroked the back of her neck under her hair, sending a slight shiver down her spine. "You sang beautifully, ma chère, especially *'Mon Légion-naire'*." He greeted Pari warmly.

Sera rested her hand on his thigh and he took it in his own, twining their fingers together. Everything felt right in the world, now that he was here with her. Though they sat in a room full of strangers, she felt safe.

"I'm glad you're here."

"Moi aussi." Marc's thumb stroked over her hand. She met his gaze.

"I'm going to get another drink," Pari announced, rising. "Back in a bit."

"She wants to talk to Julian," Sera observed. Marc chuckled.

"All the better." He leaned over again, but this time his kiss was more than a quick press of lips. "That's how much I've missed you."

"Is that all?"

"In public."

Sera glanced up at the bar, looking for Pari, who had found a seat and was chatting with Julian while he poured a pint of beer. The man next to Pari turned their way and Sera let out a gasp, her grip tightening on Marc's hand.

It was as if the man from the park—Bates—had heard her, for his gaze seemed to pick her out of the crowd, observing her with rapacious interest.

"Sera?" Marc's voice cut through the noise of the club.

"It's him again."

"Again?"

She knew she should have told him. Marc followed her gaze, cursing under his breath. He rose from his seat.

"What are you doing?" She tightened her grasp on his hand, and he looked down at her.

"When did you first see him?"

She tried to think of when she'd spotted him the first time. "A few weeks ago in the park. At the cemetery, and in the coffee shop when we moved in. And a few days ago." She shivered. "He tried to hit on me that time."

Marc's eyes went cold; he disentangled his fingers from hers. "He needs a talking to."

"Marc!" She grabbed for him, but her fingers only brushed his coat. All she could do was watch as he strode up to the bar, coming face to face with Bates.

The world narrowed as Marc grabbed Bates by the collar and pinned him against the bar. He vaguely noticed the other customers backing away from the scene, but his focus was concentrated on his former business associate. He'd never trusted Bates when he had first met the man, and he should never have trusted Royale's recommendation. Royale hadn't called off his spy, as he'd promised to do. Bates was still working for Royale.

He knew he was making a scene, but a scene mattered less than his retaliation. Bates struggled in his grasp, until Marc brought the weasel to his knees with one punch. The man started blubbering.

"You thought I wouldn't find out?" Marc growled. It was all he managed to say before he was seized from behind, his arms pinned. Julian dragged him backward, and Mayson, who had come out of his office to see what the fuss was about, gestured for them to come over. Marc didn't bother struggling. He glanced over to where he'd left Sera and saw her wide-eyed fear. David seemed to be talking to her, holding her back.

And then he was swept into Mayson's office, stumbling forward when Julian abruptly freed his arms and gave him a shove.

"Need me to stick around, boss?" Julian asked, blocking the open door.

Mayson gave Marc a once over. "No—the fight's gone out of him. Go give everyone a round on the house and tell Aaron I'll sort this out."

Julian retreated, and the door closed behind him. Mayson pressed a button and Marc heard the bolt being thrown.

"Take a seat," Mayson said, gesturing to a chair. He lit a cigarette and leaned back, tapping his fingers against the desk. "Give me a good reason why I shouldn't have you taken out back and shot for the shit you just pulled out there."

"Let me go." Sera glared at David, but he held her arm and wouldn't relent.

"Your boyfriend will have to take what comes," he said. Pari came to Sera's side.

"What is going on? I go to the toilet and miss everything."

"Let me go, David."

"Only if you come sit down." He led Sera back to their table, Pari followed behind. Sera tugged her arm free, reluctantly taking a seat.

"I don't want Marc to get hurt."

"He won't be hurt," David said, though he didn't sound especially confident.

"What happened?" Pari sat down next to Sera and David took the remaining chair.

"Marc fought with one of our regulars, but Julian managed to break it up before things went too far."

"He went after the guy who's been following me," Sera interjected. "He had reason."

"He's here?" Pari whipped around, craning her neck. "I should arrest him for stalking."

"You're a cop?"

"PCSO," Pari replied defensively.

"Christ," David muttered.

"I think he's gone now," Sera said. "I don't see him anywhere."

"Why would Aaron follow you?"

"Aaron? He told me his names was Bates."

"Aaron Bates," David clarified.

"I don't know why. I don't know him, but he's always around. In the coffee shop near my flat, in the park, at the cemetery—everywhere." She half-rose out of her chair, but David clamped a strong hand on her arm.

"Just wait. It wouldn't be a good idea to interrupt Mayson."

Marc weighed his words. "Bates was stalking Sera; he made a pass at her. I couldn't let it lie."

"I can't have you beating up my associates," Mayson said. "No honour among thieves, and all that. If I don't demonstrate my authority, they'll think I'm a pushover. And I can't have that."

"Bates works for you? Doing what?"

Mayson snorted. "I would tell you, but then I'd have to kill you, really. Bates does things for me, if you get my meaning."

It wasn't hard to read between the lines. "He's trustworthy?"

"Damn right he is. I saved the bastard's life. He's my man." Mayson frowned, stubbing out his cigarette to emphasize his next words. "I don't like what you're insinuating."

Marc knew if he let this matter drop now, he could get out of this with a beating, and count himself lucky. It rankled him that Bates could get away with it—the spying, and playing both sides. He took a chance.

"I'd like to tell you a story," he said, taking his cigarette case from the inner pocket of his jacket. He watched Mayson carefully as he lit the cigarette, seeing the anger sublimated by curiosity.

"What about?" Mayson linked his fingers and put his hands behind his bald head, rocking backward in his chair.

"About a man who serves two masters," Marc said. "I owed Royale, and until I paid up, he kept tabs on me, and on Sera. I paid up and he promised to call off his spy—except, once I get here, I find that he hasn't done that at all. In fact, his spy has threatened my lover and tonight she pointed him out to me."

"Bates?"

"The same. Did you know about his little side job?"

Mayson's eyes narrowed and though he didn't say anything, Marc could tell that he hadn't known.

"I wonder what else he hasn't told you," Marc said, casually taking a drag of his cigarette. He couldn't be too confident, but perhaps the tides had turned.

Mayson scowled. "All my men know not to have dealings with Royale."

That didn't follow. "Except for Jeremy Gordon?"

Mayson fixed him with a glare. "Except for him."

"Special dispensation?"

Mayson's glare didn't soften, though he seemed speculative.

"What was your reason?"

"That's none of your concern," Mayson ground out.

"Let me take a guess, then." Marc recalled the conversation he'd overheard when Jeremy was on his phone. "Royale was causing trouble for you and Gordon was going to solve that problem."

"Why would you think that?"

"Intuition, perhaps. Wishful thinking, even."

"You'd want to be rid of him?"

"I certainly wouldn't mourn him. I doubt you would either."

Mayson snorted. "I'd piss on his corpse."

"If only he were a corpse." Marc let the words sound like a casual musing, but in truth it was something that had crossed his mind more than a few times in the past years.

"You trying to set me up?" Mayson half-rose from his chair, planted his hands on the desk, and leaned forward.

"Not at all." Marc stubbed out his cigarette and lit another. "Just commiserating. Of course, if I'd been you and known Royale had a hand in Gordon's death…"

"How do you figure that?"

Marc shrugged. "If you have your friend's right-hand with you, one would think you'd make sure he didn't end up dead."

CHAPTER 17

Pari had kept the cab ride home light hearted, but Sera found it hard to focus on her conversation. She wanted to be alone with Marc, curled up in their bed, and was relieved when the cab pulled up to the flat.

"Was Mayson furious?" she asked, after Marc shut the door of the flat and they were alone together at last.

"Not after I explained."

"And who was that man?"

"I don't know." Marc went into the kitchen and she followed. His answer was inexplicably terse. He poured a glass of water and then hooked his arm around her waist. "I'll make sure he doesn't bother you again."

They went back through and into the bedroom where Marc shed his jacket, laying it on the bed. "I'll be back in a moment." He kissed her cheek, and then went into the bathroom. Sera took up his jacket and went to hang it in the closet. It vibrated under her hand, and she fumbled for his phone, pulling it from the inside pocket. The display read 'Aurore Belcastre' and Sera frowned. It was so late, almost 4 a.m. Why would Aurore be calling, except in an emergency? Sera answered the call.

"Is Marc there?" Aurore's voice was a sob.

"Is it Fournier?" Sera's throat tightened and she could barely get the words out.

"Non, non. That client, that Royale, he…"—Aurore's voice shook.

Sera nearly dropped the phone. Her stomach curdled with fear. "Royale?"

"He's furious—please, I need to speak to Marc."

"Hold on." She felt as if she were pushing through molasses, against the fear and worry that churned in her.

Marc came to the door of the bedroom, his eyes on his wrists as he undid his cuffs. When he glanced up, she held out his phone in a trembling hand. He took it from her and cupped her cheek.

"Sera?"

"It's Aurore."

"Aurore? What's happened?"

Sera sank onto the bed. She could hear Aurore's strident, frightened voice, though she couldn't make out the words. Marc paced the room, then, as if realizing she was there, went out into the reception room. She followed him, slowly.

"He won't harm you, Aurore, I'm sure of it," she heard him say. "Stay at home, lock all your doors. Call your brother to come stay with you if it will make you feel better. I'll call Royale. Don't worry." He listened to her again, and then repeated his words. "I promise, Aurore, you'll be okay."

When he finally hung up, Sera was waiting for him. "What did she mean by Royale, Marc? Why is he a client of yours? Did he hurt her?"

"C'est rien." He flicked through his contacts and Sera closed her hand over the phone.

"Don't lie to me, Marc, even to protect me. Especially not about Royale." She tightened her grip on the phone when he tried to tug it away. Finally, he pried it from her grasp. Furious, she shoved him.

"Dis-moi!"

"Royale had demands I couldn't meet," Marc said, his voice flat, angry. He turned away from her and she heard his phone ring a second time. He cursed. "Not a word. Promise me."

Sera opened her mouth to speak, but he laid a hand over her lips, stifling her words.

"Perron."

"You thought I wouldn't know the difference between a fake and a Monet?" Françoise shrieked at him. "My husband might not have known the difference, but I knew as soon as I saw the painting."

Marc was speechless. He'd never met Royale's wife. He'd thought Royale kept her tucked away at a provincial chateau, not acting as his secretary.

"And where do you think I would find a Monet?" he snapped back, the surprise receding as anger took over. "It was impossible."

"That doesn't matter. I want a Monet."

"There aren't any."

"Not good enough."

Sera's lips moved against his hand and he shook his head, stilling her words once more.

"There's nothing I can do," he said, glad that Françoise was on the other end of the phone, on another continent.

"Wrong answer. I told my husband he should never have trusted you. And if you think you'll get away with this, you haven't seen anything yet."

Françoise rung off and Marc lowered the phone. Sera pushed his hand aside.

"Who is she? And what is going on?"

"Françoise. Royale's wife."

That surprised her. She opened her mouth, then closed it again.

"To keep Royale from telling Jeremy's boss the truth about his death, I had to make a bargain."

Sera paled, sinking onto the sofa. "What did you bargain?"

"A Monet."

Sera gaped at him.

"I thought I'd have time to find one, and that he'd be patient until I located a true masterpiece. But Royale—and Françoise—wouldn't wait. I could have one faked, or I could take the risk of someone trying to hurt you. It was a game I had to play and a chance I had to take."

"A game? This is no game. This is our life together." Sera's voice was strident, but then she shivered, and he sat next to her, pressing her close to him. "Who would be able to follow us? They're in…"

"Bates. Royale had us followed."

Sera rose, pushing off his arm, embracing herself. "You should have told me." She went to the bedroom door and glanced back at him. "How can I trust you?" She shut the door behind her, the noise sharp in the quiet flat.

In a quarter of an hour, Sera came out, carrying a valise in her hand, and she'd changed clothes.

"Where are you going?" he asked as she went to the front door. He followed her there.

"To Pari's. And don't try to stop me." Her voice was cold, though he heard the slight tremor in her words.

"It's not safe."

"Safe? Being with you isn't safe, Marc. At least Pari's honest.

And she's a police officer. I'll be fine." She pulled open the door, stepping over the threshold, the one he'd carried her over weeks before. She didn't look back.

Sera knocked on Pari's door, her heart pounding. She wanted to cry, but her anger sublimated her tears and she gritted her teeth. Knocking a second time, she finally heard rustling movement and the door opened. Pari wore a rumpled dressing gown and her hair was in disarray.

"Sera? What's wrong?"

"Can I come in?"

"Of course." Pari opened the door wider and Sera stepped onto a brightly patterned rug in the entryway. "I'll make some tea."

Sera let her valise slip to the floor. "Thank you." She followed Pari to the kitchen, and leaned against the counter while Pari filled the kettle and put it on to boil.

"Do you want to talk about it?" Pari asked, sympathy in her voice. Her deep brown eyes were sad.

Tears pricked Sera's eyes at the gentle question. Instead of answering, she glanced down at her hands, picking at the edge of a nail. She blinked hard but couldn't keep the tears at bay. As they spilled down her cheeks, she tried to wipe them away.

"Oh, don't cry." Pari embraced her, the silk of her robe warm against Sera's wet cheeks. Pari stroked her back in a slow, soothing caress, much like Sera's mother had done when she was a girl. Sera swallowed down the sobs, wiping the tears away with her sleeve. Pari loosened her embrace and stepped back.

"You don't have to talk about it if you don't want to."

"He lied to me," Sera said, her voice hoarse and shaky. "About"—she paused, remembering that Pari was a police officer—"about something important. Something he should have told me."

After the kettle came to a roiling boil, Pari poured steaming water into two cups, plopping in tea bags. "It's chamomile—it won't keep us awake." She led Sera into the living room. "Did Marc have a good reason to lie?"

"He thought so." Sera took a sip of her tea and it burned her tongue. She winced.

"But his intentions were good?"

Had they been? Sera thought of Royale's lascivious gaze, his threats. Marc might have been trying to protect her from Royale in part, but that was only an accidental bonus. He'd really tried to protect himself, and maintain their relationship on that lie. He'd promised to go clean, to only work for legitimate clients, but it had taken only a few months to fall back into his old habits. She wasn't sure he'd ever meant to keep that promise.

"I don't think so. He'd sworn to me not to do something, something important, but he did it anyway."

Pari clasped her hand, giving her fingers a gentle, reassuring squeeze. "What will you do now?"

"I don't know." Sorrow choked her, becoming a sharp pain in her chest.

"You can stay here as long as you need to," Pari said loyally. "I only have one bedroom, but I'll make up the sofa for you."

Marc let Sera go, though he went to the top of the stairs and heard her talking to Pari. He waited until he heard Pari's door close before he retreated back into the apartment. Once in bed, which seemed barren without her, he couldn't sleep. His mind wouldn't stop thinking of scenarios, what he could say to her in the morning, whether he could convince her to forgive him. No matter the variation of his apology, the imaginary scenes always ended with him alone.

The night dragged and he must have slept, but it didn't feel like he had. Exhaustion weighted his limbs and his eyes felt gritty, like the rasp of sandpaper on wood. He dragged himself from the bed and went to shower, checking the time.

After his first espresso, he called Dawson. It was Sunday, but if Dawson was anything like himself, he'd be working.

"Dawson."

"Perron here. Sorry to call you on a Sunday."

Dawson chuckled. "No rest for the wicked, after all. I'm just finishing up some work. It never ends."

"About that—would you be able to take over the remainder of the Lancaster file?"

"I'd be delighted, but I thought you were handling that your-self."

"I was, but after Fournier was in that car accident, there's too much to handle on my own. Easier to pass that one off since you've already been working with Mrs. Lancaster."

"She'll be disappointed," Dawson teased. "I think she has a crush on you. She went on and on about 'that lovely French fel-low'."

"Did she? I'll have to call and give her my regrets, personally."

"I'm sure she'll be agreeable."

"By the way, any word on any Monets? That client of mine just rang, and was insistent that someone somewhere had to be selling one." Or rather, that Marc himself was desperate for there to be one.

"Nothing," Dawson replied. "I've set up an alert so I can be notified if that changes here at the auction house."

"Thought so, but I had to ask."

"Some people are never satisfied."

Marc was quite sure that Dawson had never had to deal with clients such as Royale and his wife Françoise. If only he could be rid of them, but it wasn't as easy as deleting them from his address book.

"Dissatisfaction keeps us employed," Marc replied dryly.

"That it does. I'll call you if anything comes up."

Marc tossed his phone on the coffee table and slumped back against the sofa. What he wouldn't give to be free of Royale. But to change things, he'd have to invent a time machine to go back, and try to keep his uncle from consorting with gangsters. Perhaps impress upon his younger and much more naive self to hold fast against temptation and corruption. When his uncle died it had been easier to keep the firm in the black with that blood money coming in while he tried to handle the business on his own in those early days.

His phone vibrated on the glass and he leaned forward to scoop it up, hoping it would be Sera.

It wasn't.

"Royale has found his Monet," Françoise said, forgoing any greeting.

"Has he?"

"It's in the Musée Marmottan."

"You have got to be fucking joking." The words slipped out before he could stop them.

"Royale assures me that you're able to get it for us."

"He's wrong."

"Why is it that you think you're in charge here, Perron?" Françoise asked, her voice cool.

"I won't steal anything for you, or for him."

"But would you do it for her? Your lovely companion is on her own quite a lot these days. And it's far cheaper to arrange a hit than the theft of a painting, as you well know."

Françoise's meaning was clear. And he knew exactly how easy it was to put out a hit.

"I'll need time." He kept his tone steady, confident, though it felt as if a vise had squeezed his heart.

"You've had months. That should have been time enough."

"I don't steal paintings."

"You don't? That's not what I heard. And leopards don't change their spots so easily."

"Mine have."

"Then give your little petite amie a kiss goodbye." Françoise's words sounded like a decree, the judgment of a vengeful deity.

"Wait."

The line was silent, but she hadn't hung up the phone.

"Has the leopard taken back his spots?" Françoise inquired, her tone wry.

There was a bitter taste in Marc's mouth. Defeat.

"Yes. I seem to have my spots after all."

CHAPTER 18

The pounding on the door woke Pari and Sera. Sera came groggily awake, rising on her elbows on Pari's sofa with her hair in a mussed halo around her head. Pari hurried to the door, her truncheon in her hand.

"Get back," she hissed at Sera in an undertone. "Into the bedroom."

Sera took the bedclothes with her and they dragged over the floor. She stumbled into Pari's bedroom and closed the door all but a crack, enough to just see into the hallway.

Pari looked through the peephole. "What do you want?" she called through the closed door. She lifted the truncheon to the ready.

Marc's voice was muffled. "I need to speak to Sera. I know she's with you."

Pari glanced to the bedroom door, giving Sera a questioning look. Sera opened the door a fraction and shook her head. She didn't want to see him. It hurt too much to think about his betrayal.

"She doesn't want to see you. Go away."

The door shook, as if Marc had hit it with the flat of his hand. "It's important." The doorknob rattled.

"Go away," Pari repeated, "or I'll call the Old Bill. She doesn't want to see you."

"I need her."

Sera heard the emotion in his voice, even through the wood. She sank to the floor in a pile of sheets.

"She doesn't need you. Now leave, or I'm calling 999." Pari pressed her ear to the door, but all was silent. She double-checked the lock, then came over to Sera.

"Are you all right?"

Sera didn't answer, just shook her head again. Nothing about her life was all right, now that she had lost Marc. Maybe she'd never really had him in the first place.

Marc left the building; looking back, his gaze roamed over Pari's windows, which were muffled in bright drapery. For a moment, he thought he saw movement, but no one came to look out, and he turned away. He didn't know how he would get that Monet for Royale, and he knew he'd be condemning himself to prison if he even tried to steal it himself. But if he didn't act...

He took out a cigarette and lit it as he walked down Highgate Hill towards the Archway tube station. There might be one person that could help him, though the man was likely to be as brutal as Royale. He could be exchanging present problems for future ones.

He walked briskly from Leicester Square into Soho. The neon sign had been turned off, making the doorway for Sanctuary almost indistinguishable in the row of storefronts. The metal handle was cool under his hand as he tugged, but it didn't budge. He pressed the buzzer at the side and waited. When there was no response, he pressed it again.

Still nothing.

Marc stepped out of the doorway, turning back to the street. Maybe Mayson was at the Dalston. He had time to take the train out there. Pulling out his phone, he looked up a map of the Underground.

"Oy! Whaddya want?"

Marc glanced back. A man in a dark suit with his hair shorn short in a military-style had stuck his head out the now open door.

"Mayson in?" Marc put his phone away.

"Yeah. Who are you?"

"A business associate. Is he available?"

The man gave him a once-over, as if judging his worth. "Name?"

"Marc Perron."

The door swung shut. Marc waited with his hands in the pockets of his leather jacket. Time seemed to drag, though it couldn't have been more than a few minutes before the man was back. His pale cheeks had gone pink and Marc wondered if he'd taken the stairs at a run.

"Come in."

Marc followed the man down the stairs and through the velvet curtain. Mayson's office door gaped open, but the man walked him right to the doorway.

Mayson looked up from a stack of papers, the overhead light glinting on his bald head. "Thank you, Alan."

"Boss," Alan grunted and retreated.

"Come in."

Marc stepped inside, closing the door. "Do you have a few minutes? My apologies for the lack of notice."

Mayson closed the file folder over the stack of paper and gestured to a seat. Marc took that as a yes. "I'm not especially busy today." He leaned back in his chair. "To what do I owe this visit? Your performance with Sera went well. One of the regulars, a man who works with the London Opera, was quite impressed."

"Is he looking for musicians?" Marc inquired, his tone light, showing Mayson he wasn't serious.

"You never know." Mayson lit a cigarette. "So what brings you here on a Sunday afternoon? I'd have thought you'd be headed back to Paris by now."

"By this evening most likely," Marc said, "but there's been a snag."

"What sort of snag? I have people who specialize in those." Mayson chuckled.

"A royal snag."

"Come out with me for dinner before you go to work," Pari urged, hovering by the sofa where Sera had curled up, not watching the television that played a mindless talk show with shrill, giggling hostesses.

"I'm not hungry," Sera said, even though she felt her stomach rumble. She would have to eat something, but when she thought of the past few days, her appetite vanished.

Pari sighed and ceased her hovering, going into the other room. At first Sera thought she had gone out, even though she hadn't heard the door. Pari came back, placing a plate and glass on the coffee table.

"I'm going to head into the office," she said. "I'll be on my beat after that, but I'll come by the club later."

Sera looked up. "I'm sorry I'm such a bother."

"No bother," Pari assured her. "But don't let him ruin your life, all right? You have a job, a place here now—you'll make it without him if you have to."

Without Marc. Again.

She gave Pari a weak smile, but it was enough to satisfy her friend. Once Pari left, her smile faded.

She'd been on her own before; she could handle being on her own again. She could survive, even in London, in a place where she was still unsure of the language. She had a friend or two, and people to worry about her. But without Marc, what would really keep her here? She ached to have tea with Colette in her flat in Montmartre, to go out to the market and greet the butcher, and buy her cheese and fruits. She could go to Saint-Germain-des-Prés. The pangs of homesickness intensified at the thought of the church.

Sera fumbled in her bag for her rosary. She hadn't prayed since they'd been in London, and hardly at all since she'd been with Marc. With him, she had no need to pray; she'd felt secure, and he'd kept her worries at bay. She'd relied on him too much, even when they'd been apart, her last thought was always of him.

The beads were cool in her fingers, their smoothness familiar, comforting. But the prayers wouldn't come. Her stomach growled insistently and she couldn't ignore it any longer. She would eat, then go to work, and when she came back, when Marc had gone to Paris, she'd decide what to do.

Marc pulled his silver cigarette case from his pocket, tapping the cigarette against it momentarily before putting it to his lips and lighting it. "I hate to admit this," he said, knowing Mayson would value the admission, even as it galled Marc to admit it, "but I need your help."

"With Royale." Mayson sat back in his chair, looking interested, but skeptical.

"Yes."

"That bastard." Mayson snorted. He tapped the ash from his cigarette into the crystal ashtray on his desk. "What sort of help?" When he raised his gaze to meet Marc's, it had changed to a predatory gleam.

"He wants a Monet and I can't give it to him," Marc said simply.

"I'm not giving you my Monet to give to that cunt," Mayson said. "He's always wanted it."

"He what?" Marc couldn't hide his surprise.

"He's always been jealous of my Monet," Mayson replied. "We were friends once, ages ago." His expression darkened.

"If I don't get him a Monet, he's threatened Sera, and I can't let anything happen to her."

"Your lovely chanteuse." The French word had a bitter tone. "Love like that makes you weak."

"Nevertheless." Marc took a drag of his cigarette. "I need to quell that threat."

"Only one way to do that," Mayson replied, stubbing out his cigarette and lighting another, "And you know as well as I do what that is."

Marc leaned forward and stubbed out the remains of his cigarette, but he didn't light a second. He rested his hands on the arms of the chair, the wood cool under his palms.

"I do, but I'll need help. He's never alone, and I won't be able to take him on in his own club."

"I can help you," Mayson said, "but for a price. You know how this game is played, Perron. It's the same in London as it is in Paris, after all. And I am not cheap."

"Name it," Marc said, the tension curling in his stomach. He knew the wood under his palms had to be damp.

"I have someone who can assist you, but in return, you work for me. I want a portion of your profit from Perron et fils, let's say fifteen percent of your gross. And when I say jump—you jump."

Marc forced his voice to calmness, and managed to keep his tone even. What Mayson proposed was outrageous, especially knowing how Mayson hated Royale. Marc had hoped to get a much better deal. "For how long?"

"A year," Mayson said. "When you first came here, I made inquiries, Mr. Perron. I know your firm's gross income is in the range of ten million euros a year, thanks to the work of your staff and your connections, connections I want access to. Introductions, when needed, and access to auction houses. Bona fides, you might say."

It was Royale all over again; his uncle's wheeling and dealing with gangsters, but what choice did he have? Royale had protection, henchmen, and he couldn't survive on his own against them.

"I agree, but on one further condition."

"I'm listening."

"That Sera knows nothing of this, and that you will protect her if anything goes wrong in the aftermath."

"She won't hear of it from me or my staff," Mayson said easily. "There's no point in having women involved in these things. But as to protection—I doubt she'd accept it from me. She's not entirely clueless as to what I do. But I can promise you that I'll do what I can."

"Thank you." The words tasted bitter on his tongue.

"How will this go down?" Mayson inquired, lighting yet another cigarette.

"I don't know yet," Marc replied. "How much notice do your people need?"

"Very little. There's always someone." Mayson gave a satisfied smile, like the cat who'd swallowed the canary. "Call or come here, and I will have someone at your disposal." He stood, holding out his hand.

Marc took it, and they shook firmly. "And if I don't need assistance after all?"

Mayson shrugged. "Then our agreement is null and void. However, I would be much obliged if you'd let me know when that bastard's breathed his last. I have a bottle of Macallan I've been saving especially for the occasion." He released Marc's hand.

"What do you have against Royale?" Marc wondered if Mayson would deign to answer the question.

"Aside from Royale's involvement in Jeremy's death, which I know, even though the arsehole denies it, we have a long history, much like your own, I suspect. He's had this coming for years, and I'll be satisfied when the cunt's six feet under."

Marc wished Royale had been six feet under for years.

Mayson's attention shifted. "Sounds like your girlfriend's here."

"Not a word to Sera."

"None. Nor a word of this from you to anyone but me," Mayson warned. "I'll be expecting your call."

Mayson returned to sit behind his desk, and Marc headed to the door.

"It's a dangerous game you're playing, Mr. Perron," he heard Mayson say.

"A necessary one," Marc replied.

CHAPTER 19

Sera came into work early, having grown tired of staying in Pari's flat. She'd gone upstairs to grab some fresh clothes, but Marc hadn't been there. His things were still there though, his suitcase open on the bed, waiting to be filled. Pausing beside the bed, she considered leaving him a note, but decided against it. Better to have the time apart; the jealousy and anger surged in her, and she knew she'd scream at him if she saw him.

Inside Sanctuary, it was quiet, though David came out from the dressing room a few minutes after Sera arrived. He was dressed to perform, and he adjusted his cuffs as he came towards her.

"You're early," he observed. "If this keeps up, you'll end up a lifer like the rest of us."

"Will I?" Sera smiled, though she couldn't picture herself staying in London forever. Even six more months seemed too long.

"If I have my way, you will," he quipped. "Your boyfriend was here when I got here, so perhaps I should say the same thing about him."

"Marc was here?" In her surprise, the words slipped out before she could stop them.

"He didn't tell you?" They moved up to the bar, taking stools.

"No, he didn't mention it."

"He might be gone by now, but he's been here a couple of hours," David said. He reached over the bar top for a glass, and filled it with water.

Mayson's door opened and Marc emerged. He was dressed casually, in jeans and a leather jacket. When he saw her, his neutral expression slipped a fraction. Sera ignored him, focusing on David.

"I was thinking we could do up a setlist for next week, perhaps work in some more modern songs."

"I have a few arrangements I've been working on," David replied. "I was thinking we could do a themed evening later this fall. Mayson and I were considering a James Bond theme, perhaps."

"I'd need a lot of practice," she said. "I'm not very familiar with…"

"Sera, could I talk to you for a moment?" Marc stepped up beside her, cutting into their conversation with no apology, though he did acknowledge David.

"I'm busy." Sera turned to David. "As I…"

"Seraphina, it's important. Please excuse us, David." He took her elbow, but she shook him off.

"Use the dressing room," David offered. "There's lots of time yet before we have to start." He left them at the bar and went to talk to Mayson.

"I have nothing to say to you," Sera said mulishly.

"Then I'll talk," Marc said, taking her elbow again. "In private."

"This isn't private enough?" She gestured to the empty bar.

"Not hardly. I know you're unhappy, Seraphina, but hear me out."

Once in the dressing room, he leaned against the closed door.

"What is so important?" Sera stood opposite him, against the vanity.

"You're important. I want you to come back to Paris with me."

"Why?" She snapped out the word, her voice a whiplash of anger.

"So I can protect you." He took her by the shoulders, forcing her to look at him. "I don't want you here on your own, not when Bates is still around."

"I have Pari," she said stubbornly.

"She can't protect you all the time." Marc gave her shoulders a gentle shake in emphasis.

"Neither can you." The words were meant to wound, and she saw they hit their target. Marc's grip tightened, his fingers bit into her shoulders.

"Bates is working for Royale. You really think you'll be safe?"

"He has no interest in me. I paid my debts."

Marc's gaze cut away from her.

"Marc, what have you done?"

"It's not about what I've done," he said, fixing her with a worried gaze. "It's about what I tried to get you out of."

"What do you mean?" She stared up at him. He wasn't making any sense.

"You're walking a fine line here. Jeremy's boss demanded blood money for his death, and I had to pay the price to Royale. And Royale still has me by the balls. If he lets our secret slip to Jeremy's boss that you were with Jeremy the night of his death, and spent a lot of time with him before that, you could be forced to tell what you know. If Royale makes him think that what I told him isn't true…"

"I wouldn't tell anyone." Sera folded her arms over her chest, partly to hide the shiver that went through her at the mention of Jeremy's name. The gun had been heavy in her hand, the retort more than she'd expected. After the first shot, he had charged her like a bull, rage in his eyes, and in that moment she'd seen her own death.

"It's precarious here," Marc said, interrupting her bloody reverie. "Did Jeremy ever tell you about his boss?"

"Nothing. Why?" What could Marc possibly be driving at?

Marc clasped her hands tight. "Watch yourself while you're here, if you won't come back to Paris with me."

"I always do."

"And stay clear of Mayson. Don't say anything about Le Chat Rouge, or about Royale. Don't invite Mayson, or any of them, to speculate."

The pieces fell into place. "Mayson is…"

"Jeremy's boss. Yes, he is. And though he can be kind, he's every bit as much of a gangster as Royale."

Sera sucked in a breath. Sanctuary wasn't a sanctuary after all. "Is it just Mayson? Or are David and Julian involved too?" Her cheeks flushed as she remembered Julian's lips on hers, his body pressed intimately to her lips as they danced.

"I don't know, but it's quite possible. Stay away from Sanctuary when you're not working; don't go out with anyone." He paused and she wondered what stopped him from saying more. "Don't let Julian get any closer."

Sera's cheeks flamed and she pulled away from him.

"I saw photos, Sera." Marc's voice was tired; there seemed to be little judgement of her, no condemnation.

"But, how…"

"That's how close Bates has been," he said. Sera turned away from him, but with the vanity mirror in front of her, it was no escape. Marc brushed her hair away from her neck, pressing a kiss on the skin he'd exposed. Had he kissed Madelaine like that?

"Don't touch me," she said harshly, jerking away from him. "I ran into Madelaine, Marc, and she had an awful lot to tell me."

Marc's features hardened and grew forbidding.

"And what did she say?"

"You should know."

"I don't. Dis-moi."

"Remember a phone call we had, a bit of fun play while you were in London? You were alone in your hotel room?" The words didn't seem to spark any recognition and her fury grew. "You were on the phone with me when you came in her mouth!"

Her words echoed in the tiny room, then faded into silence. They stared at each other in the mirror, the tension crackling.

"What do you want me to say?" Marc said finally.

"There isn't anything you can say." The words came out stilted and stiff.

Marc shifted until his chest settled against Sera's back, his warmth sinking into her, taking away the chill. "I know I've made mistakes, but I always came home to you." His warm breath feathered over her ear.

"Did you?" Her reply was faint; she could barely hear her own words.

"Every time," he said. "Remember Christmas, walking in the snow on the Champs de Mars? I can't ever stop thinking of you, Seraphina." His hand rested on her belly, the heat burning through the thin fabric. Stroking her through the cloth, his lips pressed against her neck once more, and though she tried to stay angry, she felt her fury fading under his touch.

"It was the event after Christmas that hurt," she reminded him, trying to stoke her anger and keep it burning.

"But Christmas, cosy in the café, our quiet evening…"

Sera turned in his embrace before she could stop herself. If only she could get back to that moment in time, freeze it and linger there, safe from everything and everyone. She rested her head against his shoulder, hearing the beat of his heart under her ear. His hand slid under the curtain of her hair, gently cupping the back of her neck. Goose bumps scattered down her spine as his thumb brushed against the hollow of her clavicle.

She wanted to stay like this forever, but she had to know what came next.

"When does Royale want his painting?" She raised her head to look at him.

"Soon. He has it picked out from the museum already."

"But that's impossible." She could hardly draw a breath.

"He didn't expect that I'd pay for it at an auction, of course, since there are none."

The implication was clear. "Stealing a Monet could put you in prison. That's a million-dollar price to pay." Sera took a shaky breath. Marc stroked the delicate skin under her ear.

"I know."

"Can't you—" She broke off, realizing the folly of what she was going to say. He couldn't go to the police. The police meant that prison would be real, and not just a theory.

"I only see one way out of this," Marc said finally. "And I want you to come back with me. That way, I know you'll be safe before it all goes down."

"What—but there is no way to solve this." Money or theft, that was all that could be done, all that Sera could see.

"I tried to solve the problem," Marc said, "With a fake, but it didn't work. It might have worked, if only Royale had seen it, but it was for his wife, and she knew instantly."

"So now what?" She dreaded the answer.

"This is why you need to come back to Paris. You can be safe in a city you know, surrounded by friends who can help you if something goes wrong." His voice was serious, but flat, as if he'd rehearsed the words in his head before he told her.

"If what goes wrong?" This time, the shiver down her spine wasn't from his fingers in her hair.

"I can't tell you. Not yet."

"But—"

"Trust me, Sera."

She wavered. He had taken care of her from the moment they'd met, and throughout their break-up too. But now, too much had happened. She saw a darker side to him. He accepted methods he'd once despised.

"Tell me, Marc. I need to know what will happen next."

"Not yet," he said again, "but I will."

"When?"

"Soon. Just not yet."

"Then I'll stay here," she said decisively. If he couldn't tell her, she wouldn't give up her new life. "That's the end of it. Until I know the dangers, I won't give up everything I've worked for." She swallowed. The words formed in her mind, hovered on the tip of her tongue, waiting for her to blurt them out.

She didn't have to say them. Marc saw it in her eyes and he loosened his embrace, stepping back from her just enough that they weren't skin-to-skin.

"You won't come to Paris, not even for me," he said, the words almost exactly like the ones that had come into her mind. He bent his head and pressed a tender, gentle kiss to her lips. "I can't blame you."

"Je suis désolée," she whispered, biting her lip.

"Je comprends." Marc cupped her cheek. "Be safe. I'll be back in London as soon as I can. And remember, watch yourself here, around Mayson and the others. Not a word about Jeremy."

Sera nodded. " And when you get back to London, you'll tell me?" When he didn't answer, she pushed for more. "Promise me, Marc."

"I will."

The Eurostar back to Paris was half-empty, and it gave Marc too much time to think, sitting alone in his row in the quiet carriage.

Sera would choose her career over him.

It stung, though he'd tried to hide the pain from her. But yet, he couldn't fault her. He couldn't see any way out of Royale's spider web without squashing the spider himself. The silk clung to every move he made, forced him into immobility the more he struggled. The web had begun years ago, and this was the endgame, where either the spider or his prey had to die.

Marc didn't want to be the prey.

At Gare du Nord, he caught a cab, and ignored the chatty overtures of the driver. Marc found himself reluctant to snatch at the last cards Mayson held; the cost was too great, the gamble too high. He would be exchanging one difficult situation for another—Mayson could use his leverage as readily as Royale.

But he didn't know if he could act alone.

He'd never killed a man, though he'd ordered a hit once—not that it happened in the end. The blood on his hands was a mere splatter—after Royale, he'd be drenched in red.

It would have to be a gun. Royale's grotesque bulk would make any knife absolutely useless. His pistol, still concealed in the bookcase in his apartment, would do. Sera had felled Jeremy Gordon with it, though it had taken three shots. He imagined it might take as many to down Royale and send him crashing to the ground.

But how to do it—and where? Marc tapped his fingers on the armrest, barely noticing as the cab turned onto the traffic circle at the Étoile, heading to Avenue Wagram.

Le Chat Rouge was a veritable rabbit's warren; he'd never escape detection if he attempted it there; the shots would carry, the club itself was too central to make a swift escape. Would Royale consent to meeting elsewhere, if Marc could promise a Monet? He didn't know.

Marc took out his phone after he paid the driver and got out, sending Aurore a quick message. She replied before he'd gotten into the door of his flat and he read her text as he poured himself a glass of wine.

Fournier awake, but still poorly. You have time to see him before your first appointment tomorrow. Schedule in email.

He sent her back a short reply, feeling a modicum of relief. It had seemed that Fournier would never wake. Marc only hoped that he would continue to recover. He tucked the phone into the pocket of his jeans, and walked through to the living room, where he cracked open one of the floor to ceiling windows, perching on the sill. He drew out his cigarette case and lit a cigarette, the flash of the lighter bright in the darkness.

His thoughts turned back to Royale. And Françoise. He realized that to forget Françoise would be to orchestrate his own downfall. But who was she, really? Any woman could walk past, and he'd never know. He'd never met her, or even seen a photograph. To him, she was a voice on the phone, and in a crowd at Le Chat Rouge—if she even went to the club—her voice would sound as common as any other.

He needed to meet her.

The doorman tipped his hat to Sera as she passed him, pushing through the revolving door and into Claridge's. She paused in the lobby, unsure of her next steps. Why was she here? Asking Edwards about Marc might lead to more upsetting revelations of the sort Madelaine had told her. As she hesitated, her decision was made for her. Edwards crossed the expanse of marble towards her.

"Madame Durand," he said, greeting her with a warm smile. Some of the tension she'd felt lessened. "How nice to see you again. Is Monsieur Perron with you?"

"Hello." She mustered a smile. "Marc isn't here, just me."

"Your English is much better," he remarked. "Are you here for tea? Or a late lunch?"

"Neither. Do you have a few minutes, Edwards?"

"Of course." He seemed to reassess her, as if judging her state of mind. "Come with me. I know where we can talk in private."

He led her along a hallway off the lobby, to a back stair, and took her up a floor. With a small flourish, he swiped his key card and opened a door. "This room is unoccupied at present," he said. "Make yourself at home and I'll go fetch some tea."

Sera stepped past him into the room, a small suite done in a modern style. She sank down onto the sofa, crossing her legs at the ankles, her dark jeans and derby shoes seeming very casual against the hotel's easy luxury.

Edwards returned with a tray, which he set on the coffee table in front of her. "May I?" At her nod, he poured for them both, then sat in the armchair positioned to her left. Sera took a sip of her tea, nearly scalding her tongue, but the familiar taste of bergamot was comforting.

"Is this…?"

"Mariage Frères," Edwards confirmed.

"It's my favourite," she said with some surprise. "How did you know?"

"Monsieur Perron mentioned it in passing on your last day here, so I made a point of picking some up from Selfridge's on my day off, just in case you'd return."

"Merci beaucoup." Sera felt her cheeks heat.

"But you didn't come here to talk about tea," he said.

"No." Sera thought of how she might phrase the question, wondering if he would even tell her the answer. "Has Marc always stayed here?"

Edwards took a sip of his tea before answering. "For quite some time, at least fifteen years. He told me once that his uncle preferred the Dorchester, but that he didn't want to be anywhere near the man if he could help it."

"His uncle was…" She didn't know the word for it in English. "Not a good man."

"I thought that might be the case."

"I met Marc's petite amie"—she hated even saying the words—"at the bookshop. She said she came here with him."

Edwards frowned, his gaze dropping to the cup in his hands.

"I know, hotel guests' activities are private," Sera said haltingly.

"Madelaine Wells. She was here only three times, over perhaps as many months. Most unlike him," Edwards said, leaning forward to lift the teapot and refill their cups.

"Unlike him?"

"He was always working, and very hard. Just before Christmas, he was here and looked especially morose. I asked him why, and he said that he missed someone dearly, a woman back in Paris." Edwards shrugged. "But later that evening, she was with him, and he seemed happy to see her."

Sera's heart, hopeful at the mention of 'a woman in Paris', sank once more at the mention of Madelaine.

"She returned twice more," Edwards continued, "like she was walking on air. Monsieur Perron's enthusiasm didn't match hers, but he didn't turn her down. He wasn't very happy."

Sera had to clear her throat before she could speak. "How do you know?"

"I see a lot, madame," he said simply. "I'm speaking to you now because I saw how he was with you here. I wouldn't do this for any other guest."

"He never told me about her," Sera tried to explain, biting at a nail.

"And you're worried that he loves her?" Edwards asked. "She may have been in love with him, but his heart was already taken." His words were gentle, but confident.

Sera's teacup clattered in its saucer and she set it on the table before she spilled. "It was a shock to meet her," she said. "Awful. To know he had been…" She pressed her lips together.

"Prior to her, he rarely ever had anyone round to his room," Edwards said. "Not in the fifteen years I've known him."

"I don't know what to think," she admitted.

"Do you trust him?" Edwards asked. Such a simple question should have a simple answer, but she didn't know what that answer was.

She took a sip of tea, but it caught in her throat and she choked, momentarily sputtering and coughing. Edwards sprang to his feet, snatching up a napkin and patting her gently on the back until she recovered. Sera dabbed at her lips and then at her watering eyes. Edwards perched on the edge of the sofa.

"When you figure out the answer to that question," he continued, his voice soft and nonjudgmental, "then you can decide whether or not you can forgive him for Madelaine."

Sera dabbed at her eyes again, this time swallowing back the sobs that threatened to rise. "I worry," she began haltingly, clearing her throat, "that he'll choose her over me, in the end. She's younger, prettier…"

"She doesn't hold a candle to you," Edwards replied. "Not even close. And Monsieur Perron doesn't think she does either."

"I'll have to talk to him," she said.

"He'd want to hear from you, I'm sure of it."

"But there are things I need to hear from him before I decide," she replied, glossing over the details.

"Call him," Edwards said resolutely, "or go see him. It's not that far to Paris these days."

"If I go, I'd miss work," Sera said. "And I can't miss work."

"Is work so important?"

"It is."

"The only job you'll ever have?" Edwards kept his tone light, but the question stung. She knew she was being stubborn. Five thousand euros still sat untouched in her bank account. She wouldn't starve while she looked for a new job.

But if Marc took the fall for her and stole a Monet for Royale—or whatever his plan was—she couldn't rely on him for help, and that five thousand euros would become very dear indeed.

Edwards patted her knee and rose. "Think on it. Sleep on it, even. You'll know what's right in the end."

"Merci, Edwards." She gave him a grateful smile and he returned it, his eyes kind. When she moved to rise, he held out a hand.

"Stay as long as you need to. I'll send a housekeeper in to clear up later."

Sera sank back onto the sofa. "Merci encore."

CHAPTER 20

When Marc arrived at the hospital, the doctors had just moved Fournier from intensive care into a regular room, and it took some time to track him down. He lingered in the hall until the nurse had finished.

"Only a few minutes," she warned Marc when she came out. "He's still quite poorly."

Fournier looked awful; the bruises on his face and elsewhere had become multi-coloured hues of purple and yellow, and the sallow shades of the bed linens didn't help matters.

"Ça va, Guillaume?" he asked, stepping to the foot of the bed. Fournier gave him a weak smile.

"Pas mal." He lifted a hand, rattling the tubes still attached. "I just want out of here. It's a crime against all taste." He gestured to the linen, the dull walls.

"Want me to bring you the tapestry from my office?" Marc quipped. Fournier chuckled, then winced.

"Too big for this place. It would never fit."

"True. And they might not appreciate it." When Fournier grimaced, Marc wondered if he ought to beckon for the nurse. "Do you need painkillers?"

"No, I'll be fine," Fournier said hoarsely. "The ribs are healing, but not fast enough to suit me. And I'm trying to ignore the cast on my leg." He rubbed the dressing over his chest, then let his hand drop back to the bed.

"Do they know how long?"

Fournier shrugged, the movement barely noticeable but for his wince. "A few weeks yet. The nurse said something about having scans done. They're worried about my brain. I'm not, though. I can think just fine when I'm not doped to the eyeballs." He smiled, but it was brief. "How's Aurore holding up? And you?"

"We're managing. I'm back here until you're fit again. Aurore is—well, Aurore. Without her, I think the firm would sink."

"It would," Fournier agreed. "Is Sera back with you?"

"She's in London."

"Without you?"

"She has a job there now," Marc replied. "Singing in a club. She likes it."

"But still," Fournier persisted, "you've hardly been apart since the spring."

"We need this time."

"What for?"

Marc sighed and pinched the bridge of his nose. He turned away from Fournier, pacing to the window to look out into the hospital's central courtyard. "It's a story not worth telling."

"Marc, this is me you're talking to." Fournier's voice regained some of its old life. "I've had no stories or gossip since I've been here. Humour me."

"It's…" Marc broke off. "I don't even know where to start." With Royale? Or Jeremy Gordon? Or even further back, to his uncle and the mess the firm was in.

"Start with why she's mad at you," Fournier suggested. Marc turned. "She is, isn't she? She'd be here with you if she wasn't. I'd bet my paycheque on it."

Marc sighed again. "I don't think I ever told you about Madelaine, did I?"

"No. And I'm hurt that you didn't. Who is Madelaine?"

"Madelaine worked—works—at a bookshop in London. I met her there just before Christmas. She's a lovely girl, a bit young, but pretty. A redhead," he added. Fournier whistled, but the sound was faint.

"Go on. So this Madelaine, you and she…" Fournier wiggled his eyebrows.

"I've never known you to be so circumspect," Marc quipped.

"I'm on drugs. Keep going."

"And Sera and I regrettably ran into her while we were out."

"Coincidentally? In a city of how many millions?" Fournier snorted. "You couldn't have chosen another bookshop?"

"Don't start."

Fournier laughed, then clutched his ribs with a pained grunt. "It's really your own fault then. I'm guessing there was a scene?"

"Not as much as there could have been," Marc admitted.

"Then what? This doesn't seem like enough for a row."

"I don't want to talk about it."

"Talk. I promise this once that I won't tell Aurore. She idolizes you, you know."

Marc took the chair beside the bed. "All right." He told Fournier everything, except for the parts about Royale, Bates, and Mayson. Fournier listened with interest.

"Bad move," he said when Marc had finished. "The only way out that I can see is to grovel. A lot. Maybe treat her to dinner, champagne, roses, the theatre…"

"And if that doesn't work?"

"It's always worked for me," Fournier said. "Mind you, men are much easier to please."

"That's not very helpful." Marc chuckled despite himself.

"I never said I was a miracle worker," Fournier countered. "You could always go back to London and get down on your knees before her. You know, with a fine piece of jewellery."

Marriage.

Absolutely the last thing he had expected Fournier to suggest, and the last thing on his own mind.

"She'd say no."

"Would she?"

The nurse bustled in. "Time's up. You've been here long enough, monsieur."

Marc rose, checking his watch. He had an appointment to get to.

"If you decide to take my advice, I know a good jeweller in the 5th who has some lovely pieces."

At the break between sets, Sera approached David with some trepidation, pulling him aside before he could go up to Mayson's office.

"Do you think Mayson would give me a couple of days off?"

"He might. What for? You'd miss our busiest nights if you're gone longer than two days."

"I need to see Marc," Sera replied, knowing full well how weak her reason sounded, like she was a lovesick girl who couldn't be without her man for even a day.

David frowned and she could see those thoughts running through his mind. "Come with me and you can ask."

She followed him toward Mayson's office, walking past the bar. Julian leaned over. "Your friend Pari coming in tonight?"

"She's working," Sera replied, "but I can tell her you asked after her."

"Do." Julian winked before he turned to take down a bottle of whiskey from the shelf behind the bar.

David ushered her into Mayson's office. The man himself sat behind his expansive desk, typing away on a laptop, frowning in concentration. She hadn't seen him since her conversation with Marc, since she'd learned who Mayson really was. He didn't look like her idea of a gangster, at least not with his brow furrowed and the tip of his tongue peeking from the corner of his mouth. They waited until Mayson had ceased his typing. He glanced up and surprise flashed briefly over his features.

"Ms. Durand," he said, his gaze flicking to David's. "What can I do for you?" His voice was kind and Sera's nervousness abated. He gestured to a chair. "Please, sit."

Sera sat, spreading the long black dress carefully so she didn't wrinkle the fabric. She clasped her hands in her lap. "I don't wish to bother you, but..." She dampened her lips. "I wondered if I might take the next two evenings off."

"That wasn't our deal," Mayson said, his voice even, reasonable, though his expression seemed to harden.

Sera didn't know how to explain, not without making herself vulnerable. "I know, and I wouldn't ask, but it is important."

Mayson considered her, leaning back in his chair, tapping his fingers on the arm rest. "You may, but there are a few things I'd like to know first."

Sera stiffened, then forced herself to relax, to unclench her fingers. "What would you like to know?" She heard the rustle of cloth as David moved.

"I'll just get myself a drink," he said. She turned in her chair but he was already out the door.

"You don't need to be so worried," Mayson said when she turned back. "I'd never hurt a woman. I just want to know a bit more about you. How long did you work for Monsieur Royale?"

Sera drew in a breath. She hadn't expected Mayson to have known that, but she had no idea what Royale had told him. "Longer than I wanted to."

"Were there other singers while you were there, at Le Chat Rouge?"

"A few." There had been many, though after her first six months, there had only been her. Royale, through Jean, had sent the other ones packing.

Mayson nodded to himself. "Did he ever confide in you?"

"Who?" She was genuinely puzzled, and he must have seen that in her expression, for he took a different line in his questioning.

"Did you ever see anything untoward? Violence? Couriers at all hours, that sort of thing?"

She'd seen violence, done to herself by Royale's hands, but that was likely not what Mayson referred to. "No, not that I can remember. And I've never been one to deal with couriers. The maitre d', Jean, would have done so, or maybe one of the bartenders."

"Do you remember an Englishman there recently? One who would have known Royale?" He stared hard at her.

"There were always tourists," Sera said. "What did he look like?"

"Blond, tall, well-dressed. Jeremy Gordon was his name."

She made a show of pondering his identity, however, just the mention of his name was enough to bring him to life in her mind.

"I saw him around, I think. He told me he liked chanson."

"He always had a thing for the French," Mayson remarked. "I'm surprised he didn't get to know you better—you're just his type."

"I don't date customers," she replied, a bit too sharply.

Mayson raised a brow.

Sera flushed. "Some men seem to think that being a performer means you're also a…" She searched for the word in English.

"Whore?" Mayson offered. Sera nodded. "Did Jeremy flirt with you?"

"Some. He seemed nice." She hated to say anything, especially after Marc's warning, but she couldn't think of any way around it. A few words of truth might satisfy Mayson.

"Jeremy died, and Monsieur Royale wasn't very clear on how he died, you see, but I've begun to get information from other sources." He leaned forward, resting his elbows on the desk, his hands clasped in front of him, making her his entire focus.

Sera threw him a puzzled glance. "I know little of what Monsieur Royale does."

"And I'm sure he likes to keep it that way, but I'm pretty sure you're not telling me everything you know."

"I don't understand." Sera's stomach churned and she felt nervous perspiration trickling down her spine.

"I know what Jeremy was," Mayson said. "He would have done far more than just flirt."

She couldn't help the heat that rose to her cheeks, and she cut her gaze away. She heard the flick of a lighter and smelled the sharp scent of a newly lit cigarette.

"Nothing to be ashamed of. You're not the first. His girls weren't all willing, unfortunately."

A shudder overcame her and she wrapped her arms about herself. She didn't want to remember. It was blood and pain, the cold metal of the gun in her shaky hand.

"You're protecting someone, aren't you?" She glanced up in surprise. Mayson took a deep drag of his cigarette and let the smoke out slowly, like he was a dragon at rest. "Thought so." A smile quirked at the corners of his mouth.

"I…"

"Go see your boyfriend," Mayson interrupted. "And tell him that he'll owe me."

"Owe you what?"

"I'll let him tell you."

Sera couldn't suppress the shiver of dread. What had Marc agreed to?

Marc lingered at Le Petit Pergolese, sipping a glass of Moscato as he reviewed his notes and files from the day. The restaurant bustled around him, but he hardly noticed. He read until his eyes watered. Catching the glance of the maitre d', he gathered up his work and paid the bill.

"Merci beaucoup, monsieur. Bonne nuit."

He took a short stroll in the cool night air, down Rue Pergolese. He cut through the small streets to avoid the bustle of the Étoile. He came out onto Avenue de Wagram and headed towards the Place des Ternes. He was in no hurry to return home. The apartment would be empty and the less time he spent there, the better.

The Place des Ternes was busy with a steady stream of traffic and people that emerged from the metro stop into the square. The Brasserie La Lorraine had a full terrace, and the noise of dining and conversation carried onto the sidewalk as Marc passed by.

His name came through the clatter, but he ignored it. After all, lots of men were named Marc. But then a female voice called again, this time more insistent, and suddenly familiar. He stopped dead, causing the couple behind him to veer out of the way. He turned on his heel. At a table on the edge of the terrace, under the crimson awning of the brasserie, sat Sera, a suitcase at her feet, which were clad in their usual black lace-up shoes. She was clothed entirely in black, and her face was pale above the delicate scarf wrapped around her neck. A tentative smile graced her features as he took the half-dozen steps towards her. He didn't bother with formalities, drawing her into his embrace as she stood. She swayed against him, off-balance on her toes, her face tucked into his shoulder, clinging to him as if she'd never let go.

Marc cupped the back of her head, his fingers carding through her silky dark hair. "What are you doing here, ma chère?"

Sera loosened her grasp on his neck and lowered herself to a more stable position, but she didn't let go. "I took a couple of days off," she said breathlessly, and he realized that in his surprise, he'd held her much tighter than he'd meant to.

"I thought you had decided not to come."

"I changed my mind." He embraced her again and she laid her head on his shoulder, relaxing into him. The tension inside him that had built since he'd talked to her at Sanctuary cracked and fell away.

A waiter behind them cleared his throat and they broke apart. Sera slid her hand into his.

"Monsieur, would you like something to drink?"

"Non, merci."

"L'addition, s'il vous plaît," Sera added, and the waiter gave them an understanding smile.

"D'accord, madame." In a moment, he was back and tucked the bill underneath the edge of her glass.

Marc glanced at it and dug into his pocket, handing the man twenty euros for the cost of the cocktail she'd been drinking, and a large tip. The man began to move away.

"I'll get your change, monsieur."

"No need," Marc said. He bent and lifted Sera's suitcase with his free hand. "Bonne nuit."

"Vous êtes très gentil," he heard the waiter say as they left.

They didn't speak as they turned the corner towards Marc's apartment, though they slowed their pace as if by agreement, meandering along. Sera clung to his hand, the tips of her fingers chill against his skin. Instead of taking the stairs, they squeezed into the small elevator. The top of Sera's head brushed his chin and he dropped a kiss on her hair.

Once they were inside, Sera turned her serious, unhappy gaze on him. "Mayson said to tell you that you owed him one."

Marc's whole body went cold and he struggled to hide his surprise. Sera continued speaking, her dark eyes fixing him with a worried stare.

"At first I thought he meant letting me off work. But then, on the train here, I realized that he didn't mean that at all—why would he even care about us?"

There was no getting around it. He'd tried to think of ways to explain the situation that would be palatable to her, but he'd drawn a blank.

"He doesn't care about us, not really," Marc replied. The words echoed in the entryway where they stood. He took Sera's hand and led her through to the kitchen. She leaned against the counter while he made two espressos and considered his next words.

"Merci. Sera sipped from the porcelain demi-tasse he gave her.

"Mayson loved Jeremy," Marc said. "Like a son, or maybe a lover, or a bit of both."

At that, Sera's head jerked up in surprise.

"But he wants revenge on Royale, partly for Jeremy's sake, but also because they have a long history."

"Why would he tell you all this?" Sera's voice was barely a whisper and she clasped the demi-tasse in both hands to hold it steady.

"He doesn't want to be the one to get his hands dirty."

Her face drained of what little colour she had left, and he looped an arm around her waist. She sagged against him. "You can't. Mon Dieu, Marc, that's worse than stealing."

He knew it; he'd always known it, but there still seemed to be no other way out. "Royale won't ever stop," he said. "He and Françoise, they'll take their pound of flesh one way or another."

Sera shook her head.

"If we ever want to stay in Europe—here, or London, or any-where—we won't be able to do it if they live. He's threatened

Aurore and Fournier, and that's only the start. If I snub them again, I have no doubt that there will be hell to pay."

"It is hell either way." Sera's voice had no power, as if all hope had deserted her. In his arms she was dead weight, and they sank to the floor in a heap. Her empty cup clattered to the tile. He stroked her hair as she shuddered in his embrace. "To kill or be killed." The words were so soft he barely heard them. Her fingers tightened on his arm, digging into his flesh hard through the sleeve of his suit jacket and shirt.

"But without Mayson, I don't know if I'd succeed," Marc said after a long, silent moment. "If I attempt to meet Royale without bringing a painting, a proper Monet, I'm dead the moment I step over the threshold."

"How can Mayson help?" Sera asked after an equally long pause, lifting her head from his shoulder. "Would he steal a painting?"

"No, but he'll supply someone to help. For a cost, of course, but needs must."

Had his uncle ever faced this quandary, after he'd begun associating with criminals? Did he know—or care—what his choices would do to his nephew, twenty years later?

Sera cupped his face in her small, delicate hands. Her fingers were icy on his skin and she gave him a long searching look, her dark eyes troubled.

"You'll do it anyway, won't you?" she said, "Even if I begged you not to."

Marc didn't answer her right away, but he didn't need to. His gaze cut away from hers and that told her all she needed to know. Sera struggled to her feet and didn't wait for him to rise. She went into the darkened living room, looking out the window and down into the street. It all seemed so ordinary. She heard his voice, angry and curt, but only a few words came to her.

"I won't, Françoise." There was a pause, and then she heard the low growl of his response.

In front of her, the window shattered, so sudden that she couldn't throw her hands up fast enough. She stumbled back, feeling the glass shards hitting her, hearing them striking the parquet at her feet in a tinkling rush, spreading over the floor in glittering ribbons. Her legs hit the back of the coffee table and she fell, crying out in surprise.

Marc rushed out from the kitchen, his phone still in his hand, the glass crunching under the soles of his shoes as he scooped her up, carrying her into the entryway. Away from any windows, she realized.

"You bitch," Marc snarled into the phone as he set her on her feet, shielding her body with his own. Sera heard the tinny laugh in response. Something wet slid down her cheek and she brushed it away.

"That was a warning," she heard a feminine voice say. "You know what to do."

Marc stabbed at the button on his phone to cut off the call. Sera rubbed at her face again. It was still wet. She held up her hand. Stars danced at the edges of her vision. Marc shoved his phone into his pocket and pulled the pocket square from his suit jacket, pressing it to her forehead. Pain shot through her temple and she couldn't stifle the gasp she made.

"You're hurt, ma chère," he said, picking shards of glass from her hair, letting them fall to the floor. They shuffled into the windowless bathroom and Sera sank onto the closed lid of the toilet.

"I didn't feel anything," she said, putting up a hand to where Marc still held the pocket square. He took her hand and placed it over the now sticky fabric.

"Hold that there," he said, and when she complied, he stepped back, reaching for the hand towel hanging beside the sink. Wetting one end, he came back to her, cleaning the blood from her face before he lifted her hand from her forehead. It stung when the towel touched the wound, and she winced.

"What was it?" she asked as he inspected her forehead.

"Someone took a shot at the window—at you," he said, "but they missed."

A warning, that's what the woman on the phone had said.

"They meant to miss."

"The cut will heal," he said, avoiding her statement.

Sera rose unsteadily to her feet, moving the few steps to the mirror. Blood still faintly streaked her cheeks, but as Marc had said, the cut on her forehead, right at her hairline, would heal. It had stopped bleeding, but a nasty, reddened gash remained.

Sera turned on the taps and washed her hands, the water pink as it swirled around the drain. Glass glinted in her hair and she bent forward, running her fingers over her scalp, hearing the tiny pieces ping against the porcelain before they caught in the running water.

When she lifted her head and turned to Marc, she saw the worry in his eyes.

"I have to do it." He sounded resigned, regretful. "I have no choice."

CHAPTER 21

Marc convinced Sera to rest, but he couldn't follow his own advice. He found a piece of cardboard to place inside the broken window pane, and then he closed the shutters and drew the curtains. The shutters wouldn't protect them, not the way he wanted, and he wished for steel instead of wood. He paced from the window into the living room, his eyes falling on the dark rent in the light-painted wall. When he ran his fingers over the hole, he couldn't feel the lead. The bullet had embedded itself into the plaster.

It had been too close. The next time, the damage wouldn't just be a cut from glass, it would be a bullet in the head. The shooter—the sniper, he amended—could have done it tonight if they'd wanted to.

Marc went and closed the bedroom door, then took out his phone.

"Mayson."

"It's Marc Perron. I've had a chance to consider your offer, and I will need assistance soon. It's the only way."

"I thought you'd come around," Mayson replied with a chuckle. "I can have my man there in a couple of days with everything you'll need."

"Not earlier?"

"He has work to do for me," Mayson said. "Monday at the earliest."

"That'll have to do," Marc replied, though he wished he could finish Royale off tonight.

"Arrange things with Royale, find out where he'll be, then call me with the details," Mayson directed. "I'll advise my man here and get him ready."

"Consider it done."

Mayson rang off and Marc dialled the number that had called him earlier.

"How is your poor girl?" Françoise asked, her voice syrupy sweet, not even bothering to say hello.

"She is fine."

"Pity. I'd hoped I could convince you."

"You have," Marc said, "and I've been making arrangements."

"Have you now?" she purred.

"I'll have the painting for you on Monday or Tuesday."

"It had best be real," Françoise said sharply. "But Monday won't work. It'll have to be Sunday."

"Monday," Marc replied. "I'll bring it out for you."

Françoise was silent, and for a moment he thought the call had dropped.

"Monday, then. And bring your girl," she commanded.

"Sera stays here."

"No. She comes. Consider her your guarantee of good behaviour. Besides, my husband's always had a thing for her. Best to indulge him, don't you think? I'll send you the address and your appointment time. À bientôt." She rang off.

Marc swore, wishing he could do real harm to the woman on the other end of the phone. Instead, he called Mayson back. "It's on."

Sera woke midmorning, curled up under the duvet, cosy in a cocoon of warmth. For a moment, she didn't know what was different, but then Marc shifted behind her, his legs cradling hers, his hand resting on her belly. She closed her eyes and relaxed back against him, determined to enjoy the time they had together.

Marc's thumb brushed the curve of her breast and she drew in a breath, goose bumps prickling her skin as he slowly lifted his hand, tracing his fingertips up her sternum. But though she waited for him to cup her breast and pinch her nipple, as he often did, he continued his slow, teasing caress. She shifted against him and felt his erection press between her thighs, but still he took his time, though he began to touch feathery kisses to her naked shoulder laid bare by a slipping bed sheet.

Reaching back behind her, under the covers, she grasped his cock. His entire body stiffened against her and his fingers ceased their caress, stuttering to a halt between her breasts. She stroked him from root to tip, once, twice, before he grasped her wrist and pulled her hand away.

"Not yet, ma chère," he murmured in her ear. "But there is this." He guided her hand between her thighs, his touch joining hers against her clit, a teasing caress that Sera deepened, arching in demand against their paired hands.

"More," she whispered, and he pressed down in small circles against her clit. At the same time, he nibbled at the line of her neck, firm nips that made her shudder, sensitizing her body to every tiny brush of his limbs against hers.

"Toujours." Two fingers sank into her and she whimpered as her own hand pressed snug against her clit, caught between his hand and her body. He slid a third finger into her and the whimper became a cry. Marc pressed up into her and the orgasm rushed through her, stars exploding behind her closed eyes.

In the haze of her pleasure, she felt him moving, withdrawing from her. She gave a small moan of protest. Marc nudged his knee between her thighs, spreading her legs. He sheathed himself inside her, his fingers wet on her belly as he held her against him. Sera arched her back, taking him deeper. Tilting her head back against the pillow, she opened her eyes. He took her mouth in a passionate kiss, and she wanted this moment to last forever.

As Marc drank his second espresso, and Sera nibbled on a croissant from the boulangerie down the street, his phone rang. He scooped it up from the coffee table and glanced at the number. Aurore.

"Bon matin, Aurore."

"It is a good morning, monsieur," Aurore said, somewhat breathlessly. "Guillaume has been moved into the regular ward and the doctors say he is out of danger."

"I'm glad to hear it." And he was. For all the man's quirks, he was fond of Fournier.

"He wants to see you," Aurore said. "I think he wants to work. I told him you'd want him to rest, but he wouldn't listen to me."

"I'll go in the afternoon," Marc replied, "then into the office. And I'll convince him to rest for at least a few more days."

"The file for the Thompson deal is on your desk, monsieur, ready for your trip and the auction on Wednesday."

"Merci, Aurore." Marc hung up and let the phone drop to the sofa.

"What is it?" Sera asked, picking up her demi-tasse. He told her the news about Fournier. "And what else? You look—startled."

"I have to be in Brussels on Wednesday," he said. "There's an auction of rare books."

"Must you?"

"A client hired me to go on his behalf. I can't bow out."

"I want to go with you," she said. "I don't want to go back to London if you're not there."

"You've had a change of heart," Marc noted. "I'm glad. Though Mayson would expect you back at Sanctuary by then."

Sera's brow furrowed and he reached over and smoothed away the wrinkle.

"I don't know," she said, frowning.

"It's a good job."

"Yes, but…" Sera broke off.

Marc waited patiently for her to continue, clasping her hand when she reached out for him, their fingers intertwined, and he raised her hand to his lips.

"But you won't be there," she said finally. "You'll be here, or in Brussels."

"I'll always come back to you."

"It's not enough. We'd be back where we started."

"If we even get that far."

Her grip tightened. "What do you mean?"

"I'll have to see Royale—and Françoise—on Monday." He bit back his next words that she had to be there too. He'd press Royale directly, and get him to back down. Until it was certain, she didn't need to know.

"I'll come with you."

"No." He wouldn't allow it.

"I'm involved too. I killed Jeremy, not you."

"Not in their eyes—and Mayson doesn't know. It needs to stay that way."

"You'd leave me so soon?" Her voice cracked.

"I won't leave you for long."

"You can't know that—what if…" She swallowed hard and he was surprised at the emotion in her voice, the intensity. What had changed between now and the other day, when she'd been so determined to stay in London?

He pulled her close, tucking her under his arm as he'd done on the train to London. "I'll be fine. I always make it out all right in the end." The words were forced bravado, exposing a confidence he didn't feel, but she didn't seem to notice.

That evening, Sera paced the length of Marc's flat. He sat on the sofa, reviewing a file, but she couldn't sit still. The window was fixed now, thanks to a handyman who had accepted a higher fee to come outside his regular hours. She looked through the glass, staying out of sight from the street, hovering behind the dark drape. The streetlights were coming on and the setting sun gave everything an orange tinge while deepening the shadows.

"Sera."

She turned. Marc had set aside his files and now he held out his hand to her. She retraced her steps to the sofa.

"We don't have to stay in," he said.

"I don't know." She wasn't sure she wanted to leave the apartment, to make herself vulnerable.

"Benoît's playing tonight at that club in the 4th. We could go."

The thought of seeing Benoît brightened her mood. She pushed her fears aside, because to hear him play again—

"How did you know?"

"I hear things." He smiled. "Sophie mentioned it to Aurore. Shall we?" He rose, leaving the file folders where they were.

"All right."

They took a taxi to the club, one expense Sera didn't mind this time, and it dropped them on the Rue de Renard, a few steps away from the tiny side street where the club lay. The heavy wooden door opened at street level, but inclined downward to a steep stairway hemmed in by brick walls. For a moment it reminded her of Sanctuary, though the ambiance was different, warmer somehow, despite the cool damp air. As they reached the bottom, they could hear chatter and the strains of a piano. She recognized the song immediately. Benoît was playing 'As Time Goes By.'

Marc settled his hand on the small of her back as the hallway widened, leading her into the club. He gave her a gentle nudge forward. "Find us a spot and I'll get the drinks." She smiled up at him and he dropped a kiss on her cheek before heading to the bar.

Sera scanned the room, spotting an empty table set back in an alcove near the stage. As she crossed to it, she caught Benoît's attention. He grinned and gave her a nod. She took a seat, keeping her back to the wall. Marc soon joined her, carrying a carafe of wine and two glasses. He slid in next to her, angling his chair so he could see the stage, their knees snug together under the table. She rested her hand on his thigh, feeling secure with him so close.

He poured the wine and they each lifted a glass. "To us," he said. "Santé."

"Santé," Sera echoed. She took a sip of her wine and the familiar, almost mineral taste of the Sancerre vintage, one of her favourites, flowed over her tongue.

"Ce soir, mesdames et messieurs," Benoît began, the music tapering off, "We have a special guest. While our lovely Solange performs for those fortunate crowds in Lille, Daniel Marceau is here to take her place."

A blond man stepped onto the stage. His bow tie was undone; draped rakishly around his neck, and his crisp tuxedo shirt unbuttoned at the throat. He threw a glance to Benoît and Sera saw the pianist's cheeks pinken.

They began with a classic, *'À Paris'*, and then went straight into *'Rien de rien'*, warming up the crowd with ease. Just before the break, Benoît began a song she'd never heard, a romantic lament. Daniel shifted, moving from the centre of the small stage to lean on the piano, his gaze locked to Benoît's as if they were the only two people in the world. His voice dipped to a seductive whisper, and Sera found Marc's hand under the table. He gave her fingers a gentle squeeze as they listened, and Sera swallowed against the thickness in her throat.

It was a song of love and loss, and love found once again. Although Benoît had likely written it for Daniel, it could have been written for her and Marc.

The music tapered off and in the pause that followed, Daniel straightened, giving Benoît one last look before he returned to centre stage. Then the applause began. Benoît rose from the bench and gave a small bow to the audience. Daniel did the same, and then they retreated.

Marc leaned close. "With that talent, we should start our own club with them," he remarked. The comment was a throwaway, but it resonated with Sera.

"We should." At Marc's look of surprise, she reiterated her comment. "Maybe that's what we need to do, instead of performing at Sanctuary, or you working for the firm."

"Peut-être." He looked thoughtful. "It's too soon to say."

Of course. Until they sorted things with Royale and Françoise, everything was at a standstill.

"What if we went to Marseille, or Lyon? Truly started over?"

Marc didn't get a chance to reply. Benoît pulled out the chair across from them and they rose to greet him; Sera bestowed affectionate bisous. She'd missed Benoît, missed performing with him.

"How are things in London?" Benoît asked. "I didn't think you'd be back in Paris so soon."

"I had business that couldn't wait," Marc answered before she could say anything.

"I have a job," Sera added, "and it's better than at Le Chat Rouge."

Benoît's expression darkened at her mention of the club. "Anything's better than there."

"But we're all here now, away from it," Sera offered, attempting to dispel his dark mood.

"We are," he conceded. Daniel came over, setting a glass of water in front of Benoît.

"A gift from Fabien," he said, taking the free chair next to Benoît. "So, you're Sera. I've heard a lot about you. You have a lot of fans here, you know."

"I do?"

"I'm not surprised," Marc said, nudging her. "I'd wager that you could sing tonight and you'd make a lot of people very happy."

Benoît seemed to perk up. "I'll go talk to Laurent. I'm sure he'd be amenable." He rose from his seat and disappeared into the crowd before she could stop him.

"What would you like to sing?" Daniel asked, leaning forward on his crossed arms.

"I don't know—I hadn't expected..." Her mind went blank.

"Do the Gainsbourg and Birkin song." Marc took a sip of his wine.

"Parfait," Daniel declared.

"Does Benoît know it?" She didn't remember ever singing it at Le Chat Rouge.

"He'd better," Daniel quipped. Benoît returned, dropping into his chair.

"Laurent's delighted. What should we perform?"

" '*Je t'aime...Moi non plus,* '" Daniel said immediately.

"Do you know it?" Sera asked.

"I can muddle along. I've done it before."

"You're a talented muddler," Daniel replied, and he and Benoît shared a laugh.

"Just one song?" Sera took a fortifying sip of her wine.

"How about three?" Daniel suggested. "We could do *'How Little We Know'* and another, your choice."

"All right." Her stomach quivered with a touch of nervousness, but it was overruled by the anticipation of performing again in Paris.

"Let's give *'Je t'aime'* a quick run thru in the dressing room," Daniel said. "It'll help you warm up."

"I'll see you on stage in ten," Benoît said as Daniel stood.

Marc dropped a kiss on Sera's cheek before she too rose. "You'll be fantastic," he murmured.

"I hope so." Sera squeezed his hand, then followed Daniel back behind the stage.

Marc watched Sera go, disappearing into the crowd. Benoît lounged in the chair across from him, his hand loosely cupped around his glass of water. Marc leaned forward.

"Tell me about Le Chat Rouge. Sera told me that Royale fired you."

Benoît snorted. "I punched out Jean. The bastard. I only wish I could have done more."

"I would have liked to see that." Marc thought Jean needed it; as Royale's right hand, the maître d' was always so smug, and secure in his position.

"I would have punched Royale, too, if I hadn't been so worried about Daniel. I wasn't sure he was going to make it."

Marc frowned. "How's that?"

"He overdosed," Benoît said, his tone matter of fact. "He got the drugs from Jean, who knew of his problem."

Marc wasn't surprised. Mayson had mentioned Royale's interference in his drugs trade. "You're lucky you were only sacked."

"I know." Benoît's voice dropped. "I realized it later, but I'd been furious. Daniel nearly died." He shuddered. "I don't ever want to see that again."

"Is he clean now?"

"Since that night. But staying clean is a struggle." Benoît checked his watch. "Break's over. I'd better go get them. See you later."

Marc sat back, relaxing into the banquette. The trio came out onto the stage a few minutes later and Daniel introduced Sera to the crowd, who applauded with vigor.

"Prêt?" Benoît asked. At Daniel's nod, he began. Marc blew Sera a kiss and she winked at him.

"She's pretty," said a feminine voice beside him. A woman slid onto the banquette next to him, her perfume tickling his nose—a scent of jasmine and musk, her body soft where it pressed against his. In the low light her face seemed ageless, but he could just see the slight sag of skin at her neck and the beginnings of lines at the corners of her mouth. Her dark hair was done up in an elegant chignon and she wore a crisp, expensive suit and conservative jewellery. She was the perfect Parisienne.

"She is," he agreed. Something jabbed his ribs but when he tried to twist aside, her steely grip came down on his arm, digging into him.

"Pretty, even with the mark on her forehead," the woman said. "Come with me, Monsieur Perron, and that's the only damage she'll suffer." She dug the gun further into his ribs.

"Who are you?" he asked, not moving. She laughed, a low amused chuckle.

"I'd forgotten, Monsieur Perron, that we've never been introduced. I'm Françoise Royale."

CHAPTER 22

At the end of their second song, Sera glanced over to Marc. He'd always liked *'How Little We Know.'*

But, he wasn't there.

She glanced at Benoît, who gave her an encouraging nod and began the third song. Daniel sidled up beside her and rested his arm on her shoulder. She looked up at him as they sang, their voices in a charming harmony, but the niggling feeling at the back of her mind wouldn't cease.

When the song ended, she bowed to the audience, her gaze going back to their table. Marc still wasn't there, but an almost empty carafe still sat on the table, along with their glasses. She barely heard Daniel's words to the crowd as he thanked her for performing with him. After another bow, she left the stage, weaving her way through the tables.

The banquette sat empty, and when she placed her hand on the seat, it was cold, as if Marc had not sat there for some time. She took out her mobile. No messages. Dialling his number from memory, she held the phone to her ear, straining to hear over the music and conversation.

Marc's phone rang once, and on the second ring, it cut abruptly to voice mail.

"Merci pour votre…"

She hung up and tried his number again, and for a second time it went straight to voice mail.

"Marc?" She wasn't sure if her words would carry, so she spoke as clearly as she could. "Where are you? Where have you gone? Call me."

Clutching her phone in her hand, she rose, turning towards the bar. He wasn't there, but she went over anyway.

"Did you see a tall man, dark hair, blue eyes, wearing a black leather jacket in the last little while?" she asked the bartender, raising her voice to be heard.

"Non, madame," he replied, readying a snifter of brandy and a pint of beer for the waitress who waited at the end of the bar.

"Merci." Sera made a round of the club, lingering near the door to the toilets, hoping he'd stopped to fix his hair. After another ten minutes of waiting, and continuously scanning the club for him, she wasn't sure what to think.

"Madame? Are you…?" A young woman gestured towards the toilet door.

"Ah, non. Pardon." Sera moved away, heading back to their table.

She checked her phone again, but there was nothing. Calling him brought the same result. Taking her seat once more, pushing back the wine glasses so she could hold her phone in front of her on the table, she kept her eyes fixed on the screen, hoping for a call, or a text, or anything.

By the time Benoît and Daniel finished their set, her neck ached from the tension, from craning to see through the darkened room, from staring at her phone. Her knuckles were white where she clutched at the slick plastic and she felt the dampness of perspiration on her palms. Her stomach churned. It took all she had not to bolt from the club, or to cry.

It was so unlike him. He wouldn't have just left her. Unless…

Sera's thoughts abruptly went to Madelaine, though she knew it was illogical. It couldn't be. She bit her lip, then dialled his number once more.

Voice mail. Again.

"Do you want another glass of wine?" Benoît asked, stopping in front of her table. "And does Marc want anything?"

Daniel settled into the chair across from Sera. "I'll have my usual."

"Sera?" Benoît reached out and his fingers were warm on her arm. She flinched. "What's wrong?"

She didn't have words for it. Meeting his gaze, she tried to think of what to say. "I don't know—he's gone."

"To the toilet, right?" Daniel said. "He'll be back."

"No, not there," she managed to reply. "Gone."

Benoît sat next to her on the banquette. His nearness was reassuring, but he wasn't Marc. "He must have just stepped out."

Sera shook her head. "No, it's more than that. He's not even answering his phone." She held up her mobile.

Benoît frowned and glanced at Daniel. A look passed between them and if she didn't know better, she'd think they were having an unspoken conversation.

"The bar closes in an hour," Benoît said. "We'll have a drink, and if he's not here by then, we'll take you home."

"And then?" Sera heard her voice rising to a panicky pitch and she pressed her lips together.

"I don't know," Benoît admitted. "It doesn't seem like him, not at all. We could go to the police?"

If only it were that easy, but to involve the police might put Marc in more danger than he was already. She shuddered.

Daniel disappeared for a few minutes and came back with three brandy snifters. He set one down in front of Sera and passed Benoît the second.

"Are we calling the police?" he asked, settling back into his chair. Both he and Benoît looked at her.

"I can't. It isn't that I don't want to, but I can't." Benoît opened his mouth to speak, but she pressed on. "I can't tell you why. I'm sorry."

"Does it have anything to do with Royale?" Daniel asked, his voice low, hardly audible over the noise of the club. Sera sat back in her seat, the name feeling like a slap.

"Because," Daniel continued, "if that's the case, you can tell us. We've had our own run-ins with him, and lived to tell the tale."

"Barely." Benoît shook his head. "Don't speak too soon, Daniel. We got off easy. I'm sure of it, and that's only because we weren't worth pursuing. Somehow I don't think this is the same."

"It's a long story." Sera took a large sip of her brandy.

"We have an hour, at least," Daniel said. "Tell us."

Benoît nodded. "Tell us, Sera."

"I can't. I just—can't."

"Why are you doing this?" Marc asked as Françoise directed him towards a dark sedan that idled at the top of the narrow street. She nudged the gun sharply into his side.

"Get in."

Marc reached for the door handle, debating whether or not he could overpower her before she got a shot off.

"In. If you don't, I'll let you bleed out here, then send someone after your pretty little chanteuse."

Marc did as he was told, but gritted his teeth and swore to himself that he'd get his revenge. Françoise got in next to him, keeping the gun steady. His phone buzzed in his pocket and he wanted to reach for it, yet he hoped she hadn't heard.

"Give it to me." Françoise held out her free hand and he reluctantly extracted his phone and placed it in her palm. She glanced at the number before cutting the connection, turning the phone off and sliding it into the pocket of her blazer.

"Poor Sera," she taunted.

"Why are you bothering with me?" Marc asked. "In a couple of days, you'll get your painting."

"I have my reasons."

"Did Royale put you up to this?" The statement provoked a wry, amused chuckle from Françoise.

"You don't know much about me, do you? My husband's never been able to compel me to do anything I didn't want to do."

The car sped up and Marc glanced out the window, then over to the driver. He seemed familiar, but it wasn't until their eyes met in the rear-view mirror that he realized who it was.

Jean.

Jean changed lanes swiftly and Marc realized they had reached the Périphérique.

"Don't keep me in suspense," Marc replied. "Where are we going? And since when are you a driver, Jean?"

"The villa," Françoise said as Jean laughed. "The city's just too crowded. Too many ears. And Jean's often my driver. It gives him a break."

"Why don't you tell me what you want?" Marc tried to keep his tone relaxed, but the words came out sounding terse and angry.

"Soon," Françoise said. "Over drinks at the villa. We have all night, Monsieur Perron."

"I don't have that kind of time."

Françoise laughed. "I don't think you're in too much of a position to argue. Do you?"

Marc glanced down at the gun, then up at Jean, who met his gaze with a steady, amused silence in the rear-view mirror. He settled back into the seat. It would be a long night.

CHAPTER 23

By closing time, Sera could not sit still. She thought she'd go mad waiting for a call that never came, straining her eyes in the dim club, hoping for a glimpse of Marc, that somehow he'd return. But he didn't call, and he didn't come.

Benoît took her arm when they reached street level, gentle and solicitous. When they stepped out onto the Rue Renard, Sera pulled Marc's coat closer around herself, the scent of his cologne a poor substitute for the man himself. Just having his coat with her worried her; he'd never have left it behind.

"Back to our place?" Daniel asked, buttoning his coat.

"I want to go home," Sera said.

"We'll get a cab—it's a long way to Montmartre," Benoît said.

"Not the garret—Marc's apartment in the 17th." That was home now.

"Do you have keys?" Daniel asked, stepping off the curb to hail a taxi.

Sera sucked in a breath. Marc always took his keys; so she rarely needed the set he'd given her and she couldn't even remember if she'd put them in her purse. She opened it, rifling through its contents and coming up empty.

"No." Her shoulders slumped.

"You can stay with us," Benoît said. "It's all right."

Sera pulled Marc's coat more tightly around herself. "Merci." Her voice sounded lifeless, even to her own ears. She let go of Benoît's arm and buried her hands into the pockets of the leather jacket. Her fingers hit metal and she heard a jingle. When she pulled her hand out, Marc's keys glinted in the streetlight.

"Home it is," Benoît observed. He ushered her to the cab. On the way home, she sat in silence, listening with half an ear to the nostalgic chansons the cabbie played on the radio, and Daniel's conversation as he asked the man about his evening.

At the apartment, she let them in, flicking on the light in the entryway. The place was quiet as a tomb. Benoît strode ahead into the living room, the heels of his shoes loud on the parquet. Daniel made sure the door was locked and he and Sera followed Benoît.

The living room was empty.

Benoît emerged from the bedroom. "No one here," he said. Daniel gave him an incredulous look. "You never know," he added somewhat defensively. "It was possible."

Sera went to the window and stepped cautiously to the side, all too aware of her vulnerability. The street below was empty, the apartments across the way dark as they would be at this time of night.

She didn't know what to do, had absolutely no idea. Never in her life had she felt so helpless. She could hear Benoît and Daniel talking in low voices behind her; she couldn't make out the words but she was sure they were at as much of a loss as she was. Sera pulled the curtain over the window and turned back into the apartment.

Benoît and Daniel looked at her and she could see the pity and sympathy in their eyes. She cut her gaze away, her eyes pricking with tears. Benoît sighed. She heard his steps and she turned away so they wouldn't see her cry. His hand rested gently on her shoulder and he turned her, his embrace solid and unwavering. She rested her head against his shoulder and the sobs, once caught in her throat, burst free. She heard Benoît's heart beat against her ear and felt the rumble of his voice as he spoke to Daniel, but he didn't move.

Finally, her tears ceased and she pulled back, wiping her eyes and digging into her purse for a tissue. Benoît pulled out an old-fashioned handkerchief from his pocket and pressed it into her hand. He led her over to the sofa and without urging, she sank down onto the cool, dark leather.

Daniel came into the room bearing three cups of tea, and placed them on the coffee table in front of her, while Benoît settled into the armchair across from them. She picked up her cup, but her hand shook and she had to use both hands to keep from spilling.

They sat in silence, no one willing to be the first to speak. Sera's thoughts raced, but she couldn't make sense of Marc's disappearance. How could this have happened? Who could have done it? What on earth could she do? She didn't want to have Benoît and Daniel involved, even if they were willing. They didn't deserve that.

Benoît was the first to break the silence that stretched painfully between them. "Did Marc anger someone?" he asked, sounding hesitant. "Can you think of anyone who might want to do him harm?"

"Only Royale."

Daniel swore, rising to his feet to pace the living room. Benoît took a deep breath, rubbing his eyes.

"Mon Dieu."

"He won't bargain," Daniel said harshly, his hand clenched around his cup.

"You don't know that for sure." Benoît's brow furrowed, as if he was trying to think of a solution.

"I know," Daniel replied, "and you know it too."

"So do I," Sera said. The debt she had owed Royale had kept her under his power too long. He had not budged an inch, except for when he propositioned her. She put her hand to her mouth, her stomach churning. If that's what he asked for now, could she do it?

The car pulled past the open gate, and bumped lightly over the rutted road, travelling up a long gravel drive to where a small manor house sat, with its courtyard illuminated by wrought-iron street lamps. A circular fountain in white limestone dominated the centre of the courtyard, the water a still pool, with the fanciful cherubs patiently waiting for the morning. The car drew up in front of the house and Marc saw the double doors open; a shadowed figure waited just inside.

"Out," Françoise commanded, motioning with the gun. "And don't even think about running."

"Where would I go?"

When Marc heard the door locks disengage, he opened the door. The gravel crunched underfoot. Françoise came around the boot of the car and Jean circled around the front, boxing him in. He squared his shoulders.

"Inside." Françoise seemed to have resorted to one-word commands, her voice sharp, inflexible.

"You used to be so pleasant on the phone," he remarked as he moved towards the marble steps, matching his pace to hers. "I thought you might have been fond of me."

"Hardly," Françoise scoffed. "You're as arrogant and insufferable as my husband."

Marc entered the chateau, the butler at the door moved aside to allow them entry.

"You wound me," he said, pressing a hand to his heart as he turned in the impressive, high-ceilinged entryway. The lights were low, but the pale-painted walls soared up two levels, enhancing the stark presence of a double staircase, its railings dark and made of wrought iron, much like the lamps outside. At the top of the staircase, a large canvas faced the entryway, its dramatic splatters announced its provenance.

"I didn't think you'd be a fan of Pollock," Marc said. "You do know there are a lot of fakes, n'est pas?"

"It's real," Françoise sneered. "I can't be fooled, unlike my husband."

Marc's gaze flicked to the closed doors on either side of the entry. Parlours most likely, and not a means of escape.

"You don't much like your husband," he observed, "so why are you even married to him?"

"I have my reasons," she replied, a trace of irritation showing in her tone. Finally, he'd begun to crack that cool veneer. "Jean, put him in the guest room."

Jean's hand fell onto his shoulder and a gun—another one—jabbed into his back.

"You only had to ask," Marc chided.

Françoise gave a nod and her lips widened into a satisfied smile. He registered the movement out of the corner of his eye, but couldn't move fast enough. Stars burst into his vision and then the world went black.

Sera fell into a restless half-sleep after they had been unable to come up with a solution. Benoît wouldn't hear of her going to Royale, and Daniel had pressed her to rest.

"There's not much we can do now," he'd reasoned, "but in the morning, we'll think of something. Best to have clear heads."

"J'espere," she'd said. She'd made them take the bed and had curled up on the sofa with a pillow and a thick knitted quilt.

The sun woke her several hours later and she felt muzzy-headed and bleary-eyed. She rose slowly and made her way to the kitchen, still dressed in the previous night's rumpled clothes. Her phone lay charging on the counter, but there had been no calls. She dialled Marc's number again, but the call went straight to voice mail. Again.

Instead of giving in to her tears, Sera forced herself through the motions and made a cup of espresso. Usually Marc made coffee for them, and the small kitchen felt barren without him. She stared out the window into the courtyard, watching the gardienne putter about, her hair still in curlers under a cap.

She wished Pari were here. Surely as a police officer, she'd know what to do. But Pari was back in London, probably having spent the evening flirting with Julian if she hadn't been working. The thought of Sanctuary triggered a memory, of Mayson in his office.

"Tell your boyfriend he owes me."

Her espresso in one hand, Sera reached for her phone. The number at the club rang, and kept ringing. Her heart sank. As she went to end the call, the line clicked and a gruff male voice answered.

"Sanctuary."

"Could I speak to Mayson, please?" The words came out weak and shaky.

"Who wants him?"

"This is Sera Durand."

"Sera, who?"

"The new singer he's hired," Sera said, feeling exhaustion creeping in after such a poor sleep.

"Hold on." The line clicked again and a slightly tinny and old jazz classic played in her ear. She finished her espresso as the music played for a time, and began to pace the small room. Surely, she'd been forgotten.

The music clicked off and she started and almost dropped her phone. "Miss Durand?"

"I'm sorry to call you so early," Sera began.

"Save it," Mayson said abruptly. "Why are you calling, Miss Durand?"

"You had an arrangement with Marc," she said. "I want to take you up on that arrangement."

"You?" She heard his incredulous laugh. "Let me speak to your boyfriend."

"If he could, I wouldn't be calling," Sera replied, her voice catching in her throat.

"Say that again?"

Sera repeated herself. "I know you had some sort of arrangement, but I…" She swallowed, knowing she was putting herself at risk. "I need your help. Marc's been taken by Royale."

There was silence on the line for a long moment, and Sera wondered if he'd hung up on her and left her on her own.

"Things are already in motion," Mayson said finally, "but I can have my man there tonight. It will cost you."

"How much?" She could barely say the words; her chest was tight with dread.

"A favour," Mayson said. "I haven't decided what yet, but when I ask, I'll expect an immediate response. And this is in addition to what your boyfriend owes me, mind you."

"I won't sleep with you."

Mayson laughed in her ear; the sound went on for half a minute before petering out. "Sorry love, but you're really—really—not my type."

Sera flushed, glad he couldn't see her embarrassment.

"It might be money, or it might be something else," Mayson said, "but whatever it is, you or your boyfriend will do it. Are we agreed?"

Sera swallowed. She had little other choice; the police wouldn't help without putting Marc in more danger, and she couldn't do it on her own. "Agreed."

"David can be on the four o'clock train to Gare du Nord, which I suppose would put him in around seven. You'll need to pick him up and tell him the details, however, he'll come prepared."

"I don't know where they've taken him," Sera admitted. "There have been no calls, no ransom demands, nothing."

"Really?" Mayson sounded surprised. "That doesn't bode well at all, not in my experience. Does David have your number?"

"No, I don't think—" She stopped. "David Santiano, you mean?"

"What other David could there be?" Mayson chuckled. "He's not just a pretty face, you know."

Sera didn't know what to say to that.

"He'll fill you in when he gets there," Mayson said. "Seven at Gare du Nord. Don't forget." It sounded like he'd stifled a yawn. "Don't call me again—I'll talk to David when he gets back. If he doesn't return safe and sound, then you and your boyfriend will owe me a lot more than just a favour."

With that, he hung up on her. Sera set the phone down before she dropped it, her hand trembling. Twelve hours to wait. She needed to talk to Françoise, needed to know if Marc was still alive. She stared at her phone, willing it to ring.

Marc woke with a splitting headache and a mouth that felt like it was filled with cotton wool. He cracked open his eyes, squinting into the darkened room. He tried to cough, but soon realized that something filled his mouth—and a gag, or perhaps a handkerchief, had been tied snugly over his mouth. He tried to move his hands, to bring them to his face to drag the gag away, but he couldn't move. He managed to flop onto his back, though his arms were pinned beneath him, only to stare upward into the canopy of an old four-poster bed. The mattress protested against his body weight while his torso settled into the springs.

He was able to bend his knees, though his ankles were bound, and after a series of attempts, he slipped his bound wrists under his buttocks and brought them in front of him. He tore at the gag, but it was too tightly bound and wouldn't move.

Lifting his bound wrists over his head, he fumbled ineffectively with the knot, wincing every time his arm bumped the goose egg that had risen where he'd been struck. The knot was small, bound so tightly that he had to pick at it with his nails, feeling it repel every attempt. His forehead prickled with sweat and he closed his eyes, trying to focus. He felt the shape of the knot, the bumps that might indicate where one part looped over the other. An irrational panic rose inside him, but he forced it down, slowing his breathing, counting each inhalation and exhalation until the panic subsided. He brought his hands back to rest on his chest, eyeing the plastic zip ties that held them fast. He wouldn't be able to get out of these—he didn't carry a blade.

He lifted his hands again and fiddled with the knot. A wrinkle in the fabric seemed to give a little and he seized upon it like a dog with a bone, worrying it intently.

Footsteps echoed in the hallway and he froze. They came closer and he tore at the knot, desperate to get it undone, not that it would help him much with bound hands and feet.

The footsteps paused and there was a quiet click. Light spilled across the floor and into the room from the hallway before a slim figure was silhouetted in the doorway. Marc squinted at the brightness.

Françoise laughed, a short burst of sound that was both amused and disdainful. "Did you sleep well, Monsieur Perron?" She came further into the room, moving to stand at the foot of the bed, her hand grasping the bedpost. He stopped struggling with the gag, slowly lowering his hands.

"Ah, well, I'll assume you did," Françoise continued in the same tone. "I've always liked this four-poster. Rather classic, don't you think? I have so many memories." She leaned against the post. "I would have had more, if not for you."

Marc stared at her, puzzled. He'd never met her, never interfered with her life, nothing at all.

Françoise's amusement faded as swiftly as it had come. "Of course, you wouldn't know. But you'll regret it all the same." She came around the side of the bed, climbing onto the mattress, resting her hand on his ankle. Her touch was warm, but then she shifted and a pain shot up his leg. He gasped in surprise, but the gag muffled his voice. He grimaced as her fingers dug into his flesh. The pain felt worse than when he'd broken his arm as a boy.

She let go.

Marc breathed as deep as he could through his nose and turned his head, using his arm to wipe the perspiration from his brow.

"Such a little thing," she said, stroking his leg, "but not for long. Soon you'll wish that would be all I'd do."

Marc growled with frustration. He lifted his arms and began to work once more on the gag, choosing to risk her wrath.

"Jean!" Françoise called. The maitre d' came to the door. "Hold him down." She rose from the bed as Jean strode in, smirking as he seized Marc's arms, pinning him to the mattress. Marc struggled, but he had no leverage, not being bound as he was.

Françoise came around Jean's form and pushed Marc's face away from her. He heard a snick, and the gag loosened. He pushed at the cloth in his mouth, choking a bit as he managed to spit it out.

"I can be nice, can't I?" she crooned, stroking Marc's forehead. He jerked away from her touch, as much as he could with Jean holding him down. "But if you don't behave, Jean will correct you."

Jean let go of Marc's arms and laid a heavy punch into his solar plexus. Marc gagged and gasped, his eyes watering, the breath stolen from him.

"You may go, Jean," Françoise said calmly, "But stay close. I may need you again."

"It would be my pleasure," Jean said, shooting an amused glance at Marc. "Just to see him in agony once more." He retraced his steps to the door, and left.

Françoise settled at the end of the bed, leaning against the post, one leg crossed over the other, her dark tailored skirt wrinkling slightly where it rode up on her knee.

"That really wasn't necessary." Marc's voice was barely more than a croak after so many hours gagged.

"Oh, but it was," Françoise replied. "You've denied me one of my favourite indulgences, and Jean was itching to punish you, anyway."

For the life of him, he couldn't think of what she meant. What indulgences?

"You must be mistaken."

"You are the one who is mistaken, Monsieur Perron," she said sharply, cutting him off. "Several months ago, I enjoyed my last evening with my lover, here in this bed."

"And what does your husband think of that?" Marc found his voice returning, though it was still hoarse.

"That's a rather old-fashioned viewpoint, especially coming from a man like you," she replied. "Arnaud has no say in what I do. It was he who begged to marry me, after all. He wanted money. I wanted connections. She smiled tightly at him, her eyes narrowing. "I'll fuck whomever I please."

"I still don't understand how any of this involves me." Marc shifted on the bed, wincing as the zip ties cut into his ankles.

"Jeremy Gordon was my lover. And you killed him."

CHAPTER 24

"You're not doing this on your own," Benoît insisted.

"You and Daniel can't be involved," Sera retorted. "I wouldn't do that to anyone."

"I wish Colette were here—she'd talk some sense into you," Benoît muttered.

Sera was glad Colette wasn't here to give her opinion—she already disliked Marc. "It doesn't matter—I won't let you risk yourselves."

Daniel shifted on the armchair, where he'd listened in silence to their argument. "Sera's right," he said. "I want to help, but I'm already known to the police, thanks to Marseille. Any other trouble for me would be very bad. Sorry, Sera."

She gave him a grateful smile. "Benoît, if I need to be bailed out of jail later, I'll need someone to call."

"Very funny." Benoît frowned, his insistence subsiding.

"But how will this English guy help you, exactly?" Daniel leaned forward, resting his elbows on his knees. A lock of blond hair fell over his forehead and he pushed it back.

"Marc had things arranged," Sera said, though she knew how uncertain that sounded. She'd find out all too soon what those arrangements were. Her stomach roiled with nerves and she rose from the sofa to pace to the window. She could hear Benoît and Daniel muttering to each other, but she tuned them out, taking her phone from her pocket. Although she knew it was hopeless, she tried Marc's number again. Hearing his voice recite the usual message made her vision blur with tears. She hung up before the recording ended, blinking hard.

"All right, Sera, we'll leave you to it." Benoît sounded reluctant as he came up beside her. "But if you need anything, call me. I don't care what time it is, or where you are." He laid an arm over her shoulders and she turned in his embrace. He held her tight for a long moment.

"I will, I promise."

Benoît let her go and stepped back. "Take care."

Sera walked them to the door, and accepted a hug from Daniel and Benoît before they walked down the stairs. She retreated into the empty apartment and shut the door. If only she had a phone number for Françoise, or knew where Marc had been taken. She stared at her phone. She could call Le Chat Rouge, but she hesitated.

Instead, she called Edouard. He and Sophie were still dating, and as far as she knew, he continued to work at Le Chat Rouge as a bartender.

Hopeful, she dialled the number.

"Sera! I'll have to tell Sophie that you're on the phone—she'd love to talk to you."

"Not yet, Edouard. I need to ask you something first."

"Ask away," Edouard replied amiably.

"Do you know where Royale lives?"

Edouard was silent. Whether he was shocked or just pondered her question, she couldn't tell.

"I've never asked," he said. "And I don't think I'd ever want to know."

Sera was stymied, her last idea a failure. "Merci, Edouard."

"Why do you need it?"

"I can't explain. I have to go. Tell Sophie hello for me, and that I'll call her in a few days."

"Sera, are you all right?" Edouard pressed.

"I'm fine. Don't worry, Edouard."

Once she hung up, she paced back into the living room. Glancing at her watch, she gathered her jacket and purse from where she'd left them, draped over one of the straight-backed dining chairs. Time to meet David at the Eurostar terminal. She passed the bookshelves on her way out, and her gaze darted to the stack of books, which hid the metal box with Marc's gun, assuming it was still there. She stopped, removed the books carefully and pulled the box from its hiding spot.

The gun was there, and heavy in her hand when she lifted it. She placed it in her purse, tucking it at the very bottom, along with a small box of ammunition that she found with it. She didn't want to confront Royale without protection.

"Dieu." Marc breathed the word. Why did everything come back to haunt him? Jeremy Gordon was dead and buried—at least what was left of him after the fire in the rundown slum apartments—but it seemed as if the bastard would have his revenge from beyond the grave.

"He burned to death, and you did it!" Françoise's eyes flashed with fury. "I should kill you now, instead of waiting."

Marc wanted to say that Jeremy hadn't burned to death. Sera had shot him because he had abused her. How could you sleep with such a man? But he didn't dare speak. A woman like Françoise could not be reasoned with, and he would protect Sera unto death, if he must. It seemed strange that Royale hadn't even hinted to his wife about Sera's involvement.

Françoise rose from her spot on the bed. The fury in her seemed to have subsided, at least briefly. She drew his phone from her pocket and held it up.

"Before you die, I want that painting you promised me, monsieur."

"After all of this, you want a painting?" She was insane.

"You promised me a Monet," she retorted. "Make the final arrangements, or I'll have Jean come back in to assist you."

"I'll need to know where the painting should be brought," Marc said. He held out his bound hands for the phone. "There are still many details to be sorted."

Françoise's gaze narrowed. "Your thief can bring it to Le Chat Rouge."

"No." Marc's tone was firm. "I don't want to take that chance. The sooner it's out of Paris, the better. Monets are too well known, and a theft would raise alarm. Everyone in Paris would know that one was missing."

"I won't have him come here," Françoise retorted. "How stupid do you think I am?"

"Your husband expected the delivery to come here, and you did too, up until recently."

"Things have changed," Françoise replied. "I didn't trust you much before, and I don't trust you at all now. After that stunt with the fake…" She gave him a scathing look.

"I had a chance, so I took it." Marc didn't bother pleading his case; it would be a waste of time.

"Just so. It can be brought to Chartres. It's close enough to here without giving everything away." She held out his phone. "Don't try anything stupid."

Marc awkwardly took the phone, his bound wrists limiting his movement. "Could you?" He indicated the zip ties.

"No." Françoise did not waver. Marc sighed and turned his phone on. It beeped with messages and a list of missed calls. He skimmed through the list. All Sera. If only Françoise would leave him alone for a few moments.

Instead, he called Aurore. He hoped Sera would try calling her too.

"Put it on speakerphone," Françoise insisted, and Marc obliged reluctantly.

"Perron et fils," Aurore's cheery voice chirped.

"Aurore, it's Marc. I need you to do me a favour."

"Of course, monsieur. Will you be in the office later? Fournier's asking for work, even though he's still in the hospital."

"Tell Fournier he needs to rest, but if he won't listen to you, you could give him the files for the Thompson purchase."

"I doubt he'll listen to me," Aurore replied, sounding amused.

"In the meantime, I need you to call a client for me," Marc continued, seeing that Françoise was becoming impatient. "He was to deliver a painting, but the location has changed." Marc skimmed through his contacts for the number Mayson had given him. He read it off, and then gave Aurore the location.

"Got it."

"Merci beaucoup," Marc replied, while scouring his mind for a way to get a message to Aurore about Sera without Françoise realizing. "And give my best to Sophie. I know she and Sera were supposed to meet up."

Françoise snatched the phone from him, levelling the gun at his head. "Say goodbye," she mouthed.

"À bientôt," Marc said, and Françoise stabbed the button to cut off the call.

"That was incredibly stupid of you, Monsieur Perron," she said, her dark eyes glinting with fury. Marc shrugged, casual in his defiance.

"I've never been short in my conversations with Aurore," he said. "I thought you wanted me to have a normal conversation in order to not arouse suspicion."

Françoise didn't reply. Her gaze narrowed and she lowered the gun. The retort from the gun echoed in the room and rang in his ears, and for a moment, Marc thought she'd just meant to frighten him into submission.

An agonizing pain, fiery and hot, overtook him, spiking upwards through his right leg. His jeans darkened over his calf, the blood soaking through the heavy fabric. Awkwardly, he pressed his hands down on the wound, gritting his teeth as the pain spiked again.

"Best keep pressure on that," Françoise said coolly. "You won't die from it, at least not yet." Marc heard her amused laughter as she strode from the room. He glanced up, but she'd taken his phone with him. He could only hope that his communication, however vague, would get through to Sera.

Marc lifted his hands from the wound, tugging up his pant leg to see the damage. He wanted to groan, but he wouldn't give Françoise that satisfaction. His leg was streaked with blood, but it had slowed somewhat, though not enough for him to let up the pressure. Bunching up a section of the coverlet on the bed, he pressed it into the bullet hole, wincing. Even if he'd been able to run, hobbled as he was, he wouldn't be able to walk now.

Sera stopped at Saint-Germain-des-Prés, even though she knew she had to be at Gare du Nord shortly. Her favourite church looked the same as always, and as she walked inside, heading to the chapel of the Virgin behind the main altar, she felt a tremor of hope. Soon David would be here, and they would find Marc. After placing five euros in the donation box, she lit a large candle, and then drew out her rosary, moving forward to the pews, finding a spot to sit. She knelt and began the Ave, her fingers tightening around the beads.

She'd recited two decades of the rosary when her phone vibrated. Fumbling in her bag, she drew it out, answering it with a hushed whisper. "Hello?"

"Sera, were we going to have coffee?" Sophie asked, sounding puzzled.

"Coffee?" Sera echoed in confusion.

"I told Aurore that she must be mistaken," Sophie said. "It doesn't make any sense."

"When—when did you talk to her?"

"Just now," Sophie said. "She called to talk about work and mentioned that Marc had asked her to pass on his best and that we would be having coffee soon."

"She talked to Marc?" Sera felt as if the breath had been knocked from her.

"She must have," Sophie said. "Sera, are you okay?"

"Do you know when she talked to him?"

"No idea. I thought you were in London."

"I'm in Paris for a few days," Sera replied. "I need to call Aurore, but we should get together for coffee soon anyway."

"We should," Sophie replied. "It's been too long. À bientôt."

Sera rose from the pew, enduring the glares from the other worshippers. She clutched her phone, the beads clicking against the plastic, and made her way to the square outside, where she dropped to the stone step and called Aurore.

"He called earlier today," Aurore said in response to Sera's urgent questioning. She sounded puzzled. "He asked me to call a client for him and reschedule a delivery. I was just about to do it."

"Which client?"

There was silence on the line and Sera wondered if Aurore would plead confidentiality.

"A man named Mayson—he's not in my files and I'm not sure if Marc was giving me the right information."

"I know Mayson," Sera said, injecting some authority into her voice. "We met him in London."

"Oh, I see. Marc must have forgotten to add him to our database," Aurore mused.

"Where is the delivery to be?" Sera asked. "I know the delivery man is to be in Paris tonight. Marc asked me to meet him."

"I wonder why Marc didn't call you then?"

"He's used to calling you for work," Sera remarked.

"That he is," Aurore agreed. "The delivery is supposed to be to a pub in Chartres."

"Chartres?" Sera was surprised how close it was to Paris. "I'll make sure he knows."

"Marc didn't specify a time, but I'm sure he'll arrange that."

"We'll figure it out," Sera replied. "Sometimes these things get harried."

"They do. Merci, Sera."

Sera gripped her phone, staring at it for a long moment. Now she knew where Marc was, or at least closer to it. If he'd been taken to Royale's villa, then it wouldn't be in the centre of the town. Sera rose from the step and hurried to the metro station at Saint-Germain-des-Prés. The train would take her straight to Gare du Nord. She hoped David had a plan, because she didn't know how she'd get to Marc on her own.

CHAPTER 25

Some time after Françoise left, Jean came in. He eyed Marc's leg with grim amusement, pushing his hands aside to inspect the wound. He rolled up Marc's pant leg.

"She just winged you," he remarked, sounding disappointed. "You're lucky." From his jacket pocket, he withdrew a bottle and a handful of gauze. "This will hurt like a bitch, but for some reason she doesn't want you to die of an infection. Or not just yet, anyway."

With no further warning, he undid the cap and splashed liquid over the wound. Marc fell back, pressing his lips together. He wouldn't make a sound, wouldn't give Jean the satisfaction, even though his leg bubbled and burned and it hurt worse than the bullet itself. Jean swabbed at the skin around the wound, tossing the dirty gauze aside. He splashed the wound again and this time used fresh gauze to press down on the bloody furrow.

"Hold that," he directed, and Marc obeyed, putting a hand over the pinkening gauze. Jean set the bottle aside and took a roll of tape from his pocket, tearing off strips that he used to hold the gauze in place.

"You're awfully prepared," Marc said as the pain lessened.

"Arnaud expects me to take care of her indiscretions," Jean said, sounding surprisingly pragmatic. He shrugged.

"Is that all you take care of?"

Jean snorted. "As if I'd tell you. Now, get up. Madame wants to see you in the parlour." He grasped Marc's upper arms and hauled him to his feet, surprisingly strong for a lean man.

Marc swayed as he stood, his vision darkening, narrowing. Though Jean's grasp was disobliging, he kept hold of Marc until the dizzy spell cleared. Marc stepped forward, forgetting the plastic that bound his ankles and stumbled. Jean caught him, muttering a curse. He pulled out a switchblade, bent downward, and cut away the zip ties at his feet.

"Don't try anything," Jean warned as he straightened. "You won't get far if you try to run."

Marc had expected as much. As they started down to the parlour, he asked, "How long was Françoise with Jeremy Gordon?"

Jean snorted again. "That crazy bastard. That he'd see anything in her, that she'd see anything in him…" He shook his head, but said no more.

They reached the bottom of the stair and Jean indicated a door. "In here." He knocked and Marc heard Françoise's command.

"Entrez."

Jean opened the door and pushed Marc ahead of him. Marc stumbled and winced, but managed to catch himself before he sprawled onto the expensive Persian rug. Françoise sat on a beautifully restored sofa, primly sipping a cup of tea. A tray sat on the table in front of her, and he could see his phone.

"It's been ringing quite a bit," she remarked, noticing his interest. "I didn't bother answering. Sit down. Would you like a cup of tea?" She indicated the sofa across from her and Marc sat, wary at her change in mood. His stomach growled and he wished for far more than a cup of tea.

"Please," he said, and she poured him a cup, adding milk and sugar as if she were a hostess at a garden party. She pushed the cup towards him and he picked it up gingerly, his bound hands making the simple gesture awkward and uncouth. The tea scalded his tongue.

"I think we've given your assistant enough time, don't you?" Françoise remarked. "I had thought to call her, but then, why would I give myself away? Arnaud will be here soon anyway, so perhaps I'll make him talk to her the next time. He likes young women like her."

"Make him?" Marc echoed. Françoise gave him a scornful look.

"Without me, he wouldn't be where he is. He takes direction very well, most of the time. You could learn from him."

Marc drank more of his tea, trying to imagine Royale being controlled by this woman, his wife. He'd never seemed like the sort to let anyone take control.

"What do you give him for his obedience?" he asked, knowing the question was cheeky but determined to find out more, hoping to discern the dynamic between them and use the knowledge to his advantage. He had little else to rely on.

Françoise smirked. "Whatever his pathetic little heart desires. Isn't that right, Jean?" Marc glanced up at Jean, who wore a matching smirk, and nodded his assent. "In fact, I think I know just the treat for him." She lifted Marc's phone from the table and held it out. Marc put down his tea cup.

"What do you want me to do?" He took the phone from her, seeing the missed calls, wishing he could talk to Sera.

"Set up a meeting for tomorrow," Françoise said. "And tell your deliveryman that he's going to be bringing two pieces for delivery."

"Two?" Marc stared at her.

"A present for me, and a present for Arnaud. He'll love it when I give him la petite Durand."

Marc placed the phone on the edge of the table. "No."

"Pardonnez-moi?" Françoise arched a brow.

"I would never do that." Marc rose from his seat. Françoise didn't move. She was eerily calm.

"As you wish." She shrugged. "Jean, take care of him for me, will you? It seems that I have a phone call to make." She took up Marc's phone, dialling a number.

"Bonjour, mademoiselle," she said sweetly, sounding little like herself. "I'm calling about the delivery you spoke about with Monsieur Perron earlier. Oh, he asked me to call, he's been so busy here…" At that, Marc lunged for her, but Jean was quicker, seizing him around the throat, his strong arm stifling Marc's breath as he hauled him back. Blood roared in Marc's ears as he struggled. Although he could see Françoise's lips moving, curling into an amused smile as she spoke to Aurore, he couldn't hear a word she said.

Marc's legs gave out and Jean followed him down, his grip snug, but not deadly—not yet. He managed a gasping breath as Jean loosened his hold a fraction, and felt a surge of hope, a surge that was stifled once more. Clawing at Jean's arm, he kicked out with his feet but hit nothing but carpet. The fine weave muffled the thumps of his heels on the hardwood floor.

His vision shimmered and narrowed, and he saw Françoise laugh.

Sera slowly paced the length of Gare du Nord, glancing at the arrivals boards every time she passed one by. She paused inside the Tabac shop and flipped idly through a fashion magazine, glancing up often to scan the concourse.

A calm female voice came over the public address system to announce the arrival of the Eurostar from London. She set the magazine back on the rack, and cut across the centre of the concourse to wait near the platform. She didn't wait long.

David strode down the platform towards her, looking professional and anonymous in a dark suit and muted grey tie, a rolling suitcase in one hand and a boxed parcel in the other. Sera greeted him and fell into step beside him. He gave her a nod as they walked purposefully through the station, then outside to the taxi rank. A beggar woman, her kerchief grime-stained, shuffled down the line, begging for money. At David's cold glance, she drew back her hand and shuffled past.

They didn't speak until they were inside the taxi, heading down the boulevard du Clichy, rushing past the sex shops with their garish storefronts.

"A friend of mine will lend me his car," David said, as if he were in Paris on holiday. The corner of his mouth quirked upward.

"That's generous," Sera replied in the same casual tone. The cab driver tapped his hands on the steering wheel, singing along to the song on the radio.

"Quite, but very useful, since I won't be here too long." David's gaze fell on her directly and his expression seemed to soften. "It's not quite the same without you, you know. You're coming back, right?" He spoke in English.

"I don't know," she said in the same language. "I would like to, but…"

"Understandable." He gave her another nod. The driver sped down the street, pausing only a moment before plunging into the traffic circle at the Étoile and careening out onto Avenue Wagram.

Sera paid the driver and she and David entered the apartment building. She motioned for the ancient elevator, but David shook his head. "We will take the stairs."

She let David precede her into Marc's flat. It felt strange to have another man in the flat that wasn't Marc. She shook her head at her irrational feelings. Benoît and Daniel had been inside, but David was different. His intentions were different.

"I don't know where the villa is," Sera began, "but Aurore called to tell me the delivery location for the Monet, which Marc has supposedly arranged."

"And?"

"In Chartres, not far from Paris, at a pub on the main square. I've been there only once before."

"I haven't, but I'll look it up on my phone." David set down his luggage, resting the parcel carefully against the wall.

"We're to be there tomorrow at midday."

David frowned. "That doesn't give us much time to prepare." He rubbed his jaw. "I'll get in touch with my friend, and while we wait for him, I could use a coffee. You need to tell me everything you know. I quizzed Mayson, but though he knows Royale, he doesn't know everything."

"I don't know how much more I can tell you," Sera replied, entering the small kitchen. "But I'll try if it will help. Marc and

Royale have a long history, a bad one, and I have my own history with the man as well. He's never forgotten me, and I'm not talking about my singing." She shuddered, remembering Royale's fleshy, damp fingers pawing at her. And at his request, directed through Aurore, that she would have to see him again.

"Tell me."

Sera turned the empty espresso cup in its saucer and leaned back against the sofa, the leather creaking.

"I still don't understand how it's come to this," she admitted, "but Royale won't let things go. He's obsessed with having a Monet, and doesn't seem to think of anything else."

David shrugged. "That's why he does so well," he said. "Like Mayson does. Every favour owed, every euro in the pot…"

"Mayson doesn't seem anything like Royale," Sera blurted out. David gave her a glance both exasperated and pitying.

"They're more alike than you think, but Mayson's always been able to put a good face on things. And he likes you, believe it or not."

"He does?"

"You'll still owe him," David said bluntly, "but he wouldn't have sent me if he didn't have some fondness for you. He has lots of hired hands for this sort of thing."

"What have I done?" Sera almost didn't want to know.

David cracked a grin. "You sing like an angel, and you've increased the club's take. I'd be jealous, if I wasn't so certain of him."

"Have you been with him long?" Sera wasn't exactly sure what David and Mayson were to each other, and she didn't know how to ask without seeming to pry.

"Three years," David said. "He's lovely in private." He smiled a small, secret smile. "We met on a job I did for him, introduced by a colleague."

David's phone rang, interrupting the question Sera had been about to ask. David rose from the sofa, the phone at his ear, pacing to the window as he talked. How did a pianist become a hit man? And how had he met someone like Mayson? David was lean, lithe and almost delicate in comparison to what she imagined a hit man would be: either a man like Jeremy Gordon, tall and commanding, or a burly intimidating sort like some of Mayson's other men.

"Taken care of." David turned back to her, interrupting her train of thought. "We'll have to meet him; he won't bring the car into the city."

"Where?"

"We'll take the RER out to Nanterre-ville."

"It's not far." Sera rose from the sofa and took up her jacket where it lay draped over one of Marc's straight-backed dining chairs. The light wool of her jacket was comfortingly warm and she tied the belt around her waist and picked up her purse.

"Prête?" David asked.

"Oui."

The walk to the Étoile was quick and Sera paid for their tickets in cash from the machine while David waited nearby. They took the stairs down to the platform and stood there waiting. The air in the tunnel was warm but not oppressive, smelling of the Metro grime—a combination of perfume, machine oil and a staleness hard to identify. She could hear the faint strains of a busker in a hallway on the other side of the tracks, his saxophone echoing in the tunnel. He played a rendition of *'Hymne d'amour'* and Sera took a deep, aching breath to stifle her sadness. If only everything that had happened in the last year could be undone.

The rumble of the approaching train drowned out the saxophone. David hooked his arm around her shoulders as the train glided up to the platform. "Come on."

They boarded and he found them seats together, opposite an older couple who ignored them completely as they bickered over the evening's chores. David leaned close to her.

"You and Marc in forty years?" he teased. "I can see it now."

"I wish." The words caught in her throat. Would they be like that in forty years? Would they even make it that far? She swallowed, her gaze lowering to her clasped hands.

"Je suis désolé," David murmured, resting his larger hand over hers. He was warm and she realized then how cold she was. She pulled her jacket close with a shiver.

David let his hand rest on her leg. "Almost there," he said. She nodded, and they sat silently until the train pulled into the station. Sera hadn't been to Nanterre before and she felt lost as they left the station. She took David's arm and he led them across the street, passing a bank, and a Monoprix with its glowing, rosy-coloured sign. Several turns later, they came upon a nondescript dark blue car, a Peugeot sedan.

All its lights were off and Sera started when the driver's side door opened. A man stepped out and she could just see his face in the dim light from a nearby street lamp. He was swarthy, but young, of average height, and he took a cap from the car and put it on.

"Bonsoir." He held out his hand and David shook it. Sera heard the click of keys.

"All there?" David asked. The man nodded.

"Oui, c'est tout la." Without another word, he loped off down the darkened street.

"May—err—your boss really has connections," Sera remarked, changing her words as a woman passed near, laden with shopping bags from the Monoprix.

"That he does," David said. "Shall we?" He walked around to the passenger door and opened it for her. Then he walked around to the back of the vehicle, quickly opening the trunk to inspect it before returning to slide into the driver's seat.

"Back to the apartment?" Sera asked, buckling her seat belt.

"Yes. I'll have a few things to get ready," David replied. "Then sleep. Tomorrow will be a busy day."

CHAPTER 26

Marc woke slowly, his head aching, his body stiff and sore. He shifted and felt the warmth of a coverlet spread over him. The dim glow of a lamp illuminated the room enough so he could see that he was back where he'd started. His hands were still bound, and when he moved his feet, he found that they had been tied again, but he had more range and couldn't feel the bite of the plastic zip ties.

He threw back the coverlet to rise, but a hand slid over his side; a cold, feminine hand scraped its nails across his stomach where his shirt had untucked and risen up.

"Where do you think you're going, mon coeur?" a voice purred. Marc jerked away from the touch, from the voice.

Françoise laughed, stretching out on the bed while he stumbled to his feet, bracing himself against the bedpost. She slid from the bed in a sinuous motion, the delicate lace of her negligee draping her hips. She was a handsome woman, curved in all the right places, fit and toned, and the light made it nearly impossible to guess her true age. Her dark hair was fixed up in an elegant but slightly mussed chignon, which made him wonder how long she'd been in bed with him. She reminded him of Catherine Deneuve in the film Belle de Jour.

"Come here," she said, taking advantage of his gaping to move closer. He glanced at her hands, scanned her body. "I'm unarmed." She spread her arms, the lace pulling snug against her breasts, the shadows of her nipples becoming visible.

A man cleared his throat and Marc turned. Jean stood near the door, a Glock in his hand, held loosely down by his thigh.

"But he isn't," Françoise continued. She grasped Marc's lapels, pulling him against her, beginning to undo the buttons of his shirt. He pushed away from her, but didn't get far. The click of Jean's shoes on the parquet caught his attention, and in his peripheral vision, he saw the gun rise.

Marc stopped. Françoise laughed again, a husky, satisfied sound. "I haven't had much fun since Jeremy died," she said, continuing to unbutton his shirt, spreading it open and running her hands down his chest before she pushed the shirt down his shoulders. "It seems only right that you should be the one to have to please me now."

Her hand snaked downwards, and she grasped his cock through his trousers, her grip hard, demanding. Despite his inner vow to stay unmoving and unfeeling, Marc, winced, his eyes tightening shut for a brief moment. Françoise twisted her hand.

"It's not worth it for you," he rasped out, but his words had little effect.

"Isn't it? It's only fair—your petite amie with Jeremy, and me with you." Her grip on him loosened and she stroked him instead, purring with delight when he twitched under her hand despite himself.

Françoise undid his belt and unbuttoned his jeans. She paused with her fingers at his zipper, drawing out the moment.

"Embrasse-moi," she commanded, tilting her face upwards, parting her lips expectantly. Marc looked down at her, trying to control the anger that surged in him, still vitally aware of Jean's hovering, dangerous presence.

"Jamais." He met her gaze, steeling himself into silent rebellion.

Her foot moved faster than he could follow, striking his leg, unerring in its target, the bullet wound through his calf. The pain knifed through him and he stumbled. Françoise took him down as easily as a lion might a wounded gazelle. Without his hands to break his fall, he hit the parquet hard.

Before he could scramble to his feet, a blow from her foot kicked him in the ribs, knocking the breath from him. He gasped like a fish out of water, but she didn't let up. Marc curled into a ball as the blows rained down on him, doing his best to protect himself.

After what seemed like hours, he heard a commotion somewhere outside the room, and Françoise's angry voice, her steps on the parquet, growing fainter. The blows had ceased and Marc shifted cautiously. When no further blows were forthcoming, he uncurled his legs, biting back the groan at the pain the movement caused. There were more footsteps now and he flinched as a large shadow loomed over him.

"You're lucky," Jean observed. "Without that interruption, she'd have killed you." He smiled.

Marc stared up at him and Jean gave a negligent shrug. "Her husband has arrived, our glorious master." He smirked at that and turned as the door opened. Marc heard a familiar hacking cough that ended in an amused chortle.

"I never thought I'd see the day," Royale rasped, patting his mouth with a handkerchief. He wore a puce-green suit, the jacket undone over his protruding belly, the white shirt wrinkled. Françoise stood near him, but carefully separate, her expression cool as the dark robe over her negligee. Marc thought he could detect a distaste for her husband in the way she held herself stiff and still.

"You never could have done it," she said, her tone icy. "He'd have fooled you with that fake and you'd have thought yourself victorious."

Royale seemed to shrink under her scorn, something Marc would never have considered possible. Royale recovered quickly with bluster, strolling over to where Marc lay.

"Nevertheless," he said to Françoise, "this view is satisfying." He aimed a kick at Marc's midsection, but unlike his spry wife, Royale's movements were slower and Marc rolled out of the way. Royale cursed.

"Venez," Françoise commanded. "Leave him. We have things to discuss."

Royale strode back to the door where Françoise waited. Jean trailed him and Françoise moved aside to let them precede her. Jean hit the lights as they left and when the door closed, Marc was left in blackness.

Sera slept poorly and woke early. She lay in bed, listening to the sound of David's light snoring coming from the living room. He'd insisted on sleeping on the sofa, having waved off her suggestion that he take the bed.

If only Marc were here. Sera rolled over, reaching for her phone where it lay on the bedside table. No calls, no messages, nothing. Never before had she wished so fervently to speak to him, not since Royale had demanded payment of the loan she'd owed him, when he'd demanded the use of her body if she didn't have the money. She shuddered. She didn't regret Royale's upcoming demise, but without Marc, nothing mattered.

An insistent, shrill beeping came from the living room and she heard a muttered curse as the sound was cut off. She sat up in bed, pushing the covers aside. David came to the door, his dark blond hair askew, bare-chested, his jeans rumpled.

"I had a message from Mayson," he said. "He tracked down Royale's villa—he called in another favour. We'll go there instead of the meeting place. I want to catch them by surprise."

"What about Marc?" He was all she could think of.

"Royale wouldn't bring a hostage into town with them," David answered, calm and matter-of-fact. "He'll be at the villa."

Sera rose from the bed, taking up her robe and slipping it on. "Will we be able to free him? What if we can't?"

"We'll do the best we can." His tone wasn't reassuring, but Sera knew he was being realistic. "If you've handled a gun, I have one you can bring with you. I'd rather you were armed."

Jeremy Gordon's surprised and angry face flashed in her mind, and she remembered the retort of the gun, the smell, and the blood.

"I've used a gun before," she said in a steady voice.

"Good," he replied, sounding as if that was what he'd expected. He turned to go. "We'll have breakfast, then leave. I've studied the area and all is in readiness."

Sera followed him out and headed into the bathroom. She set her phone on the edge of the sink, just in case Marc did call. Her hope wasn't entirely gone, but it wavered.

A shower and breakfast did little to hearten her and Sera slid into the passenger seat of the car with a growing unease. At David's suggestion, she'd worn comfortable dark clothes, an outfit that would make her seem unremarkable to any possible witnesses.

Sera shuddered. With Jeremy's death, she'd thought the danger had ended, for both her and Marc.

David started the car and pulled out into the street, taking the turn onto Avenue Wagram and travelling quickly through the traffic circle around the Arc de Triomphe. He accelerated as they turned onto the Périphérique, merging into the morning rush.

Sera glanced into the back seat, where the brown paper package lay. "Is that really a Monet in there?" she asked. He hadn't opened it for her; they hadn't talked about it at all.

"No. It's a decoy, at best. Mayson wouldn't actually let his Monet out of his sight." David chuckled.

Sera looked away, glancing out the window, but the buildings passed by in a blur, her gaze turned inward. So many favours were owed to Mayson now.

"We'll get to the villa in plenty of time to surprise them," David said. "The meeting in town wasn't until the afternoon. They won't be prepared."

"Are you sure?"

"We'll stake the place out, figure out the best ways in and out." He reached out, resting a hand on her leg. "I won't leave without him, if I can help it."

Sera's stomach churned and her hands felt like ice where they were clasped on her purse, which held the gun he'd given her. He hadn't wanted her to use Marc's, in case it could be traced. She didn't like being armed, but he'd insisted.

"You'll only use the gun in the worst-case scenario," he'd said. "I'm good at what I do, so it should go down without a hitch. Don't worry."

Now it sat heavy on her lap and she hoped she wouldn't have to use it.

"We'll negotiate with Royale if we can," David said.

"Negotiate, how?"

The words came out more sharply than she'd intended. Marc had talked of killing Royale, but she couldn't see how that could happen. They were heading into an unknown place, just the two of them against how many more people.

"I have my ways. Trust me." David took the next exit off the Périphérique, heading out into the countryside.

Sera studied him as he drove. He didn't seem the least bit concerned; his expression was neutral, relaxed, his gaze focused on the road ahead, his hands loosely grasping the steering wheel. He looked over at her.

"Rest while you can," he advised. "We have a little ways to go yet."

Sera leaned back against the head-rest and closed her eyes, but she couldn't relax as her body shivered with adrenaline. She envisioned Marc, seeing him again, kissing him, and having him safe. She couldn't bear it if she lost him.

Jean came for Marc mid-morning. He checked the zip ties on Marc's wrists once again.

"Venez," he said. Marc rose to his feet.

"Where are we going?"

"Out." Jean took his arm when Marc's movements were too slow to satisfy him, hustling him to the door. "Madame's orders."

"Not Monsieur's?" Marc quipped. Jean gave a derisive snort. "Never his."

He escorted Marc downstairs to the front parlour where Françoise and Arnaud Royale waited. Françoise sat calmly on a settee, drinking espresso, but her husband paced, moving to the window, stifling his coughing in a handkerchief. A half-smoked cigarette burned in an ashtray.

When Françoise saw them, she took one last sip of her coffee, set the cup and saucer aside, then stood.

"Good, you're here."

Royale turned from the window. "I don't see why you're bothering to bring him," he said, shooting Marc a scornful look.

"Bargaining chip," Françoise said, sounding exasperated. Royale harrumphed and Marc could feel the tension between them rising. What had gone on between them? Royale seemed out of sorts, his usual garrulous confidence stifled. Françoise was icy cold, radiating disdain whenever she looked at him.

If Marc wasn't in such a precarious situation, he would have found Royale's discomfiture amusing.

"The car is ready," Jean said, "whenever you are."

Françoise studied the small group. "Arnaud, you'll stay behind. There's not enough room for you. Jean can take Monsieur Perron out to the car, and he will sit in the back with me."

Jean shackled Marc's arm and marched him from the room, out through a short hallway. Behind him, he could hear Royale's furious protestation and Françoise's sharp retort.

Jean chuckled. "He'll never learn." They moved into the main entry hall and walked out the door onto the gravel drive where a dark sedan waited. The back windows were heavily tinted; it looked almost like a hearse. Jean glanced at his watch, then back at the villa.

"Their bickering is going to make us late." He turned on his heel, pausing. "Don't you even dare move," he said before he headed back inside.

Alone on the drive, Marc glanced around. The expanse of lawn in every direction gave him nowhere to hide, and the trees that lined the drive wouldn't help either. His feet might be free of bonds, but he wouldn't make it far. He sidled over to the sedan, trying not to limp, and looked for keys.

Nothing.

He couldn't hotwire a car, and wasn't even sure he could do it with this one, and certainly not in time. He returned to where he'd been standing, stymied and frustrated. Jean returned, and he could hear Françoise's heels on the marble entryway.

"Get in," Françoise commanded as she came out the front door.

"No." Marc stood still, feeling his leg aching. He saw Françoise raise one brow, then glance at Jean.

"You heard her," Jean said.

Royale came out onto the step. "So much for your control," he sniped, before coughing. Françoise glowered.

Jean nudged Marc in the back, and not gently, the heavy steel of the gun obvious. "Move."

Marc took a step forward.

"Who the fuck is that?" he heard Royale say.

Dust rose from the gravel drive between the trees, and he could just spot a car. It was dark, like the sedan, and he couldn't see who was inside.

He hoped with all his heart that it wasn't Sera.

CHAPTER 27

"Marc." His name was a whisper on her lips.

David slowed the car. "Stay in the car," he said. "Let me do what I'm here to do."

"But…"

"I'll get Marc out safely," he assured her.

"How?" At first, she could only tell Marc and Royale were there, but as they got closer and David pulled the car aside, she saw Jean, and a woman. She'd never seen the woman before; she stood tall, elegant in her dark suit. Who was she?

David bent and took a gun from where it had been tucked underneath his seat. She didn't know what kind it was, only that it was larger than the one he'd given her, larger than Marc's. He slipped off the safety.

"Stay down."

Then he opened the door and stepped out.

A shot echoed through the car, loud enough to deafen her and she ducked, her hands over her ears.

Marc saw the car drive close, then stop. The sun glinted off the windscreen and he couldn't see the occupants, but Jean stepped up beside him, gun at the ready.

"Friends of yours?" he asked.

Françoise had stepped back, into the shade of the doorway, but Royale hadn't moved.

"What games are you playing?" he barked at his wife.

The door to the car opened, and a familiar man emerged, keeping the door between him and the villa. Before Marc could react, David brought a gun up and a shot rang out. At first, it seemed like David had missed. Jean laughed and Françoise stepped forward, but then he heard Royale's wheeze.

"Franç—" he coughed out, but this time his words were followed by blood, not spittle. The large man staggered and fell, his bulk hitting the marble with a sickening thud.

"Check him," Françoise snapped. Jean left Marc's side, but Marc didn't see where he went, for he took his chance.

A pain knifed through his leg and he lost his balance, falling to his knees. A hand in his hair wrenched his head up and he felt a trickle of blood slide down the back of his neck from the torn out follicles. A gun nudged his ear.

"Try that again and he's dead," Françoise called out from above him. He looked out across the drive. David stood where he was, a solemn, dark figure. He lowered his gun.

"Let him go, or you won't ever see the Monet," he called.

Françoise's grip tightened. "Give it to me or he will die," she called back. "I don't need him."

David bent his head, appearing to be listening to someone. A few words turned into a heated moment, from what Marc could see of David's expression.

"Marc!"

He'd been so focused on David that he hadn't seen the movement. The passenger door of the car had opened and Sera stood there, her dark hair around her shoulders, looking more beautiful than he'd ever seen her.

"What perfect company," he heard Françoise murmur.

"Dammit, Sera."

"Marc in exchange for the painting," Sera snapped over the roof of the car at David.

"We do that, he's dead. She won't let him go until she's examined it. We have nothing to give her but an obvious fake," David replied.

"Then you take her out."

"Not with the gun to his head."

"Mademoiselle Durand can bring the painting," Françoise called out. "Unless she wants to see her lover dead."

"That's it then." Sera felt nauseated; her head ached, and her stomach churned. She moved around the car and took out the wrapped parcel from the back seat. It felt light, too light to contain anything of value. Her steps faltered.

They were all dead. Marc would die as soon as Françoise opened the parcel, and she would perish after, having first watched Marc being shot in front of her eyes.

"Hurry up," Françoise called. "I haven't much patience."

Sera came around the car and up beside David. "I'll cover you," he said. "We're evenly matched now; Royale's dead."

Sera's gaze flashed to the rotund man, prone on the marble. He wasn't moving, and Jean had come to his feet. All of them ignored Royale.

"Remember, you have a gun, and can use it," David said in a low voice. Sera hitched her purse on her shoulder and took a step towards the villa.

Marc watched Sera as she came towards them, moving slowly, a bulky parcel in her hands.

"Finally," Françoise crowed. She let go of him, pushing him aside. "Jean, watch him." Jean stepped up beside him, though he seemed relaxed.

Françoise came down the stairs towards Sera, and they met in the open. Marc glanced to David, who watched the scene carefully, but did nothing. He lifted a phone to his ear and Marc frowned. What was he doing?

Marc shifted, trying to get to his feet.

"Don't even think about it," Jean said. Marc ignored him, bracing his hands on the marble and shoving himself upright. He tottered, then steadied. Jean smirked. "As if you're in any shape to help. If Françoise wanted to hurt her, she could."

"No one could stop me," Marc retorted. Jean shrugged.

"If you say so."

Françoise turned and came back up the stairs, bringing Sera with her, the painting in its parcel. She gestured to Sera to walk in front of her.

There was a crunch of gravel and Sera turned, almost losing her balance. The car that had brought her here, and David, backed away and he executed a perfect three-point turn before heading down the driveway at a fast clip.

Françoise started to laugh. "Looks like it's just us, mes amis."

Sera had gone frighteningly pale and she met his gaze.

They were done for.

Sera forced her knees into a locked position before her legs gave out under her. David was gone. Their one chance to escape had vanished. Betrayed. After all those nights performing together, after Mayson's promises—nothing. She should have expected it, but she'd considered David a friend, someone who would have her back.

"Come inside," Françoise said, laying a hand on her shoulder. "Have a cup of tea while we look at the painting you've brought. Is it as beautiful as you'd expect?"

How to answer that? Sera swallowed. "I haven't seen it."

"You haven't? Then you'd best hope it's incredible."

As they went through the door, Sera twisted around, her gaze falling on Royale's body. "Is he dead?"

"He is," Jean said, bringing Marc with him, a hand grasping his upper arm. Marc limped next to him, his hands bound in front of him. They were dead, the pair of them, once Françoise opened the parcel. She sought out his gaze once more, and he met it.

Maybe not done for, not yet. His gaze flicked down to his hands and she puzzled over how she could free him.

"He's no loss," Françoise said. "I've been wanting to rid my-self of him for years."

"But he was your husband," Sera said, "wasn't he?"

"He was. But never a good one."

They went through the entryway to the front parlour, and Françoise directed Sera into a chair. She took the parcel from her and set down her gun on a side table.

Marc eyed the gun, wishing he could make it to the table, and knowing he couldn't.

Beside him, he heard Jean chuckle. "The moment of truth," Jean muttered. Marc felt Jean's grasp on his arm loosen as he watched Françoise.

The brown paper came off the parcel, revealing a cardboard box. Françoise sighed and tore off the tape that held the thin top end of the box closed. She glanced inside, and then laid the box on the coffee table, knocking her empty espresso cup onto the floor. The carpet muffled the sound, but the cup cracked in two. Françoise eased the painting from the cardboard, slowly, carefully. Time seemed to slow, and the silence deafened him.

All eyes were on the parcel, but Sera's hand was in her bag, gripping the gun. She drew it out, and didn't bother with a warning.

The retort was stronger than she'd expected and it jarred her; she nearly dropped the gun. A wet stain spread across the shoulder of Françoise's jacket and she dropped the painting, clutching at her shoulder, her screech of pain deafening.

Jean started to laugh. He lashed out at Marc, catching him by surprise, and Marc fell heavily, but Jean didn't bother with him further. He picked up Françoise's gun from the side table, looking down at his boss with a mix of amusement and pitiless derision.

Françoise finally straightened. "You bitch. Jean, kill her."

"Should I?"

Françoise grasped blindly for her gun, but her hand met empty wood. "Give me my gun," she snarled.

"No, I don't think so." Jean stepped back easily as Françoise lunged for him, missing and falling to her knees.

"But don't you move," he said, his cold gaze fixing Sera in her seat. He strode over and took the gun from her before she could recover from her shock. "And you don't need that."

From the corner of her eye, Sera saw Marc slowly rising to his hands and knees, but she didn't say anything, keeping her gaze fixed on Jean. He was the danger now.

"I like you there, like that," he said to Françoise, as if they were having a casual conversation. "You really should be there more often, on your knees."

"Give me my gun," she snarled again, grasping the settee with her uninjured arm and trying to rise. "You work for me."

At those words, Jean's expression seemed to shut down, and he kicked out, catching her arm so that she fell back against the settee.

"You think so, do you?" he sneered. "I have listened to your complaints, listened to your bastard of a husband cough and wheeze for so long that I wanted to strangle him."

Marc reached Sera's side and she fumbled inside her purse, hoping to find something to break the zip ties that bound his wrists.

Neither Jean nor Françoise seemed to notice.

"Hurry," Marc whispered.

"I made you what you are," Françoise argued.

"I made me what I am," Jean corrected. "A venal whore like you couldn't make anyone anything. You were so in love with Jeremy Gordon that you would have supplanted me."

"With Arnaud dead, Le Chat Rouge is yours," Françoise offered.

Sera dug out her keys, the only thing she could find that might possibly work. Marc held up his hands.

"Don't try to break it, shove it in here." He indicated where the zip tie laced through the locking mechanism. She took the most slender of her keys, pressing it in, working to shift the plastic and lift it away from the tie. Marc twisted his wrists, putting pressure on the tie, and it slipped. Not a lot, but enough to give her hope.

"Hurry."

"The club is mine already," Jean retorted. "The deed is mine; your husband signed it over."

"What?" Françoise screeched.

"You have nothing more to offer me," Jean told her. "And no one will miss you."

Marc slipped free of the zip ties and Sera shoved her keys back into her purse. "We have to make a run for it," she whispered, rising and tugging him to his feet beside her.

"I can't," he said, swaying on his feet beside her. Perspiration broke out on his brow.

Sera hooked his arm around her shoulder. "You can."

They only made it a few steps before there was a shot. Sera glanced back wildly, but there was no pain, and Marc still stumbled along beside her.

"Go, go," Marc urged. "It's Françoise who's been shot, not us."

They made it into the entrance hall, with the Jackson Pollock painting and the cold marble floor.

"And where do you think you're going?"

Marc and Sera turned as one, and he saw Jean standing in the doorway to the parlour, an amused smile quirking his lips.

"You don't need us anymore," Marc replied. "You have what you need."

"Do I? I don't think so."

"Then just kill us," Sera said, sounding angry for the first time. "Stop playing."

"Tempting. It's easier to kill someone than you might think." He looked inordinately pleased with himself.

"Françoise trusted you," Sera retorted.

"She did. A silly thing to do, but then people often underestimate me. Royale did, to his detriment." Jean shrugged. "But no matter, he's not here to complain about it either."

Although they outnumbered him, Marc knew they were outmatched. "What do you want, Jean?" he asked, shifting to take more weight off his injured leg.

"I wouldn't mind you dead," Jean said calmly, "but at the moment, that's not my main concern. Let's handle this like adults, shall we?" He stepped aside, indicating the open door. "Entrez."

CHAPTER 28

"Purse on the table, if you please, Sera," Jean said pleasantly. Sera obeyed, but it was easy to see she was reluctant. Marc propped his leg up on the table, relieving some of the ache. He needed a doctor, and soon. He hadn't looked at the wound lately, but from the pain, he knew it wasn't healing, not the way it should.

"I have a proposition for you both," Jean said, looking relaxed, Françoise's gun and Sera's resting on the settee beside him, and his own resting in his lap, his hand curled comfortably over the butt, a finger close on the trigger.

Sera shuddered beside him and Marc knew she'd looked too long at Françoise, sprawled on the floor, her blood soaking into the delicate Persian rug.

"What is it?" Marc asked. He held Sera's hand tight in his. "I won't steal any paintings for you."

"I don't need paintings," Jean replied. "Couldn't care less about them. What a waste of time."

"You can't be serious." Sera sounded shocked.

"Art is a waste," Jean said. "Look at where it gets people. The Royales, you, your boyfriend. All in trouble."

"What do you want?" Marc persisted.

"An introduction," Jean said.

Marc heard the surprise in Sera's voice. "What?"

"It shouldn't come as a surprise," Jean said. "Royale was always at odds with Jack Mayson. I want to build an empire, not tear it down."

"You want an introduction to Jack Mayson?"

"I do, and not just any introduction. I want bona fides from both of you."

"Bona fides for a murderer?" Marc snorted. "You've got to be joking."

"Do I look like a joking man?" Jean's gaze narrowed. "I plan to link my people with Mayson's, and if we're not fighting each other, the profits will grow for both of us."

If they ever wanted out of here, there was no other answer they could give.

"We'll introduce you," Marc said. "And I'll even give bona fides, however, I can't guarantee Mayson will believe me."

"I'm sure he'll make sense of the situation," Jean said. "They usually do. And he likes you, doesn't he, Sera? Or at least, that's what I've heard. Remarkable for a man like Mayson, don't you think?"

"He'll make up his own mind, I'm sure," Sera replied.

Jean took a phone from his pocket and tossed it to Marc. "Call your secretary and have her order three tickets for the Eurostar tonight, the latest train. We're going to London."

Once the tickets were booked, Jean called a doctor to come look at Marc's leg. Sera sat nearby, watching, wincing every time Marc cried out in pain.

"He's barely hurt, you know." Jean stood nearby. He had not let them out of his sight for a minute.

She glared at him, even though she knew he was still armed. "Go to hell."

"I'm afraid you're not very intimidating, cherie," he replied. "And why Royale fancied you, I just don't know."

"Better taste?"

"If you say so." Jean smirked.

The doctor finished with his work.

"It was a clean shot, monsieur, and it should heal, now that it's been properly dressed."

"Merci, Monsieur Richard. I appreciate you coming on such short notice."

The doctor accepted the money Jean gave him, far more than what he would receive in the state health service for an appointment. "De rien."

Jean led the doctor out and Sera came to the bed. Marc was sitting up, and perspiration still shone on his brow. She sat down next to him and he put his arm around her. She leaned against him.

"Do you think this will be the end of it, after we go back to London?" she asked. She dreaded the trip, dreaded walking into the Sanctuary and being the one to introduce the pair.

"Jean may keep his word, he may not," Marc said, "but in London, we have the advantage. We know the area, and we know others there. Do you think Pari could be depended upon to help?"

"I know she could. She's police," Sera replied.

"This is beyond her experience, but if we need the police…" Marc paused, wincing as he shifted on the bed. "I don't know if I'll be able to protect you if things go badly."

"Remember what I said, back at Claridge's?" Sera asked. "You're going to end up sleeping on the sofa if you keep that up."

Marc chuckled and kissed her forehead. "We wouldn't want that. The game is still on."

"Time to go," Jean said, coming to the door.

"We'll need to stop for a change of clothes in Paris," Sera said. "Marc can't wear those trousers."

"We have time to stop," Jean said. "And I must check on Le Chat Rouge before we go."

"And I need to talk further with Aurore," Marc added. "I'm supposed to be in Brussels tomorrow."

"Brussels?" Sera didn't remember him saying anything about Brussels.

"A client, and an auction," he said. "Perhaps Aurore can go in my place."

"We'll have time," Jean said again. She found it strange that he was so pleasant compared to his usual self.

"Why did David just leave?" Marc asked her. She glanced at Jean, who looked interested, and back to Marc.

"I don't know."

She didn't want to voice it, but she knew. David had left them to die.

Once in Paris, Marc called Aurore and arranged for her to cover the Brussels trip.

"You know more about the file than I do," Marc told her. It was true, she did. She knew more than he and Fournier both. "I trust you."

"Why can't you travel, Monsieur Perron?" she asked, sounding puzzled.

"Something urgent has come up," he said. "I have to head back to London."

"Is it Mrs. Lancaster's estate?" Aurore asked.

"Something like that," he hedged. "I'll get in touch as soon as I can. I promise."

"All right. I'll go see Guillaume; he'll have advice for me now that they've cut back on his pain meds."

Marc hung up as Sera finished packing them a bag.

"This will have to do," she said.

"We still have our things in the Highgate flat," Marc said. He went to lift the bag.

"I'll do it," she said, stopping him. "Your leg needs to heal."

They went into the living room of Marc's flat, where Jean waited.

"She did nearly get you, didn't she?" he said to Sera, gesturing to the hole in the plaster where the bullet had embedded itself.

"She missed. Let's go and get this over with," Marc replied, taking Sera's hand. Her fingers were cold on his, and though she didn't say it, he knew she was worried. She'd barely said a word on the drive back to Paris, or in the lift, or even in the bedroom.

As they followed Jean to the door, Marc gave her hand a gentle squeeze. "Not much longer, ma chère."

"We'll never get free of this," Sera said. "Never."

"We will," Marc replied, his voice low. "I promise you, we will."

"We're taking the stairs," Jean said, gesturing to them to precede him. "We can't all fit in the elevator."

"But his leg!" Sera protested.

"He'll manage," Jean snapped.

Marc took the stairs slowly, leaning heavily on the rail, each step painful. Once in the car again, he sat back and wiped his brow. Their driver, a surly man Jean had called Robert, glanced at him in the rear-view mirror before returning his gaze to the road.

"All right?" Sera asked.

"No, but I'll manage."

At Le Chat Rouge, he was relieved to hear that Jean expected them to wait in the car.

"I won't be long," Jean said. "Robert, make sure they don't do anything stupid."

"I should call Pari," Sera said as soon as Jean had left.

"No phone calls," Robert grunted.

"Later," Marc said. "After this is over."

"Marc, what if Mayson wants us all dead? I'm starting to think the worst. David was my co-worker, perhaps even my friend, but he just left us like we were worth nothing to him."

"Mayson wanted Royale dead," he assured her. "If anything, his orders were to see that done, and then leave." He wanted to believe the words himself, but he didn't. What he did know was that neither of them could take anything for granted: not Mayson, not David, not anyone in London, except perhaps for Pari.

Sera huddled close to him, and he tucked her in next to him, under his arm. It was just like on the train to London, except this time, they weren't going by choice.

Jean got back into the car. "Robert, to Gare du Nord," he said. "Oh, look at you two lovebirds." He snorted, and Robert gave a short chuckle.

The drive to the station was quick, and they were through security and immigration too soon for Marc's tastes. None of the security staff seemed to notice the tension in the group, or if they did, they didn't care.

Their tickets were for a group of four around a table, and Aurore had gotten them into a quiet car.

"You and Sera in the window seats," Jean directed. He sat down beside her, leaving Robert to block Marc's path to the aisle.

"We don't have anywhere to go," Marc pointed out in exasperation.

"Can't be too careful." Jean settled back into his seat, pulling out his phone. He stopped his fiddling only long enough to eat the meal they were served, but even then, he kept an eye on the phone's screen.

Sera hardly ate, even when Marc nudged her foot under the table. She took a few bites, then pushed her plate away, leaning back in her chair and closing her eyes. He knew she wasn't sleeping, but there was little else for them to do as the train made its way through the darkened French countryside, and closer to London.

CHAPTER 29

Over Sera's protests, Jean forced them to go straight to Sanctuary. Marc gave the cab driver directions from St. Pancras.

"This is more important than going to your flat." Jean reprimanded her as if she were a schoolgirl. Sera felt the heat rise on her cheeks.

"It's too late," she said. Marc squeezed her hand.

"It's not even one o'clock," Jean said. "And it's a club."

She wanted to protest further, and tell him that he couldn't do anything now that he was unarmed, having had to give up his guns before they came on the Eurostar, but she didn't. Robert sat close by, and she knew he could hurt her even without a gun.

Once in Soho, the cab slowed to a crawl as it turned the corner, coming to a halt across from Sanctuary.

"I have always wanted to see this club," Jean said, opening the door. "Pay the man, Robert." He ushered Marc and Sera out of the cab, taking Sera by the arm. "You can come with me, cherie."

Sera, thrown off balance by Jean's grip on her arm, stumbled down the stairs. At the bottom, she pushed through the velvet curtain and stepped into her old life, or so it felt. She hadn't been gone long, but already the club seemed strange to her. Julian was at the bar, pouring drinks for a couple of men, but he saw her come in, and his eyes widened. She glanced over at the stage.

David sat at the piano, done up in his usual tuxedo, looking as if nothing had happened, as if he hadn't killed a man and left her and Marc to die. His expression was solemn, but he gave her a small nod of recognition.

"Where's Mayson?" Jean asked, his voice low, a hiss in her ear.

"I don't see him," she said. She turned towards the bar, heading for Julian. "But he will know."

"Sera, what can I get for you?" Julian asked. "A glass of Sancerre?"

"Not right now." She tried to smile, but it faltered. "Is Mayson here?"

"He's in his office," Julian said, glancing from her to Jean, who still held her arm, and then to Marc and Robert. His gaze settled back on her, questioning.

"We would like to speak with him," Jean said in English, his French accent strong.

"Could you see if he's available?" Sera asked, wanting so much to ask for help, but not daring.

"I'll see if he's free." Julian left the bar and headed to the solid door that led to Mayson's office. It opened and he went inside. As they waited, Jean glanced around.

"Nice place. Better than Le Chat Rouge, certainly, though that stairwell had me wondering."

"It is nice," Sera said, hearing the piano over the murmur of conversation.

"Now that Royale's gone, Le Chat Rouge will be getting a facelift," Jean told her. "You should come back and sing."

"No. Never." She pulled at his grasp and he let her go.

"Never say never."

Marc stepped to her side. "I'll say never."

"As you will. Not that it matters. There are hundreds of performers looking for jobs."

Julian exited Mayson's office, beckoning to them, and Sera and Marc preceded Jean.

"He will see you, but leave the goon outside," Julian said, indicating Robert.

"Have a drink," Jean told Robert airily. "But just one."

Julian pulled the door open.

"Enter."

The office was as it always was, neat and dark, and smelling faintly of cigarette smoke. Mayson gestured to the chairs; three of them now.

"Have a seat." His gaze drilled into Marc. "Why are you here?"

"I had a favour to fulfill," Marc replied, taking a seat, careful not to jar his leg. Sera took the seat beside him, leaving Jean to the remaining chair.

Mayson glanced at Jean only briefly, but Marc knew he'd taken a full measure of Royale's former maitre d'. "I see. You seem to owe many favours these days."

"Arnaud Royale is dead," Jean said bluntly in his accented English, resting his hands on the arms of the chair. "As is his bitch of a wife."

Mayson gave Jean a nod, but looked again at Marc. "Expect to hear from me."

"Of course," Marc said, ignoring Jean. "But we need to speak about that as well, a bit later."

"Noted." Mayson turned his attention back to Jean. "So Royale's dead. What of it?"

"I've taken over, and I think we could come to an amicable agreement. You want more business; I want more business. Royale was determined to undercut you, but I think we'd make more profits by cooperating."

"I didn't trust him," Mayson said bluntly, lighting a cigarette and taking a drag. "So why should I trust a conniving little thief like you?"

Jean bristled at the insult, and Marc saw his features harden. "I know every detail of the operation he ran, and then some. I know that he was bribing your men and intercepting shipments. If we worked together, we could increase our take and elbow out the smaller gangs."

Mayson leaned back in his chair, his gaze on Jean. Marc waited, watching the pair of them, aware of the tension in the room, and of Sera next to him, her breathing shallow and nervous.

"Prove that you mean it, and in six months, we can sit down for proper negotiations," Mayson said finally. "Until then, my opinion stays the same as it did when Royale was your boss."

"Mr. Perron can vouch for my sincerity," Jean noted.

Mayson scoffed and shot Marc an amused glance, as if they shared some secret. "I know Perron only marginally better than I know you, and he's not someone I take opinions from," Mayson said with a chuckle. "Six months, no sooner. How do I know that there's not some other thief angling to take you out once you are back in Paris?"

"There won't be," Jean said. He rose, straightening his suit jacket and buttoning it. The gesture made him seem almost prissy. "I will see you in six months, then."

"Stay awhile in the club, enjoy it," Mayson invited. "Julian will pour drinks on the house."

"That's very generous of you." Jean moved to leave, then paused, eyeing Marc.

"Perron and I have business," Mayson said. "He'll be out shortly."

Marc bit back a smile at Mayson's direct cut of Jean, treating him as little more than another of his thugs. Stiff-backed, Jean exited the office, the open door allowing in a murmur of conversation and the tones of David's piano.

Mayson stubbed out his cigarette and lit another. Marc took one from his cigarette case and did the same.

"So the bastard's dead, eh?"

"I saw it with my own eyes," Marc replied. Sera shuddered.

"Good riddance, and Jeremy has been revenged." Mayson looked satisfied at that.

"I appreciate David's help in that," Marc said, "but he left during a very precarious situation." The words were couched in a neutral tone, but Mayson frowned, leaning forward in his chair.

"You wanted Royale dead," he stated. "So did I. And so it was done. End of."

"We could have died," Sera interjected, speaking for the first time.

"New to this, is she?" Mayson asked Marc, rhetorically. "I suppose so," he said, his attention returning to Sera. "But that's none of my concern. Your boyfriend—and you, don't you forget—got exactly what you asked for."

Sera's hand clenched on the arm of the chair, but she didn't reply.

"To the letter, indeed," Marc acknowledged. "But David's leaving could have meant that you would never collect."

"I considered it worth the risk." Mayson shrugged. "But you're here, and alive. And you'll fulfill my favours when I need them. I'll be in touch about where to send the first payment, Mr. Perron."

"What are they?" Sera asked.

"I haven't decided yet." Mayson stubbed out his cigarette. "Now, if you'll excuse me," he pulled a stack of invoices towards the center of his desk, "I have work to do. But I'll be in touch, never fear."

Marc rose and took Sera's hand. "Let's go home," he said.

She rose with him, though her gaze strayed again to Mayson, wary.

Mayson didn't look at them as they left and went out into the club. Marc spotted Jean and Robert having a drink at the bar, but he didn't stop to speak to them. Jean turned on his stool, and behind him, Julian looked as if he would speak.

"I'll be in touch," Jean said.

"You've gotten what you asked for," Sera snapped.

Jean stood, coming face to face with her before Marc could shoulder him aside. "Not yet, I haven't. Not until the deal's inked."

"Go to hell."

Jean chuckled and patted her cheek. Marc caught his hand.

"Don't you dare touch her."

Jean tried to pull his hand away, but Marc held him fast. Robert left his stool and reached for Marc's arm, but Julian was there first.

"The bar's closed, messieurs," Julian said in French, staring down Jean and Robert. Marc let go of Jean's hand. "Since these gentlemen were just leaving, may I offer you a drink, Sera?"

"I don't think we'll stay, Julian," she said, moving closer to Marc. "Not tonight, anyway."

"Soon, though. A drink on me," Julian said.

"Bien sûr."

Marc put his arm around Sera. "Bonne nuit, Julian."

Julian gave him a nod. As they moved away, Jean went to follow, but Marc saw Julian step into his path.

"Let's get a cab," he said as he and Sera pushed through the velvet curtain.

"Back to the flat?"

"Wherever you want to go."

CHAPTER 30

The black cab took them to the flat on Highgate Hill, though to Sera it seemed devoid of the warmth it had held before. Before Mayson, and Jean, and Royale. The streetlights illuminated the living room, casting it in a cool glow. She didn't want to stay here anymore. It wasn't home.

"I don't think I want to be in London anymore," she said, turning to Marc as he shut the door behind them.

"Where do you want to go?" he asked. They moved into the living room, but didn't turn on the light. Sera sank onto the sofa.

"I don't know. But not here, not in this flat. It's not the same."

"I'll pay out the lease. Perhaps we should go to America, far away from all of this."

Sera wasn't sure she wanted to fly across an ocean, to a land where the people only spoke English.

"Je ne sais pas." She rose and paced to the window, looking out onto the street, across to the darkness of the trees in Waterslow Park. Marc came up behind her.

"Canada, then? Montréal?"

"Maybe."

There were too many memories here now, and an image of Madelaine flashed through her mind. She didn't want to see that girl again, no matter what Edwards had said. It still stung.

"Back to France?" Marc put his arm around her and she leaned into him.

"Je ne sais pas."

He rubbed her back, and it was soothing, though it wasn't helping her in making a decision.

"Let's go to bed," Marc suggested finally, urging her away from the window and towards the bedroom. "We can decide tomorrow."

Once in bed, tucked under the duvet, Sera shivered. The sheets were cool against her skin, and though the duvet was thick and warm, she was not. Marc drew her close and they were skin-to-skin, but she still felt cold. He shifted and she felt the brush of gauze and tape against her leg. If this had ended any differently, she would have been in this bed alone. She shuddered, a violent shake that went from head to toe.

"Ma chère?"

Sera tucked in closer, her head on his shoulder, his arm around her, holding her tight, her leg over his. He stroked her with his free hand, slowly running down the length of her ribcage, leaving a trail of warmth.

"I don't know what to do," she whispered.

"Tomorrow, ma chère," he replied.

"And we can put aside the game," she said after a moment, the words catching in her throat. He brought his hand up and stroked her hair, cradling her head in his hand, his fingers gentle on her neck, his thumb stroking her cheek. The touch was security, a promise of his care.

"I'll never leave you, ma chère," he whispered. "I promise."

Morning came too soon, and Marc felt as if his body had been run through the wringer. Every part of him ached, and his leg most of all. Sera slept on beside him, her face pale in the early dawn, the shadows evident under her eyes. He stayed still beside her, not wanting to wake her earlier than necessary. The game was over, and he would take care of her the best he could.

Finally, the ache in his leg drove him from the bed and he pulled on a terrycloth robe from the wardrobe. He limped to the bathroom and found a bottle of paracetamol, and downed two tablets with a swallow of water. Glancing into the mirror, he saw his own pale reflection, with dark shadows under the eyes, and lower, the mottled bruises on his chest where the robe didn't cover.

Sera was right. They couldn't stay here. London had lost its magic, and he didn't care to be near Mayson if he could help it. But where should they go? Montréal was a possibility, but he was reluctant to settle so far from Paris. What if they found a small house in Chartres, or elsewhere? He could commute into Paris for work when he needed to, but they'd keep out of the capital and life could go on. He knew now he couldn't leave the firm; it was in his blood, and he cared too much about it, more than he'd admitted. Royale was dead and now he could truly leave the criminal world behind.

Marc went into the kitchen and put the pot on for coffee, leaning on the counter and taking the weight off his injured leg as he waited. When the espresso was ready, he poured a healthy dose into a mug and took it into the living room. His phone rested on the side table by the sofa and he sat down and picked it up, flicking through his messages. Then he typed a quick note to Aurore. She could look into houses in Chartres and several of the surrounding towns, and then he'd have something to offer Sera.

He heard the bathroom door close, and the water running. Sera hadn't slept long. He sipped his espresso and replied to emails as he waited for her to emerge. When she did, she came into the living room in a black tunic and tights with bare feet. Without a word, she settled onto the sofa next to him, tucking under his arm.

"You're up early," she said, her words partly muffled by his robe.

"So are you. You should have slept longer."

"I had a nightmare," she said. "I didn't want to try going back to sleep again, not without you there."

"Our nightmares are over. Or they will be."

"What do you mean?"

"We should go back to France, but not Paris. What do you think of Chartres?"

Sera sat up, looking puzzled, her brow furrowed. "Chartres? What happened to Montréal?"

"Did you really want to move that far from Europe?" Marc asked in surprise. He hadn't thought she'd seriously considered it.

"It might be safer," she said finally. "Otherwise we're too close."

"Royale is dead," he reminded her gently.

"Jean is not," she replied.

"I don't think Jean will bother with us, not anymore. He has what he wants. We hold no value for him." Jean didn't want art, and didn't care for musicians. Whatever his motivation was, Marc knew it didn't include them.

"Still, I don't want to run into him in Paris."

"Hence Chartres. Close enough for me to go to the office when I need to, and yet far enough away that it's not on Jean's doorstep." His phone buzzed, and he picked it up. Aurore had been fast.

"Chartres, monsieur? Not Paris?" she wrote in an email. "Here are five, and since you didn't specify a price, I went from cheap to ridiculous. Does this mean you're leaving London for good?"

Marc flicked through her selections. The cheapest homes were too small, and he didn't want an apartment. Partway down the list, he spotted a detached house in the middle of a small expanse of green lawn, bordered by hedges.

"I was thinking something like this," he said, showing the listing to Sera. She took the phone from him, looking at each photograph closely.

"Peut-être." She looked at him. "But I still want to work; you have the firm, and I have... well, nothing."

"There would be clubs in Chartres," Marc replied, "or you could find something else you've always wanted to do. We have time."

"We do, don't we?" She set his phone down on the coffee table and snuggled into his side. "Except for Mayson's favour."

"He may never ask," Marc replied, but he knew it was wishful thinking.

"He'll ask," Sera said, sounding resigned. "It's just a matter of when."

"Until then, we'll build our life together." Marc stroked her arm. "Should I put in a bid on this house? I don't think it'll be on the market long."

"Not yet," Sera said. "But we can go look at houses. And I'm sure you'll need someone with you on all your work travels."

"That I will," he replied. He could see their future in his mind—a life of art and auctions, travelling to foreign capitals with Sera by his side.

"I'll start packing," Sera said, rising to her feet in eagerness. "Book the tickets."

"Hold up a moment," Marc said, catching her hand and pulling her back down beside him. "You're forgetting something."

"What?"

He kissed her.

The **LE CHAT ROUGE** Series

Take a walk on the darker side of Paris…

A jazz club on the Left Bank, Le Chat Rouge seems stuck in another era. Neglect and crime have left their mark, but the club is a haven for the desperate. Sometimes a singer whose talent is worthy of the world's greatest stages, or a patron who has wealth to spare, find their way to its smoky interior.

Gangsters, drug dealers, con artists…many occupy Le Chat Rouge's worn velvet banquettes and tread its creaking parquet floors, but all submit to Royale. The ruthless owner demands loyalty and few earn his favour. Those who do are as brutal as he is, and those who defy him might very well risk their lives.

It's a dangerous place, but fortune awaits the most daring.

BOOK 1: THE PARIS GAME

On the darker side of Paris, it's dangerous to not pay your debts…

A singer in a jazz club past its prime, Sera Durand must come up with thousands of euros to pay back her boss, a ruthless gangster. A confrontation with her ex, an art dealer profiting on the wrong side of the law, leads her into a questionable wager, but one that could solve her problems.

Marc Perron knows a winning proposition when he sees one. Seducing a shy young woman of Sera's acquaintance will be the easiest thing in the world, and the prize, to have Sera in his bed once again, is worth the chance of losing a sizable sum. What he didn't expect was the depth of Sera's desperation.

When one of his deals goes awry, Marc's solution could cost them more than money…

BOOK 2: MOONLIGHT & LOVE SONGS

When Le Chat Rouge's pianist, Benoît Grenier, meets the club's new singer, his world is turned upside down. He'd given up ever finding someone to love. His hopes and dreams of a life beyond the club are revived, while his heart heals.

Daniel Marceau has come from Marseille, looking to escape bad decisions and worse memories. He never expected to fall in love, and when his past catches up with him it could ruin the only thing he's ever found worth living for.

Daniel's fears and his reluctance to ask Benoît for help could cost them everything they've worked so hard to create.

NOVELLA: THE CHRISTMAS GAME

Alone in London on business just before Christmas, Marc Perron meets an intriguing young woman working at a bookshop. A light flirtation seems to lead nowhere, but the night before he returns to Paris, she knocks on his hotel room door.

Madelaine's taking a risk, but no one's ever looked at her the way Marc does, and she's not about to pass up a chance to get to know him better. When he suggests a game of wagers, she can't resist challenging him. And herself.

Their matchup is a fiery one and each wager tops the last, the sexual heat between them crackling. Neither want to lose the game, but Madelaine fears she might be losing her heart as well.

All of the **LE CHAT ROUGE** series are available for purchase at online retailers, including Amazon, B&N, The Book Depository, Kobo, Apple, and more.

ABOUT THE AUTHOR

Alyssa Linn Palmer is a Canadian writer and freelance editor. She splits her time between a full-time day job, and her part-time loves, writing and editing. She's currently working on several new projects, including lesbian romances for Bold Strokes Books, and more of the Le Chat Rouge series. She loves to hear from readers, and you can find her online at www.alyssalinnpalmer.com, or on Twitter @alyslinn. Sign up for her newsletter to get the latest: http://www.alyssalinnpalmer.com/newsletter/.